About the Author

Lisa Cutts is the author of four police procedural novels, based on her twenty-one years of policing experience. She works as a detective constable for Kent Police and has spent over ten years in the Serious Crime Directorate dealing mostly with murders and other serious investigations. She has been on BBC Radio 4's *Open Book* with Mariella Frostrup, part of First Fictions festival at West Dean college, Chichester, on the inaugural panel at Brighton's Dark and Stormy festival, on ITV's *This Morning* and at the Chiswick Book Festival. Her debut novel, *Never Forget*, won the 2014 Killer Nashville Silver Falchion Award for best thriller.

Lisa Cutts
Buried Secrets

**SIMON &
SCHUSTER**

London · New York · Sydney · Toronto · New Delhi

A CBS COMPANY

First published in Great Britain by Simon & Schuster UK Ltd, 2017
A CBS COMPANY

1 3 5 7 9 10 8 6 4 2

Simon & Schuster UK Ltd
1st Floor
222 Gray's Inn Road
London WC1X 8HB

Simon & Schuster Australia, Sydney
Simon & Schuster India, New Delhi

www.simonandschuster.co.uk
www.simonandschuster.com.au
www.simonandschuster.co.in

A CIP catalogue record for this book
is available from the British Library

Paperback ISBN: 978-1-4711-5314-3
eBook ISBN: 978-1-4711-5315-0

Typeset in Sabon by M Rules
Printed and bound by CPI Group (UK) Ltd, Croydon, CR0 4YY

Simon & Schuster UK Ltd are committed to sourcing paper
that is made from wood grown in sustainable forests and support the Forest
Stewardship Council, the leading international forest certification organisation.
Our books displaying the FSC logo are printed on FSC certified paper.

For my six wonderful friends –
Catherine Irwin, Eileen Yuksel, Helen Smither,
Paula Kane, Theresa Garrod and Tracey Smith.
Here's to the next thirty-five years.

Buried
Secrets

Chapter 1

Monday 5 June

Milton Bowman slammed the front door behind him, leaving his wife alone in the kitchen without so much as a backward glance. Why did she bring out the worst in him? Despite the tumble of thoughts in his head, the stifling heat of the early morning didn't pass him by, especially as he'd taken the time to tighten his silk tie and dress in his newest grey suit. Appearances were of the utmost importance to Milton. It was one of the reasons he had taken everything that was happening to him so hard. Some people walked away, some people lashed out. He simply wasn't sure how he could get everything back on track again.

He got into his car parked on the drive, bonnet facing outwards as all advanced police drivers had been taught, slammed the door, opened the window and screeched away from his ninety per cent mortgage-free house in the direction of the dual carriageway. He fought the urge to loosen his tie, not wanting to appear unkempt. Standards should be maintained.

Getting up early for work had never bothered Detective Constable Hazel Hamilton: hearing the alarm sound at half past five in the morning wasn't something she particularly enjoyed or looked forward to, but she liked the feeling of being awake and out of bed ready to launch herself into another day at the Major Crime Department.

Some mornings she needed to walk one of the dogs she fostered on behalf of a local charity, but this morning she only had herself to take care of.

On her way out, dressed in a navy trouser suit, she took her packed lunch, prepared the night before, from her fridge. She mulled over what that day's tour of duty might bring, and wondered if another murder or rape would mean that she wouldn't get home before the sun set.

As she pulled away from her modest two-bedroom house, she focused on the four-mile drive along the coast to East Rise Police Station and forced herself to save any further thoughts of double shifts until she pulled up outside the 1960s concrete building that someone had once considered a good idea. Its five floors of grey looked out over one of the South East of England's more run-down seaside towns, complete with screeching seagulls snatching food at every opportunity and making a mess of every car.

She gave a glance to the blue sky and noticed a

lack of both cloud and gulls, indicating that the sea was probably calm and peaceful. For a moment, she dared to risk the idea that her day might be equally as tranquil. There had been two days last week when she managed to get out of the major incident room on time.

As she headed towards the dual carriageway that took her most of the way, she saw that there was an unusual amount of traffic for so early in the day. It wasn't the best start she could have hoped for. She pushed her mixed feelings aside and wondered what a warm, sunny day at the seaside would bring her over the next eight hours of her shift.

'Emergency. Which service?'

'Ambulance,' said Luke Morgan into his mobile as he jogged towards the mangled Vauxhall Insignia he had watched seconds earlier drive along the dual carriageway in front of him, taking the roundabout too fast, and veering off at the last second straight at the metal barrier separating the north- from the south-bound lanes. The noise of the engine gunning behind him as the car shot into his line of vision had made him look up. Until that point, Luke had been lost in thought, off to collect his early morning paper from the shop. He'd stared incredulous as the car collided with the concrete flowerbed, poured in place by the council in an attempt to make the smog-ridden dual carriageway easier on the eye.

That car contained a person. Perhaps more than one.

This thought hadn't escaped Luke.

By the time he'd covered the thirty or so metres to the car, a Transit van travelling in the opposite direction had stopped and two people had come out of their houses to see what was happening.

Luke reached the driver's door of the Insignia at the same time as the driver of the van, a man Luke put in his early forties, got to the passenger side. Luke crouched down at the open window on his side and saw the waxy face of the sole occupant of the car behind the steering wheel.

'Help is on its way,' said Luke, glancing down at the driver's lap. Thick red liquid was flooding the material of his trousers. Glancing further down, Luke was able to see that his left leg was bleeding heavily just below his knee. Or at least, just below where his knee should have been, were it not jammed between his trapped right leg and the centre console of the car. The impact had severed the flesh and bone, and Luke could see that blood was pumping out of the man's leg at an alarming rate.

Luke concentrated on the face of the person rapidly going downhill in front of him. His first aid training had taught him only so much. Even so, common sense would tell anyone that a severed limb with such a loss of blood was limiting the man's remaining time on earth. Still aware that he was talking to the ambulance service operator, he spoke into his mobile while maintaining eye contact with his casualty.

'He's in his mid-forties,' said Luke.

'No, I'm thirty-nine,' said the man, 'but I'm having a bad day.'

Luke gave an empty smile and said, 'What's your name?'

'Milton, Milton Bowman.' He winced and screwed his eyes up before adding, 'I'm supposed to be at work. I have to tell you something. My wife—'

At that point, Luke stopped him. 'Milton, listen to me. The ambulance is coming but I have to get you out of the car. You're losing a lot of blood and I have to try to stop it. I'm going to pull you out and I won't lie to you – this is going to hurt.'

Once more Milton tried humour; it was the only thing he could think of. It was either that or shut his eyes and hope that when he opened them again he had dreamed what had happened that morning in his own kitchen, and this, the stuff of his nightmares.

'What's your line of business?' said Milton. 'Motivational speaker?'

'No. It's your lucky day. I'm a Marine. Don't worry, mate. This is a flesh wound in comparison to some I've seen.'

As he spoke, Luke leaned into the car and opened the door, reaching across for the seat-belt release. While he wasn't lying about seeing some atrocious injuries during his time in Afghanistan, he knew that his casualty was in trouble. In only the few seconds they'd been speaking, Milton's colour had turned greyer than his suit. He now wasn't talking but he was at least breathing. That much Luke was certain of, as he could hear his breath as he removed the seat belt and got ready to pull him from the car. All the time Luke was trying to save the stranger's life, totally oblivious of the man, other than his expensive taste in clothes. He was however, very aware of his surroundings: he knew who else was in the street, where they were, what they doing, that the van driver had finished talking to the police operator and that he still couldn't hear a siren in the distance. For now, Luke was on his own.

He glanced over to where he'd last seen the van driver who was now standing a few feet away from the car. Even though he'd distanced himself from the crash, he was still straining to see what was going on. Luke took advantage.

'Hey,' he shouted over, 'give me a hand here?'

The van driver gave an involuntary jolt in the direction of the car wreck as if his impulse upon being asked for his help, like his initial reaction, was to rush to assist, but then he checked himself and paused.

'Could do with a strong pair of hands,' said Luke. He saw it now: the apprehension in the man's eyes at watching someone's life blood drain away. He understood yet he didn't have time for it.

'You take his shoulders. His name's Milton.'

That seemed to propel him forward. His gaze drew level with Luke's as he reached the car door.

Between them they carried Milton from the car, Luke all the while talking to him. The rush-hour traffic was stacking up in both directions, some vehicles because they couldn't get past, and some whose drivers had a morbid fascination and were trying to watch.

'What were you saying about your wife?' said Luke, trying to keep Milton conscious for as long as possible as he tried in vain to use his T-shirt to stem the blood seeping onto the concrete.

'When I left her earlier, it wasn't good,' Milton gasped.

His speech was getting harder to decipher and Luke had to move from the mangled mess of his lower left leg, where he'd been kneeling in blood so thick that against the pavement it appeared black.

'I'll make sure she knows which hospital you're going to,' said Luke.

'No, you don't understand.' Milton tried to swallow, his strength leaving him now. 'It's probably too late.'

Luke moved back out of the way as the ambulance crews and police took over. He glanced up and down the street, took in the traffic and was very aware of how he must look, naked but for a pair of beige shorts and most of his body speckled with blood.

Above everything else he couldn't fail to notice the worried glances that the two police officers were exchanging and their looks of concern at the Vauxhall Insignia and the now unconscious man on the ground.

Luke saw more police vehicles arrive and, amongst the uniform officers, a woman in a crisp navy trouser suit. She had an identity card on a lanyard around her neck and held out a police warrant card to one of the officers. He watched her give a nod and a greeting smile she didn't mean to the patrol officers, and then take in the scene as she made her way over to him. She made him feel very much that she was one of the more senior in service and experience. He felt sure that she was going through a mental checklist and working through her priorities. In her position, he would have done the same: ensure there was no imminent threat or danger to anyone present, then move on to those injured and in shock. Only once they were being taken care of find out what happened and who caused it.

'Sir,' she said, glancing down at his blood-spattered legs and clothing. 'Thanks for helping out here. I'm Detective Constable Hazel Hamilton. Are you injured?'

'No,' said Luke, 'I'm fine.'

'Can I ask you what happened?'

She had her pocket notebook out and cheap black biro with its chewed end poised above the page. The photograph of her on her ID card around her neck was of her unsmiling face, something Luke felt was her habitual expression.

Luke told her what he'd seen, then added, 'And the man in the car is Milton Bowman.'

He returned his gaze to the police officer as he said the last part, taking in the strand of blonde wavy hair that had come untucked from her ponytail. He saw the badly applied foundation on her cheeks which probably meant she'd rushed to get to work. Now she'd found herself at the scene of an accident, possibly before she had even got as far as the police station.

Last of all, he saw her bite her lip and steal a sideways glance in the direction of the casualty.

What he didn't know was that she was fully aware who the figure on the ground was.

One of the bosses from Major Crime, Detective Inspector Milton Bowman from East Rise Police Station.

Chapter 2

DC Hazel Hamilton led Luke away towards one of the patrol cars and had a quick word with its driver, who handed over the keys and left them to it.

'I'll be back in a minute,' she said as she opened the car door for him, handing him a blanket from the boot. Hazel Hamilton had spoken to Luke for less than sixty seconds, but that was plenty of time for her to assess him and come to the conclusion that he would stay put when asked to, wasn't about to faint on her, and would cooperate. And almost as important would sit in the back of the car and not steal the kit or play with the blue lights.

He took the silver-foil blanket from her without a word.

'Would you mind sitting on this?' she said. 'I've checked with the driver and it's all she's got in the car. I don't want to sound insensitive, but being honest with you, if you get in and leave blood on the back seat, we'll have to get the car deep-cleaned. We can't afford for it to be off the road. There's always a distinct lack of fast-response patrols. I'd appreciate it.'

He put it on the seat and climbed in.

'How are you feeling?' she asked. Hazel didn't have any concerns about his welfare: one of the things that made her a very competent officer was her ability to talk to people and get them to tell her things. In her twenty years as a police officer, it had never ceased to amaze her that some of her colleagues seemed incapable of conversation. She very much got the impression that the six-foot solid man sitting in the back of the patrol car would tell her what she needed to know yet would not volunteer information without being asked the right questions.

'I'm all right,' he answered. 'More than I can say for Milton Bowman. The van driver's not looking too good either.'

She sighed and tucked the loose hair behind her ear. 'You're right there – about both of them. The van driver'll be fine but we're waiting to hear more about Milton.'

Luke watched her chew the side of her mouth and peer in the direction of the crowd of uniformed men and women battling to save one life.

'Has anyone told his wife?' said Luke.

Hazel's gaze snapped in his direction, frown creasing her forehead.

Pre-empting her question, he said, 'It was about the only thing he said to me. He told me that he was supposed to be at work and started to say "My wife" something or other, but I stopped him. I had to get him out of the car and try to stop the bleeding.'

'I'm not sure who's been told to tell her,' said Hazel. Under normal circumstances, it would be one of the PCs at the scene. Bearing in mind who the victim was, someone of equal or more senior rank would be given the unenviable task of knocking on Mrs Bowman's door to tell her that her husband was on his way to hospital. Whatever the outcome, life was never going to be the same again for anyone in the family.

Hazel steeled herself for a physically uncomfortable time, back twisted so she could turn to speak to her witness, heat of the day making her suit cling to her, as she got as much detail from Luke as she could about all that he'd seen, heard and done that morning.

Detective Inspector Harry Powell sat with his head in his hands at his desk at East Rise Police Station's incident room.

He had barely had time to sit down when he received the call that DI Milton Bowman had been flown to Sonbury city's Accident and Emergency and he wasn't expected to live.

Harry had got to work earlier than usual to catch up on paperwork, although all that consumed his thoughts now was the memory of Milton on the previous Friday evening, getting ready to leave the office before heading off home to take his wife out for a surprise meal. Harry ran his hands over the top of his head before rubbing his neck. A neck that had felt merely the pressure of an increasing workload until three or four minutes ago, and now it bore the burden of having to give the terrible news of a traffic accident to Linda Bowman.

At least that was what Harry was concentrating on – a traffic accident. When he'd last spoken to Milton he had seen the dark shadows under his eyes, watched him tighten the knot on his tie, all the while aware of a tenseness in his face he hadn't noticed before. Harry put it down to the upcoming chief inspector's board he knew his counterpart was desperate to pass, and the added burden of his drug reduction campaign.

'Special occasion, is it?' he'd asked with a hidden pang of jealousy. On the surface, Milton seemed to have it all: beautiful wife, a mortgage smaller than most people's credit card bill and he played golf with the assistant chief constable. In contrast, Harry had his job.

'No. I'm hoping it'll keep her off my back for another week or so. Things aren't too good between us at the moment.'

At the time, that had made Harry feel slightly better about himself. Only now, of course, it was churning his insides around. He stood up and made his way out of his office. He knew that no one else was in the incident room. Even the cleaners didn't come in before seven, but he'd been there to get ahead of the day, especially as he was on call for incidents in the county. A good night's sleep always eluded him when the phone could go at any minute, with a distant voice informing him there had been a murder, a shooting, a rape, a kidnap, or a ferry disaster, and asking how long he would be before he got there to take charge.

East Rise incident room was where he'd worked as a detective constable, before going away to the county town's police station at Riverstone to get himself promoted to sergeant, and then returning as a detective inspector. He paused in the centre of the room, seagulls screeching outside. The place held many happy memories for him, except he knew that when he recalled today it would bring back no positive thoughts.

Dismissing the idea of waiting for someone else to come on duty and accompany him to his destination, Harry went outside to the car park, got into his car and drove off to deliver some very bad news.

It was just before 8 a.m. when Harry pulled up outside Milton Bowman's address. He'd been there many times in the past but not for a few years. He had got to know Linda, become very fond of her and considered her a friend. Once or twice, Harry had had a glimpse of what he thought was the real Linda, one who wouldn't stand for any nonsense and could take care of herself. He hoped he was right: she would need all the strength she could muster in the next few months.

The last time Harry had been to the Bowmans' house was when he had dropped Milton home following a five-a-side match between East Rise incident room and one of the county's other incident rooms at North Downs. It had turned a bit ugly with East Rise losing by eight goals to two, riling Milton who went in for a tackle, breaking the opposition's top scorer's leg.

The irony of Milton's leg injury hadn't failed to pass

Harry by as he got out of his car and went past Linda's Mazda on the driveway to the front door. He rang the bell and waited.

Through habit, he ran an eye over the house. It might not have been enemy territory but he'd learned that it was best to be cautious. The curtains were pulled back, the upstairs bedroom window was open and the side gate was ajar. Something about the stillness of the house got to Harry. Quiet was usually a good thing, only not today. He felt a lurch in his stomach that told him things weren't right.

With his eyes still on the house, he backed down the drive, opened the car door and felt around in the glove compartment until his fingers grasped his Airwave radio and then his asp.

Because he was right-handed, the metal baton felt more natural in his right palm, although he chose not to extend the weapon; he had a feeling that the element of surprise was his best option. Radio silenced in the other hand, he made his way back along the driveway to the open gate.

It crossed Harry's mind that he might have assessed the situation incorrectly and Linda might be inside putting the kettle on, wondering what to do first that morning, with her husband on his way to work and their son away at university.

As he stood still, deciding whether to continue around the back of the house or whether to knock on the door, the sound of the landline ringing from the front room broke the silence. No one came to answer it, and the shrill noise eventually stopped when the answerphone cut in.

Harry instinctively broke into a run, hurtling through the gate, along the side of the house, past the kitchen door to the rear of the property. His breath caught and all he could hear was his heart hammering as he came to a stop and peered through the double glass doors to see Linda's body lying on the tiles, thick blood seeping from her skull.

Even though he took it all in with one glance, it was the first sight of her face with one eye closed and the other staring straight at him that would haunt his days.

Harry stared at the bloody face of Linda Bowman through the glass. He only took a second to surge into action, although it felt as though he'd stood still for minutes. He had seen bodies too numerous to recall. Some deaths were due to stabbings, some to gun shots, occasionally there'd be a drowning, once there'd been a man crushed beyond recognition by a metal skip dropped on him in an industrial accident, but not one of them hijacked his thoughts or filled his nightmares. It wasn't because he didn't care about people or his job, only that was what it was – a job. People killed each other and died horrifically every day, and frequently the bodies came his way. The difference was this body belonged to someone he knew. Harry liked Linda, he had eaten meals with Linda, he had danced with her at social functions. Harry had even admired Linda from afar, wondering why she stayed with a man like Milton. Harry had always thought that Linda was the sort of person who could have achieved anything in the right circumstances if she set her mind to it.

Now he found himself running towards her on the kitchen floor, having flung open the unlocked back door. His mind was racing. He was a professional and not a total fool. The intruder could still be on the premises. Getting himself killed wouldn't help anyone, and certainly not Linda.

He focused. He breathed. He stared at the Airwave radio in his hand and realized that at some point between reaching the back door and kneeling beside her he must have turned it on. He pressed the emergency button, overriding all other transmissions, and called for assistance.

Harry knew that as soon as he summoned help it would be on its way. His priority was Linda, but he fought the urge to sit beside her, try to stop the bleeding from her head, straighten her clothing, tilt her mouth back to breathe air into her lungs. Harry put his hand out to touch her face, and jerked it back as soon as he felt fluid beneath a swelling to her right temple. He had been to enough post-mortems and read enough pathologists' reports to recognize the signs of a large bleed beneath the skin. Although he was no medical expert, Harry's police experience over the years told him he was looking at a skull fracture.

Anger and rage gripped him as be fought the urge to charge from room to room, find whoever had done this and punch the living daylights out of them. He stopped himself for one reason only: he was good at his job and that meant someone, somewhere was going to face up to what they'd done to Linda. If he didn't rein in his feelings, he could be the one who jeopardized that.

He had to find whoever had done it.

Harry could see no signs of breathing from Linda and the black matted hair, caked in drying blood, pushed him towards the decision to leave her where she was and make sure that no one else was in the property. He felt for a pulse, even though he knew from looking at her that he was wasting his time. He couldn't ignore the risk of the offender hiding somewhere, but equally, he knew the torment he would suffer if there was someone else lying injured that he could have saved. One death in the house was bad enough: he wouldn't be responsible for leaving someone to draw their last breath whilst he lamented over Linda.

He cast his eyes over her face and had to stop himself from stroking her cheek. It would have been a kind parting gesture from one friend to another, but ever the professional, he couldn't risk contaminating the scene any further. Heartbreaking as it was, that was what she was now: a corpse and a crime scene. The woman who had offered him sound marriage advice a number of times when he'd asked her for help, the woman who had driven over to his house in the middle of the night when one of his children was sick and his wife was praying at her own mother's hospital bedside, the woman who had confided in him that her husband was having an affair and she didn't know what to do.

Harry had let Linda down, although he knew that the person who had really let her down was Milton.

Milton. If he was responsible for this, Harry could stay here right next to her. But if he was wrong about Milton, he had to move and do it fast. Any second now, sirens would shatter the suburban streets, alerting the killer that Linda's body had been discovered. That was, of course, if they hadn't seen his car pull up outside, heard him knock on the door and watched him sprint through the gate and down the side of the house.

I'm no good dead, thought Harry as he tore his gaze away. He ran his eyes over the knife block. It was full. He took this as a sign that today wouldn't be the day the stab-proof vest hanging in his office three miles away might have saved his life if he'd paused to put it on.

His heart was beating faster now, the adrenalin kicking in. In the hall Harry hesitated, briefly wondering whether he should go upstairs, or into the utility room and garage at the back of the house, or into the living room. He listened for sounds from anywhere else in the house.

All was still. Nothing stirred.

Mind made up, he was going to start with the utility room with its access to the back of the house. He took a step across the hall's thick carpet. The sounds of his movement were covered as his foot sank into the depths of grey wool. The sound he did hear, however, was the brushing of the front door as it was pushed open from outside, rubbing against the pile.

Harry spun on the spot, asp in hand, arm pulled back, about to extend the metal baton in his fist straight into the face of a uniform PC.

'Sorry, sir,' said the young lad, instinctively moving his head out of the direct line of his superior. 'We were told to make it a silent approach and the door was on the latch.'

Not wanting to waste time, Harry said, 'Get in the kitchen. Don't move her, just stand guard until we've checked the rest of the house. And tell one of the two officers who have just pulled up outside to stand by the front door, and the other to search the utility room that leads to the garage.' As he said 'utility room', Harry pointed at the back of the hallway.

The PC neither asked how he knew it was the utility room nor showed any signs that he found it interesting that the DI knew what lay beyond the door. He did as he was told and trained to do, and went to stand next to a woman who had been dead for some time.

Chapter 3

DC Hazel Hamilton had one ear tuned to the car's police radio as she took notes of Luke's version of the accident.

'I heard the car before I saw it,' said Luke. 'I started to run before I thought about it.'

She looked round at him, his face visible between the headrests, neutral and curious about everything going on around him.

Despite his reassurances that he was fine, she knew all too well that sometimes people didn't like to admit that they were feeling sick because of what they'd seen. She couldn't completely rule out delayed shock or that for all his bravado he was suffering.

She waited with her biro poised above the page in her pocket notebook for Luke to continue.

'I couldn't be completely accurate, but I suppose he was doing about forty miles an hour,' said Luke after a ten- or fifteen-second pause.

Even though Hazel now had her head down and was writing, she could see the man on the back seat of the car crane his neck towards the accident. It was natural for people to be curious, although rubberneckers always made her feel uneasy.

At that moment, her train of thought was interrupted by a voice on the radio summoning all free and available patrols to make their way to an address, possible intruder on premises, woman lying injured. She had a feeling that she was listening to the sounds of Major Crime being summoned to their next investigation.

The sound of her phone ringing from her pocket told her her instinct was right and she was about to get a whole lot busier.

To give herself some space and avoid being overheard, she climbed out of the car into the early morning heat and took a call from her former uniform inspector, Josh Walker. He was someone who had been a constant support to her before she'd returned to Major Crime. She listened intently, hardly uttered one word.

She ended the call and tapping the mobile phone into her empty hand glanced over her shoulder to the marked car, windows and doors shut, witness waiting for her return. She took in Luke as he sat impassive, watching her through the glass. He couldn't possibly know that she had just been instructed to find someone else to take his statement, then go and change her clothes to avoid cross-contamination from the scene, before heading off to DI Bowman's house.

Inspector Walker's last words to her had been, 'Someone's attacked his wife in their home. We think Milton did it.'

Chapter 4

By the time Hazel had showered, changed and arrived at the Bowman home, several marked and unmarked police cars, two grey CSI vans, an ambulance and a paramedic car were outside, and metres of police tape were strung across the road, marking out a sizeable area around the house. Two police community support officers stood on the cordon, one gripping the blue-and-white scene log, making a note of everyone going in and out, along with times and roles. No one got in or out without signing and giving a reason and everyone entering wore a white scene suit with hood, white overshoes and a white face mask.

At some distance from the cordon, the media were already in the street, trying their luck with anyone who would talk to them.

One reporter saw Hazel and said hello. He looked familiar from the local news but Hazel knew better than to talk to him. He had a job to do, as did she. The difference was that hers related to identifying, arresting and convicting a killer. His involved a three-minute news story that would be forgotten when the county's next unexplained death came along.

'Hello, Sergeant,' he said. 'I've heard there have been some exciting developments.'

She had to hand it to him – it was a great line chancing that she would at least confirm something new had happened, even if she went no further.

The young, charming reporter had overstepped the line by calling her 'Sergeant', something that she wasn't, and he was probably aware of.

He didn't even look crestfallen when she replied, 'Oh really. What's that then?'

'Just heard something was happening.'

The cameraman looked up into the trees lining both sides of the avenue and shifted his camera from one shoulder to the other.

'Let me know when you find out,' said Hazel, already walking away to the mobile incident room set up outside the cordon where the inspector was waiting. She didn't give the reporter another thought.

She didn't need a two-day media training course to know when a journalist was full of crap.

At the door of the mobile incident room, which was technically speaking a van, Hazel met with Josh Walker. He winked at her as he came out with tea in a polystyrene cup.

'World and his wife are here, Haze,' he said to her when he had led her safely out of earshot. 'Thanks for getting here so fast after I called you. This is a right cluster fuck. Looks like Milton did his wife in, and then drove into a wall or flowerbed or whatever the fuck it was.' He shook his head. 'It's unbelievable. Why would he do it?'

'Perhaps he didn't do it on purpose,' she replied, pulling out her shirt to allow some air to circulate. She was already feeling clammy, despite the change of shirt and suit. 'He didn't seem the type to take his own life.'

'What makes you say that?'

'I don't know.' She paused, studying the face of her old inspector, a man she'd asked advice of so many times and who had steered her in the right direction, been a constant in her career and made her smile when things hadn't gone according to plan.

'Perhaps it all got too much. We all have our dark days, Josh.'

Before he had a chance to answer her, another figure appeared in the doorway of the incident room. This time it was Harry Powell. He looked weary yet alert.

Hazel had worked with him in the Major Crime Department for some months now, and like most of the officers and staff in their division, Harry was easy to deal with. Sometimes he swore and shouted, but he knew how to get a job done properly.

Harry's phone rang, and Hazel took the momentary distraction as her chance to discuss him with Josh.

'You think he's OK?' she asked, nodding her head at the DI's back as he ducked back into the van. 'Did he find Milton's wife?'

'Yeah. Poor bastard's been friends with them for years. Not sure how much they all saw of each other lately. There's not much socializing going on these days. You know what it's like: when you've finished for the day, there's a tendency to get home as fast as possible. Harry told me he worked over two hundred and fifty hours last month and got called out on seven different occasions in the middle of the night.'

Hazel raised an eyebrow at her mentor. 'That's a lot of overtime. Who'd be an inspector? You don't even get paid for the extra hours.'

'Yeah, true, but I get to go to meetings with the superintendent and get shouted at for being a useless twat. It's what I live for. Anyway, the reason I wanted you here was because you're a trained family liaison officer and we may need you. I know that FLOs don't usually get deployed to the scene, it's just that I wanted to speak to you about it first before I put your name forward.'

'Really,' said Hazel, running through in her mind whether she could take on a family liaison officer role on top of personal commitments. The work meant extra hours and sometimes taking phone calls in the early hours of the morning, being available whenever the family needed you, certainly in the first few days at least, despite establishing times to ring.

'I'm only giving you the heads up for now,' said Josh. 'Milton's not looking too good as you know, and from Harry's description, the wife is definitely dead, although the paramedics are still inside. They have a son, so someone within the incident room's needed to speak to their boy. A lot of the trained officers in Major

Crime and from East Rise know the family. If I'm brutally honest, we're running out of options. We asked for help from another county although, quite frankly, that's not the preferred route. And I know that you'd be the best person for this one.'

'I see what you're saying,' said Hazel, 'let's keep this in-house. We don't want everyone knowing that the chances are one of our DIs killed his wife and then tried to commit suicide.'

'That's about it,' agreed Josh, casting an eye in the direction of the gathering news crews. 'But it's going to cause a total media storm when it does get out and I don't fancy the fallout.'

Chapter 5

'You'll need to take my clothes,' said Harry to Detective Chief Inspector Barbara Venice who was in overall charge of the murder investigation.

She mulled over what he'd said. Normally, she'd get a PC or DC to talk to witnesses about seizing their clothing except this wasn't an ordinary day, and it certainly wasn't an ordinary investigation. The procedures were the same no matter who the victims of such a crime were, and police officers and their families wouldn't receive preferential treatment. However, if things weren't done correctly, there would be a review and all manner of criticism thrown at her and her team for failing to investigate. And all because the only suspect they had so far was one of their own.

'I don't need to tell you how careful we're going to have to be, Harry. I've already requested an out-of-county deputy SIO to lessen the chance of being accused of hiding anything.'

Barbara Venice paused to glance down at her policy file open in front of her.

'Tell you what, get yourself away from here. Give me your car keys and we'll take it back to the nick. In the meantime, I'll find a patrol to run you home, but it'll be best if you sit on a paper sheet in the back of the car. I don't want any contact traces dropping off you before we get your clothes off.'

In spite of how the morning had gone, Harry smirked at her.

'Pack it in, you silly great sod,' she said. 'I'm being extra cautious with this one.'

Barbara Venice was the same age as Harry although she looked years younger, and unlike Harry, hadn't had one of her front teeth knocked out playing rugby. The false tooth hid it well, but the drinking and socializing weren't so easily magicked away with a trip to the dentist for an implant.

'Seriously, Harry, how are you doing?'

He knew it was genuine concern: Barbara was a decent woman who kept an eye on her staff. Over the years she'd been at a few social functions with Harry when Milton and Linda had turned up. She had seen Harry drinking with Milton, but always watching out for Linda. On one occasion, Harry had driven his friend's wife home when Milton had disappeared from the bar, nowhere to be found.

'Yeah,' he replied, 'I'm OK. Well, it's probably time that I was sitting on crinkly, noisy brown paper and on my way home to slip into something a little more comfortable.'

He glanced down at his feet. 'I suppose that you're

also going to want my brand-new leather shoes, worn only once, and I won't be getting them back for months.'

'I'll make sure you get a receipt.'

Harry gave an empty laugh. 'Who were you thinking of to run me home? Hazel Hamilton's outside with Josh Walker. All right to ask her?'

'Can you hang on here a moment?' she said. 'I need to speak to Josh anyway.'

Harry did as he was told and stood beside the cushioned seats at the table where DCI Venice had been writing up her policy file. The A4 book was open at her last entry and Harry glimpsed the words, 'Risk assess DI Harry Powell. Contact with the inquiry?'

He couldn't blame her for distancing him from it all: he'd discovered his old friend's body for starters. Harry indulged himself for one minute, let his guard down and shut his eyes. He was alone now. He could risk it.

The image of Linda's body, rigor mortis already starting to set in, as she lay on her side facing towards the rear door. She'd had her back to the hallway.

Harry's eyes snapped open. He hadn't realized until this moment the significance of the way she was facing. How could he have missed that? She had her back to the door, meaning that someone she knew and trusted had been in the kitchen with her.

One eye had been staring straight at him.

Linda had such beautiful green eyes.

Perhaps she'd been trying to watch for him, waiting for someone to come and help her.

Harry shook his head. 'Don't think such stupid bollocks,' he said.

Barbara appeared in the open doorway of the mobile incident room and raised an eyebrow at him.

'Are you talking to yourself?'

'Barb, Linda had her back to the door – the spot where someone would have been standing talking to her. It must have been someone she knew.'

She took a step towards him, leaned forward, but stopped short of actually taking his hand in hers.

'It's been a shitty day for all of us. Go home, let Josh bag your clothes up, and someone will be over to take your statement.'

He felt worn out, but not ground down. 'I can do my own bloody—'

A hand came up from his superior officer to silence him. It worked.

'Milton is a friend of yours, Linda is a friend of yours, and you found her with the back of her head caved in. Do you really think I'm going to let you write your own statement?'

'OK,' sighed Harry. 'Who are you going to send to me?'

'Not sure at the moment.' She looked down at a list of priority enquiries on the table, blew out her cheeks and said, 'Once I've allocated the FLO, house-to-house, CCTV, Senior CSI and heaven knows what else ... I'm thinking Simone Piper?'

'You fucking what? I don't want her – she's bat-shit mental.'

'Harry, how on earth did you get through your inspectors' board? You can't say that sort of thing.'

'How about Hazel Hamilton? She's normal.'

'I think that Josh has earmarked her for FLO. Don't look at me like that. I'll see what I can do.'

Harry leaned against the side of the table and crossed his arms, the beginnings of a smile on his freckled face.

'And don't forget,' she said, 'the way she was facing may indicate she was surprised. Or of course that she was moved after she was attacked. We won't know more until the CSIs have finished and the post-mortem's been carried out.'

'Are you going to let me know the result of either?'

'Not before you've got out of my way, handed your clothes over and told us in writing everything that happened this morning.'

Harry raised his eyes to the van's ceiling, stained with something dark he hoped was coffee.

'You know where I am when you need me,' he said, making his way to the door.

He stuck his head out and saw Josh and Hazel deep in conversation which stopped abruptly as soon as he appeared.

Weary with the world, Harry made his way to Josh who had his car keys in his hand and was gesturing in the direction of a marked police car, ready as instructed to take his plain-clothes counterpart home.

Harry was fully aware that he was being escorted home by an inspector and not a constable or sergeant because he had a reputation for being somewhat argumentative. It had surprised everyone when he'd been promoted from sergeant after years of falling out with management over a variety of issues, but he was revered by the rank and file because he always stood up for his staff. No one wanted to take the chance that he wouldn't fully cooperate and hand his clothes over. No one wanted to take the chance that he might be wearing a suit and tie covered in telltale signs of blood-pattern distribution.

Anyone could be a killer. Even an old friend.

DI Harry Powell hadn't been made a suspect so far, or, irrespective of rank, he'd have found himself under arrest and dressed in police station custody-suite-issued jogging bottoms and sweatshirt.

But blood splatters were the least of his worries at this point in time: he was more concerned with what the inquiry would reveal in relation to Linda and Milton's well-hidden personal lives.

Chapter 6

Afternoon of Monday 5 June

'As if it's not fucking bad enough that I've had to sit on shiny brown paper all the way home, Josh has buggered off with my newest whistle, and I'll never see my shoes again.'

Hazel picked up her mug of tea from the kitchen table where she'd made herself at home, and said, 'If you're going to talk cockney, I should perhaps get an interpreter.'

'Where are you from? Leeds?' asked Harry.

'Manchester.'

'Why did you end up in the South East?'

'I heard how warm and friendly you all were. And besides, I had to go home and get changed too to avoid cross-contamination from being with a witness at Mr Bowman's accident this morning. Sir, can we get back to the statement?'

He drummed his fingertips on the pine tabletop and nodded at her.

He wasn't going to be obstructive, they both knew that, but he wasn't just going to roll over either. Even despite the terrible events of the morning, he wouldn't go off script and allow people to see the real Harry. He'd cry in the privacy of his own home, but not until he was alone. Any tears he shed for Linda would be done in secret.

They were both aware that Hazel had been chosen because she wouldn't leave until she had what she'd come for. That, and the stark truth that there weren't that many people available to pick from.

'Shouldn't they have sent a DS?' asked Harry.

'We didn't have one, so you've got me.' Hazel knew better than to argue, but still, DI or not, he was a witness, and a witness in a murder inquiry, so she should be treating him with the same respect as anyone else.

'Are you OK speaking to me, or would you prefer someone else?' she asked, not completely convinced this was going to work.

Harry scratched at the stubble already creeping over his face. 'Course I am. Tell me, why did you leave uniform and come back to Major Crime?'

'I heard that you were going to be my new DI,' she said, shutting down the question immediately. 'So, can we start with what time you left the incident room to go to Milton and Linda Bowman's home?'

He knew better than to keep avoiding talking about what he'd seen. He wanted the person responsible found, and found quickly, but he wasn't sure how he was going to be able to pick the right words. Hazel was a good officer, and wouldn't tell a soul outside the incident room what Harry told her. A number of officers and staff would have access to his statement, although only a few would speak to her directly and ask for her opinion on whether Harry was in some way responsible for Linda's death.

'Can you describe how Linda was when you first saw her?' said Hazel, tone even, pen poised, but eyes on Harry.

She watched his facial muscles tighten, saw him slowly blink, tighten his grip on his coffee mug.

'She was looking straight at me. Well, one of her eyes was—'

The beginnings of a sob came from Harry. It was the kind of noise someone made when their distress had built inside them, to the point of boiling over.

He put his hand out to stop her from speaking. If she gave him words of kindness now, he couldn't be sure he could stop himself. He was used to being the one who rocked up at people's doors, told them bad news, explained what was going to happen and tried to pick up the pieces. He'd done it his whole life, personal and professional. No amount of bravado he showed to his family, friends and colleagues had ever let them see how much he mourned for butchered and raped strangers with only himself for company.

He was a decent man, but his PR was all wrong.

For the next couple of hours, Hazel asked Harry questions and he answered them.

Twice Hazel pulled a small packet of tissues from

inside her jacket hanging on the back of the chair and pushed them across to him. Twice he took one and passed the rest of the packet back to her.

'OK,' she said at last. 'You know what comes next, Harry.'

He raised his eyebrows at her: firstly, because he had no idea what she was talking about, and secondly because she'd switched at some point from calling him 'sir' and was now using his first name. He'd been so caught up in what he'd been telling her, concentrating, trying to get the details correct so that anything that could help find Linda's killer would be written down and passed to an incident room of detectives, he wasn't aware of when this change in familiarity had taken place. Perhaps it was around the second or third coffee, or when he'd poured himself a large brandy.

Harry looked down at his empty glass then drained the remains of his coffee.

'Do you want to read your statement yourself to check it, or shall I read it out to you?' Hazel waited for his reply.

'I'm sure it's fine,' he said, looking around for the bottle of Martell. He pushed himself from the chair, scraping the legs across the tiled floor, setting Hazel's teeth on edge. He took a stride towards the draining board where he'd left the dwindling bottle, turned with it in his hand and said, 'Would have been a time you'd have joined me. I won't tell if you don't.'

'I'll read it out to you,' said Hazel, stifling a sigh.

'Stop me if you're not happy with the content of this,'

she said and began to read from the pages and pages of handwritten statement sheets in front of her.

Hazel concentrated on what she was reading, but was all too aware that Harry was staring at her as he heard his version of finding Linda Bowman in her own kitchen, pieces of her skull stuck to the floor, blood so thick it was no longer red but black.

Finally, Hazel sat back and said, 'All I need now are some signatures from you and I'll be out of your way.'

Slowly, he sat back up. His face was unreadable, but then it usually was.

He picked up a black pen from the table, pulled the statement forms towards him and began to sign, first the top left-hand side of page one, followed by his signature on the bottom left, then the same with each sheet up to the twenty-fourth. He only glanced up once he'd put his final signature after the last word.

'I suppose you're going to start asking me all sorts of questions now, such as my date of birth, where I was born and how tall I am,' he said with a frown.

'Or, you can turn the page and fill it in yourself.'

'No, it's your job, and besides, I'm now pissed. Sure you won't join me?'

'Is there anyone I can call for you?' It was her turn to put her hand up to stop Harry from interrupting. 'I know you're going to tell me that you're not the usual kind of witness and you've seen it all before, but I know from personal experience, not just through this job, how much these things can build up and get to you. So try to forget that you're a DI, and let me know if there's anyone I can call for you, or if you'd like someone to be here for the rest of the day.'

Harry gave a short hollow laugh, looked up at the kitchen clock, adorned with cobwebs, and said, 'No one's coming back here tonight. Not unless my luck really improves.'

He knew better than to ask her to come back to join him for a nightcap after she went off duty. Even Harry recognized that asking her to have a drink with him for a third time was crossing a boundary. He didn't need to be investigated for sexual harassment on top of everything else.

Paperwork collected and jacket back on, Hazel was ready to leave. Harry stood up to follow her to the front door.

As they got to the door, Hazel reached for the handle at the same time as Harry stretched across to open it. Their hands remained for a second where they were: Hazel's beneath Harry's. Awkwardly they stared at each other, both a little taken aback by the intimacy of the act. They'd spent hours in the same room, at the same table, yet this was the closest they'd been to each other, and it made both of them feel uncomfortable in a way neither had expected.

Hazel moved her hand away, and before she knew what she was thinking, said, 'Perhaps we'll have that drink another time.'

Her own words had surprised her, though not as much as they'd jolted Harry towards the right side of sobriety.

He stood looking at her, mouth slightly open, free hand rubbing at the stubble on the side of his face, the other still on the door handle.

He tugged the door open and said, 'Well, see you later.'

'Yes, bye,' said Hazel, stepping outside into the late-afternoon heat. She walked to the end of the driveway, turned to say something, and saw Harry close the front door.

'You idiot,' she said to herself as she got back into her unmarked car. 'Of course he wasn't asking you out.'

She drove away, face still reddened from the humiliation of misreading the entire situation.

Chapter 7

Doug Philbert, another of Major Crime's detective inspectors rapidly dispatched from North Downs incident room, was not usually a man to lose his temper. This particular day, however, hadn't got any better since finding out that one of their DIs was about to die, the same DI's wife had been murdered, and her body discovered by another DI who Doug was pretty certain had a soft spot for the murder victim. To top it all off, Doug was privy to some uncomfortable information regarding the Bowmans' marriage and history. He'd then got into a row with Operational Planning about staffing, had to explain to his own wife that he wouldn't be home any time soon, and had to cancel a lecture at Training School for the mock incident room he was supposed to be running for those on the accreditation pathway for their detective constable status. Doug could still recall the CID course when it was six weeks packed into ten, including a day at the county's brewery and another getting legless on the ferry across to France. That was soon stopped when police helmets and truncheons were found adorning the walls of pubs and cafés in Boulogne, in exchange for plain-clothes officers drinking free Stella Artois by the bucketload. He never did find out where his own police-issue headgear ended up, but he suspected if he scoured the bars across the Channel he'd find it there somewhere, gathering dust on a shelf, his force number in permanent marker pen inside its rim.

He picked up the phone and called Inspector Josh Walker. He could tell by the background noise that Josh was outside, Doug presumed still at the scene at the Bowmans' home address.

'Inspector Walker. How can I help you?'

'Hi, Josh, it's Doug Philbert. I'm in need of an FLO, and rumour has it that you've already had a word with Hazel Hamilton.'

'Yeah, she's OK to do it, I think, but as she's one of your DCs, the final decision's yours.'

'I'm going to have to allocate it to her,' said Doug with a sigh. 'She's not ideal for this one and I've already had to send her to take Harry's statement too. We simply don't have enough staff, as usual.'

'Oh, right,' said Josh. 'That's raised another issue. Can I run something else by you?'

Doug could hear the background hum lessen as Josh took himself off somewhere quieter to speak.

'Just got back into my car. I don't want anyone over-hearing what I'm about to say,' said Josh. He sighed. 'Harry's a mate, a good mate, but is he going to cause her any problems?'

Doug wasn't totally sure how he should react to the question; pausing only seemed to prod Josh into continuing.

'It's common knowledge that Harry had a thing for Linda Bowman. Everyone saw how he looked at her. Everyone, that is, except for Milton and Harry's own wife.'

'Estranged wife,' corrected Doug. 'What are you telling me here? Linda ends up dead because after Harry's been making puppy eyes at her for twenty years he finally snaps and kills her? Not only is that hugely unlikely, detective inspector or not, but he'd have found himself in a cell by now with the duty solicitor on their way if, for one second, there was any suggestion, likelihood or evidence to point towards his involvement.'

Doug rubbed his temple with his free hand, regretting not putting the call on speakerphone so he could at least try to manoeuvre his headache away. His hand hesitated over the phone, then he decided it was best if no one overheard Josh's concern.

'Hazel will be in no danger, I promise,' clarified Doug.

'Fucking hell, Doug. I didn't think he was going to do Hazel in – I was worried about him trying to shag her. Now, I'm bloody worried.'

In his temporary poky office next to the incident room, Doug shook his head at what he had heard himself say. He had too much on his mind today, and was letting things slip out.

Feeling the pain behind his eyes start to blur his vision, Doug took off his glasses and laid them on the table. He could see even less now, of course, but at least he was able to massage his temples with more ease.

'He probably will try to give her one,' said Doug, 'but chancing your arm with a woman isn't the same as being a physical menace.'

'OK then. I'll ring Hazel, tell her the news and send her to see you.'

By the time he'd taken a couple of painkillers, washed down with lukewarm coffee, and put his glasses back on, Doug glanced up to see Hazel standing at his open office door, about to knock.

'Hello, Hazel,' said Doug. 'Come in.'

She took a step inside, unsure whether to sit down. She had returned to Major Crime over six months ago after having spent years within its walls working on murders, rapes, kidnaps, even a couple of bomb hoaxes. Being there felt as if she was back within her comfort zone, although taking a statement from one of the department's DIs who had just discovered the murdered body of another DI's wife was new ground for all of them. Even Doug Philbert looked out of sorts and he was always calm and collected.

Hazel waved Harry's statement at the DI. 'Thought you'd be the best person to give this to,' she said. She was aware it was supposed to go into the tray to be registered on HOLMES but experience told her she should be handing it over to someone in person on the chance that this was an operation where the paperwork was to be kept under wraps.

He held his hand out to take the sheets of paper from her.

'Please sit down,' Doug said, smiling at her. He liked Hazel, and couldn't remember anyone having a bad word to say about her, either professionally or personally. She had always struck him as somewhat dull, yet fundamentally decent.

'Sir, I understand that I'm to be the family liaison officer for the Bowmans' son.'

'We had some difficulty locating him. He wasn't at university where we thought he was going to be, so that's a slight welfare concern, but also it suggests he might in some way be responsible for his own mother's murder.'

Hazel raised her eyebrows.

'Oh, I see,' she said. 'I guess we still aren't sure about most of the facts.'

'It's early days yet,' he continued. He was about to tell her that she definitely was going to spend the foreseeable future taking care of the Bowmans' son, despite all FLOs being told that they would only be assigned jobs after their own personal circumstances or feelings had been taken into account. He would go through the motions and ask her if she had any problems with this particular deployment, but short of ringing in sick for the next two months, she was going whether she liked it or not.

'You're up shit creek without a paddle,' said Hazel,

'and I'm being sent because you don't really have anyone else.'

Doug fought the urge to merely agree with her. He was management at the end of the day. He was aware Hazel's father had died in a car crash and her role in this investigation might well cause her anguish, yet what was he supposed to do? He had to send someone and she was the easiest answer for him.

'It's because of your particular skill set in dealing with matters like this – delicate matters, not to mention you're extremely capable. And I won't lie about this bit, we're short of trained liaison officers. You're correct about that one. You need to go and see Travis Bowman this evening. He's staying at his friend's house. See the DS on this operation. He's got the details.'

With a barely concealed sigh, she stood up to go.

'Oh, Hazel,' Doug said as she reached the door, 'can you keep me updated if Harry Powell contacts you again?'

There was something in the expression flitting across her features that he couldn't read but interpreted as concern. Doug couldn't help but think that Harry had already done something he perhaps shouldn't have.

'You will let me know if you have any issues, won't you?' he asked.

'Course, sir,' she said, turning away so that he couldn't see her face redden for the second time in an hour.

As Hazel made her way to see the incident room's DS, she took her phone out of her pocket and reread the text from Harry. 'Can you call me? Forgotten something. Even better, come over if you're still on duty.'

She couldn't help herself: this was the start of something that was only going to be trouble for both of them. Fighting it was just too difficult, and giving in seemed the more pleasant option.

Chapter 8

Whatever had happened in Hazel's past, she managed to cope and lead a normal life. Until she turned fifteen, her life had been normal, boring even. That all changed when she trotted down the stairs one night to the sounds of her mother crying to find her being consoled by two police officers. They had come to tell her mother that there had been a car accident and her father was dead.

Her life changed so rapidly and drastically, she didn't adjust to her change in circumstances, just woke up one day and everything was different.

Before she knew it, she was at her mother's cousin's house eighty miles from her own home town, sharing a bedroom with a twelve-year-old girl she was in some way related to, though had met only once and had nothing in common with, other than a few long-forgotten relatives.

Following her father's funeral, Hazel kept her head down and remained a serious and studious girl. Before long, she was a serious and studious woman working in a local hotel as a receptionist before deciding to join the police.

The image of the two officers standing in her kitchen had never left her.

Contact with her mother was limited after she left home. It was clear to everyone that Mrs Hamilton never recovered from the news of her husband's sudden death, and she failed in every way to give her own daughter any comfort and support.

Never once did Hazel complain to anyone about her mother's behaviour: she was only trying to survive and deal with it the best way she could.

Hazel loved both of her parents and always would. Now her life was about making as many positive contributions to other people's lives, whatever the personal cost.

Chapter 9

As soon as DCI Barbara Venice thought she was about to get two minutes to herself, her mobile phone rang once again.

She picked it up with a sigh and as the display showed *Number withheld*, she answered with her corporate, 'Barbara Venice. How can I help you?'

Such was the urgency of the caller's tone that when Josh Walker opened the mobile-incident-room door and made to step inside, she gave a tight smile in his direction and held up her palm to warn him off.

For several minutes she sat and listened, fighting against the instinct to write down and record in her policy file what the voice was telling her. Except she knew there was a time and a place to keep notes on something so sensitive, and indeed dangerous. There was no doubt about it, what she was hearing was the last thing she was expecting to find out, and it wasn't going to make her job or the job of Major Crime any easier.

Hunched over the table, elbows supporting her arms,

one hand clutching the phone to her ear, the other hand grabbing at her hair, was how she remained for some time. It was only when she felt a sharp pain to her scalp that she realized quite how much force she was applying and it dawned on her just how transfixed she was.

When the call ended, she remained where she was, incredulous at the new information. For a moment, she didn't know how to react.

The secrets that any marriage or relationship held were often a surprise to her, even after so many years as a police officer. The people she worked alongside were usually the same as any other cross-section of society, but how she hadn't known about the Bowmans' ability to pull the wool over everybody's eyes was beyond her.

They had seemed to be such a normal family, and now all of that was shattered. Just how had they managed to keep the truth about Linda a secret for so long?

Barbara looked up as the door opened again.

Josh's face appeared in the gap. 'I couldn't hear you talking so I gathered you'd finished your call.'

She nodded slowly at him.

'Everything OK, Barbara?'

'Not really,' she said as she blew out her cheeks and exhaled a long, slow breath. 'All I can tell you at the moment, is that this isn't going to be straightforward and from the content of the call I've just taken, this is one murder which is really going to bring the pains on.'

Chapter 10

Evening of Monday 5 June

Hazel found out what she could from the incident room's detective sergeant, got an FLO log book, and drove towards Aiden Bloomfield's house. She'd been told that Milton and Linda Bowman's son Travis was now being looked after by his friend's family, and officers were already at the house. As usual with a family liaison deployment, she wasn't totally sure what she was walking into, but that was one of the aspects of the role she loved so much. Checks would have been carried out on the premises she was going to, as well as the people in it and connected to it; however, possibly not everyone in the house had previously come to the attention of the judicial system. These were the ones who were waiting to strike, or possibly even already had, just hadn't been caught. They were usually the worst kind.

During her time at Major Crime, Hazel had been sent to work with many families, some of which were more pleased to see her than others. Rape victims were sometimes the hardest to deal with mentally, as they had their own type of bereavement to contend with. Some murder victims' families had welcomed her into their home, while some had treated her with outright hostility and distrust, only willing to meet with their solicitor present. Whatever the situation, she'd loved them all. It was dealing with people at the end of the day. And people who needed help, whether they wanted it or not.

DC Hazel Hamilton had no reason to doubt that her current deployment would be equally as interesting.

She knew that this one would also be out of the ordinary, although it was fair to say that they were all embedded in her memory: the unpredictability of dealing with people under horrendous pressure made all deployments unique. This one, however, featured a nineteen-year-old boy whose mother had been murdered and whose father was about to die. She couldn't picture Travis as anything other than a boy, even though legally he was a man. What adult wouldn't buckle under the pressure of the last twelve hours' horror, let alone a teenager?

The satnav she'd borrowed from the incident room, along with the filthy unmarked Skoda, was indicating that she was about to turn into the Bloomfields' road. It didn't escape her notice that the houses were detached, some gated and all worth at least twice that of the Bowmans' home, if not three times.

Pulling up outside number 17, Hazel glanced towards the property and saw the outline of a woman appear in the downstairs front window. The figure peered out into the street, before rushing out of sight into the darkness of the house. By the time Hazel had put the satnav away and got her paperwork together, the front door was open.

They were expecting her.

She felt an adrenalin rush as she was about to enter the unknown. There was a chance that one of the people in the house was a murderer. It crossed her mind that it might even be Travis Bowman. Still, even Hazel wasn't prepared to rush in and arrest the young lad with little more justification than her bleak view of the human race.

Checking that her Airwave radio was in her bag, her PAVA spray in her jacket pocket and her asp tucked into her trouser pocket, Hazel got out of the car and locked the doors. She was aware that she was being watched by the person at the door, and thought that it was probably the woman who had seen her pull up in the street.

As Hazel walked up the driveway, she saw in the early evening summer light that the woman waiting for her was in her late thirties, attractive face creased by a frown and an air of concern about her.

She went past the marked police car outside the house and towards the woman she assumed to be Aiden Bloomfield's mother. To all the world, she appeared to be a concerned individual, mum to a young man whose friend's own mother had been murdered and whose friend's father had been airlifted to hospital. Hazel saw something else. This was possibly a woman who knew more than she was letting on and who was covering for Travis, or more likely, her own son.

Wasn't that what parents did? They did anything to protect their own children, even if it meant assisting them to cover up a murder and going to prison themselves. It wasn't the first time, and it wouldn't be the last.

'Hello,' said Hazel, showing her warrant card. 'Are you Aiden's mum?'

'Yes, please come inside,' she said, moving out of Hazel's way. 'I'm Jenny.'

The officer stepped inside the wide hallway, running an eye over the large staircase leading to the next level, and several feet of oak flooring. While Hazel appreciated that a lot of money had been spent on the house and its furnishings, she was also aware of the family shrine of glass photo frames adorning the walls behind her.

She could hear her two uniform officers talking and voices coming over their radios.

Hazel, with her back still to the wall, said, 'I'm Hazel. I'm a police officer and I've been asked to be Travis's family liaison officer. How's he doing?'

Jenny Bloomfield gave a jerky shrug and let her hands fall to her sides. 'It's difficult to say. It's bad enough what's happened to Linda. It gives me goosebumps. I only saw her a few days ago and offered her a lift to the train station. She said she fancied a walk, and now I feel so bad that that was the last time I saw her, walking away from me.

'The two officers here broke the news and he doesn't seem to have taken it in yet. He wants to go to the hospital to see his dad but they were talking about taking him to King's College Hospital in London, into theatre, so until we know, there's no point in Travis going anywhere.'

'Well, that's one of the things I'm here to help with,' said Hazel, wondering whether to tell this woman more, then dismissing it. 'Can I meet him now?'

She was led into a room off the hallway through an open door. The room was lit only by the dying light of the evening sun and a large table lamp in the far right-hand corner. In front of that sat an armchair. Hazel could make out the shape of a man sunk back into the chair. The position of the furniture meant his features were darkened yet his size was all the more pronounced.

About halfway between her and the man in the chair was a three-seater sofa with a uniform officer perched at each end.

'Hello,' she said, 'I'm Hazel, also a police officer.'

'I didn't realize how dark it's getting in here,' said Jenny as she stood just inside the room and reached over and turned on the wall lights.

As she did so, the man stood up. From the distance of thirty feet or so away, Hazel estimated him at six foot four, early twenties, biceps the size of most men's thighs. The short sleeves of his navy-blue T-shirt were taut across his upper arms and chest.

'This is Travis,' said the uniform officer closest to Hazel. 'We were waiting on an update about his dad.'

All thoughts she'd had on the journey over about

Travis still being a boy were forgotten. She could see the resemblance to his father in his face, a man she had only worked with on two occasions, neither of which she'd enjoyed. Milton Bowman hadn't been her type of man. Harry Powell, however, was.

To her annoyance, her thoughts had flitted to Harry when she was supposed to be here as family liaison officer to the detective inspector's son whose mother had just been murdered. The job came first, always. She put her momentary lack of concentration down to the heat of the day, not to mention the end of it being nowhere in sight.

'Please, Hazel, sit down,' said Jenny. 'I'll see where Aiden's got to.'

As she turned to leave the room, Hazel glanced at her and took in her tight-fitting light blue dress and bare feet. She switched her gaze back to Travis and thought she'd caught him watching his friend's mother's retreating backside.

Hoping she was wrong, she took the seat nearest to him, waited until he sat down again, and then put her brand-new A4 investigator's notebook on her lap. Her pen was clipped to the top of the cover but she had no intention of writing at this stage. This was the part that intrigued her: meeting the family, helping them whilst keeping her distance. Watching what they did. Hazel could already feel that something wasn't right here and so far, no one had told her very much at all.

That was still to come.

Chapter 11

The black Range Rover pulled to a stop at the road leading to the twenty-storey block of flats. It was the only hideous monstrosity to blot East Rise's skyline, and it took its job very seriously. As well as the building being so ugly it was offensive, it managed to house over half of the seaside town's undesirables. This, of course, made it much easier for the police to know where to concentrate resources and early morning search warrants, and was a very useful starting point for those wishing to track down anyone who was the wrong side of the law.

The night was beginning to draw in, leaving enough light for the driver to watch for signs of hostility or unwelcome attention from rivals in the occupants' line of business. He glanced out through the window and said to the two passengers, 'It's the fourth floor and everything you'll need's in there.'

Without looking at the man next to him, the driver pointed at the glove compartment, heard it open and said, 'See you in ten minutes. If I have to drive off, you know where I'll be.'

The other two men, large imposing figures, both over six feet tall, got out and made their way to the entrance of the building.

They went in through the unlocked door and began their ascent to the flat they had been briefed to attend.

Within a couple of minutes, neither of them the slightest bit out of breath in spite of their bulk, they were standing outside number 417. They exchanged a look, a nod in agreement that it was about to begin, and one of the men lifted his hand and rapped twice on the door. A heavy rapid knock that reverberated along the corridor with its cheap shiny flooring and sounded off the bare walls. The dusk was settling in and didn't find much resistance, what with a window at either end of the narrow twenty-five metre long hallway, and only three working light bulbs to illuminate the misery.

A noise behind the door made both of them take a tentative step backwards. Those who were cornered were usually the most unpredictable.

'Open up, Vinny,' were the only words needed.

The door was flung open to reveal a weedy man, mid-twenties, although he appeared much older.

Drugs would do that to a person.

In his left hand was a carving knife.

'Bloody hell, Vinny,' laughed the door-knocker. 'Put that knife down, will you? You're shaking like a shitting dog.'

Uninvited, both men stepped inside and shut the door behind them.

'Milo,' stammered Vinny as he backed away, knife

dropping to his side. 'I'm really pleased to see you. I was really worried it was the other crew. Me and Si here were just saying that we were about to call you and find out what was going on. Weren't we?'

He glanced over his shoulder at another equally sad individual who had remained rooted to his seat on the sofa up until this point. Even now, his only contribution was to nod and look heroin-worn, Adam's apple bobbing up and down in anticipation of what was to come.

Milo moved towards Vinny and grabbed his arm, took the knife from his grasp. No resistance was met. 'What the fuck are you doing?' said Milo right in Vinny's face.

He watched the sad specimen in front of him swallow, shut his eyes and then heard him say, 'We were waiting for you. It's been really shit around here at the minute. Police are everywhere: it's the summer and all the tourists means there's a load more of them and it's getting difficult.'

'I don't give a fuck. And neither does Tandy. He's my boss, you see, so if I don't do my job, he gives me a swift kick in the bollocks. I'm your boss, so if you don't do your job, I kick you in the bollocks.'

True to his word, Milo then released Vinny's arm and in one swift motion, brought his right leg up so that his foot connected with the drug addict's testicles.

The immediate effect was Vinny dropping to the floor.

Milo stood guard whilst his associate made his way to the sofa.

'Simon,' he said as he watched the young man attempt to become invisible by sinking back into the stained cushions. 'You seem like the brighter of the two, although there really isn't much in it. Here's the mobile you're to call us on if there's any problem. It's a pay-as-you-go and it has Tandy's number in it. You lose it, flog it or use up the credit prior to our deal, you won't just get a kick in the nads, I'll cut them off and shove them up your arse. You understand?'

A frantic nodding for several seconds met his stare until he said, 'Well, you enjoy this lovely day by the seaside and we'll be in touch.'

The two of them left the flat and made their way back down the stairs.

When they reached the Range Rover, they climbed inside, shut the doors and settled back in their seats.

'All OK?' said the driver as he indicated to pull out.

'Oh yeah,' said Milo. 'The great thing about junkies is they've got no bollocks.'

'Hope they have,' was the reply. 'I've just threatened to cut Simon's off. I'd really hate it to look like an empty threat.'

Chapter 12

As Hazel sat watching Travis, she made no move to write anything down in her FLO log. That was for later when she was alone. The notebook was for times, dates, telephone numbers and the recording of the visits. The log book showed their content. That was always the interesting part. Hazel had been deployed to violent families who had lost sons through drug wars, recidivist criminals who had lived by the sword and literally died by the sword, and most recently to the family of a nine-year-old girl who had been abducted and murdered by her own uncle, a situation that almost made her hand in her warrant card and resign. It hadn't looked that way to start with, but within minutes of her arrival in their neat, middle-class house, she felt something crawling up her spine, burrowing into her brain.

She hadn't reached that point yet, although the niggling had started.

'I know your dad,' said Hazel, careful to use the right tense, 'and I'd met your mum a couple of times. I'm sorry to meet you under these circumstances.'

These weren't platitudes, but she still waited and tried to read Travis's face.

He gave a wan smile; at least he looked worn out. From an investigator's point of view, that was a good sign. He glanced down at his hand resting on the arm-rest. He ran his thumbnail backwards and forwards across the fabric.

He had tears in his eyes as he looked back up to meet Hazel's steady gaze.

'Can I go see my dad?' he asked.

Hazel heard the two uniform officers on the sofa behind her get up. She waited until they'd left and she'd heard the soft click of the door as it shut.

'Travis, there's no easy way to tell you this—'

She broke off as he threw his head back against the chair and his hands flew up to cover his face. Silent sobbing racked his gigantic frame.

As a trained officer, she knew not to try and phys-ically console the teenager although it was fighting a natural human instinct that existed within us all. Such an act of intimacy at such an early meeting gave out the wrong impression. Besides, Hazel didn't know if, in the near future, this young man would be declared a suspect in his own mother's murder, and how would it look months down the line in Crown Court if the family liaison officer had been cuddling the lad within minutes of walking in the door? Better to be criticized for keeping her distance than acting inappropriately. It was a fine line, like most of policing: damned if you did and damned if you didn't.

'Your dad was taken to King's College Hospital by air ambulance, and despite everything they did, he died.' She paused and for the first time, looked down. This part she really hated. No matter how many death messages she'd given, none were ever easy, and each and every single one remained in her memory. They jumped into her mind at random times: buying glue at the supermarket to help her eight-year-old second cousin with an art project made her think of the parents of a fifteen-year-old boy who had died while sniffing glue, and how she'd gone to their home at 6.15 one Sunday morning to ruin their lives forever.

DC Hazel Hamilton had never before broken the news to a teenager that his father was dead. Policing had its own shop of horrors.

'Travis, I can't imagine how you feel right now. Can I call anyone else for you? Family member?'

He shook his head, hands still in front of his face. Something that sounded like 'No' came out in a rasp.

The part that would come soon from the police officer was all about setting ground rules for when Travis could and couldn't call her. FLOs were supposed to have the initial family contact along with the senior investigating officer. Barbara Venice was on her way, but for now Hazel was on her own. Usually, it wouldn't be a problem in any way. Usually, however, Hazel didn't have to deliver a death message along with telling the next of kin of a murder victim who was currently lying on the mortuary table that he wasn't to call her after midnight or before 6 a.m.

'I'll let you know when I can take you to the hospital,' she said.

His head snapped in her direction as if she'd offered a glimmer of hope so she talked quickly before he thought that he'd misunderstood and his dad was alive after all.

'Your dad died about half an hour ago. The hospital will let you see him as soon as they can,' she added.

What little remaining colour there was in his face disappeared.

'There are a few things I need to tell you,' she persevered, moving forward in her seat. 'The DCI in charge of your mum's death will be here soon. You do understand that her death is being treated as murder?'

'What a fucking day this has turned out to be,' he said, biting his lip and allowing a tear to run down his face. He took a deep breath, possibly in an attempt to stop himself from sobbing again.

The door opened and Hazel turned to see Jenny's head through the gap. She hesitated, then came close to launching into a gallop across the room as Hazel beckoned her in.

She perched herself on the arm of the chair and tried her best to engulf Travis in her toned, tanned arms. His size made that impossible but nevertheless Jenny gave it her best try. Travis turned his head into Jenny's chest as she stroked his blond hair and held her to him.

'My dad's dead too,' he said.

Jenny closed her eyes tight and said, 'We'll look after you. Me and Aiden. You can stay here as long as you like.'

Wanting to give them some privacy to share their misery, Hazel got up to make some phone calls. It had been a lot for anyone to take in, and despite it being her job, she was tired. Recognizing that none of this was about her or the other officers, she still understood that this was an unprecedented event for East Rise Police Station and no one was completely sure how they were supposed to feel about Linda and Milton's deaths.

She took a step in the direction of the door. A young man was watching the scene in front of him. His expression was difficult to read. He looked dismayed though Hazel couldn't put her finger on what gave her that impression. Unlike Travis, he had no presence in the room. He stood with his hands by his sides, dangling uselessly next to him. Although he wore an almost identical T-shirt to Travis, his biceps weren't putting the short sleeves to task. He was six or seven inches shorter than Travis, and from the colour photograph in the hallway that she'd seen on her way into the house, hung slightly higher and off-centre than all the rest, Hazel assumed that the put-out young man standing before her was Aiden Bloomfield.

She watched him watching his mother clutching his best friend to her breast and thought she saw annoyance flicker over his face. She had to make herself remember that these boys were only nineteen years old. The boys of a similar age she had dated in her youth weren't in the same category as these two who clearly spent all of their spare time in the gym. By himself, Aiden would have been a good-looking man, reasonable height, well-built, but next to his best friend, he was overshadowed.

Jealousy sometimes made people behave badly.

Hazel continued towards the door, aware of the scene around her, giving them time to take in the news. That nagging feeling that something wasn't right increasing with every step she took.

Chapter 13

Doug Philbert's headache was getting worse. He had already discussed Milton and Linda Bowman's post-mortems with the DCI. The same Home Office pathologist was to perform the painstaking procedures of examining both bodies to establish cause of death, toxicology and any forensic capture. Usually, either DCI Venice as the senior investigating officer or Doug himself as the deputy SIO would attend. Neither of them relished the idea of watching their battered, naked friends' bodies being dissected. With all that Doug knew about the Bowmans, he wasn't sure he was the best person to be going along anyway. His absence at their final, albeit intrusive farewell flooded him with mixed feelings: he had tried for some time to put the knowledge he carried about with him aside, except he couldn't resist soaking up some of the blame for what had happened to them both. Sweeping matters under the carpet rarely worked. Ignoring a problem didn't make it go away.

If only Doug had spoken up earlier.

After a few phone calls, he had managed to arrange for crime-scene investigators and two detective inspectors from a neighbouring force to attend both post-mortems and then complete a handover to Doug. It had taken the pressure off any personal feelings, as well as minimizing any criticism by defence counsel at a future Crown Court trial that anyone present had contaminated the evidence in any way.

He sighed at the harsh but practical use of the word 'evidence', put it to one side and continued with the job he had to do, no matter how personally uncomfortable it made him.

A detective constable appeared in Doug's office doorway, and said, 'Sir, as you're filling in here for a few days, can I get your signature on this form?'

He took the piece of paper and ran an eye over what he was signing, as the officer in front of him, whose name Doug couldn't remember, asked, 'Has the briefing been put back from nine to ten o'clock?'

At that moment, Doug had no idea what the current time was or who had arranged the briefing. He was almost certain that he hadn't.

'I'll check with Barbara and let you know,' he said as he handed the form over, glancing at the time on the telephone on his desk. 'I'll let you all know when I've spoken to her.'

He nodded and smiled dismissively, but the young DC in front of him didn't seem to be going away. One problem with being sent to help out at the last minute was that he didn't know everyone as well as he would have liked. Doug knew all of the staff at his own incident room yet still struggled with those from East Rise, and couldn't for the life of him recall this young man's name.

'Can I speak to you for a moment?' he asked, fingering the corners of the A4 piece of paper. 'Only ...' He glanced behind him at the open door leading to the corridor. The office Doug was in opened onto a blind spot and while it had proved useful, allowing him to overhear some very interesting gossip, it was impossible to tell if anyone was standing around the corner.

'Shut the door,' said Doug. 'Have a seat.'

'I'm Tom Delayhoyde.'

Doug's face lit up. 'You're—'

'Yeah, Hugh's son. You joined up with him.'

'Where's he now? I heard he left the job.'

'He left after twenty-five years, had enough, took early retirement and he and my mum run a pub in Norfolk.'

'Well, that's great. Give him my best when you speak to him next.'

Doug left it there and allowed the lad to speak. This couldn't be the reason Tom had wanted the door shut, so he waited.

'I feel a bit bad telling you this, but I've run it past my dad, even though I realized before he told me not to be so bloody naive and just tell someone.' Tom gave a meaningless smile.

'Sounds like your old man,' encouraged Doug.

'There was a girl I was seeing a couple of years ago,

Sasha Jones. We went out a few times, only she was a bit of a problem in the end. Basically, she's a nice woman and I feel as though I'm being out of order here but this is a murder inquiry. I may be reasonably new to the department, except I can't keep this to myself.'

Tom took a deep breath and exhaled through pursed lips.

'Sasha was over the side with Milton Bowman.'

The young detective threw himself back in the chair.

'Milton was having an affair?' said Doug. He would love to have quelled all the rumours by telling the boy he was wrong, but it wasn't in his nature to lie. He could see how uncomfortable talking about it was making him by the squirming in his seat. It indicated a total lack of malice on his part yet these things inevitably got out.

'How do you know this, Tom?'

'It gets a bit worse, I'm afraid.' He paused and looked down at the all but forgotten data protection form, the one he had first come to get signed for a simple request for information on the paramedics in attendance that morning.

'After Sasha and I broke up, she started going out with someone else. I think, from what I heard, it was going pretty well. They kept it quiet, well as quiet as you can on a nick, but he thought it was going somewhere. Then suddenly, she ended it. She ended it because she was having an affair with DI Bowman.'

'Do you know this for certain?'

'Well, that's what George Atkins told me.'

'What does George Atkins have to do with this?'

'He's the one that Sasha was going out with after she and I broke up. She told George it was over when he asked her to move in with him. She told him it was over because she'd fallen in love with Milton Bowman. He was planning on leaving his wife for her.'

Doug tried not to give away how he was feeling: the pounding in his head was making his skull throb at this revelation.

What was now making his brain feel as though it was spinning inside his cranium was the name George Atkins. He was the police officer currently suspended for headbutting a handcuffed prisoner.

He was also the football player whose leg had been broken by Milton Bowman in the friendly five-a-side match.

Chapter 14

'This is not what I want to hear,' said Barbara Venice after she'd listened to Doug's update over the phone. 'Where's Tom Delayhoyde now?'

'I've sent him to speak to his sergeant,' said Doug. 'Do you want me to cancel tonight's briefing for everyone other than management? We need to have a plan for how we handle this.'

There was a pause on the other end of the line as Doug waited, giving his senior in rank time to make the decision. He knew what he would do in her position; he bided his time until she made up her mind.

'Yeah, thanks, Doug. We can get our heads together and let the rest of the team get some sleep as soon as they've done what they need to tonight. We'll have a briefing at eight in the morning for the whole incident room, but I'll be with you as soon as I've finished up here, and then caught up with Hazel.'

They said their goodbyes and Doug walked to the tiny grubby kitchen to make himself a coffee before walking into the incident room. The bank of twenty desks was filled bar a few.

'Evening,' said Doug. Heads turned to look at him, a few said hello, a few were on the phone, the exhibits officer was rustling bags behind a mound of seized items.

'From DCI Venice, the briefing is cancelled this evening but full attendance tomorrow at eight o'clock in the conference room. If we need to, we'll move it to a bigger room. For the time being, check with the DSs as there are bound to be outstanding urgent enquiries that need doing before you go off. We're having a management meeting in a bit to sort out a few issues.'

Doug scanned the room for Tom Delayhoyde as he said the word 'issues'. His old friend's son was nowhere to be found, as he was no doubt off speaking to his sergeant about how this was going to be handled, recorded and eventually formed into some sort of evidence, be it good or bad. Right now, it looked very bad.

He left the officers and civilian investigators to it. With the exception of Tom, they'd all worked on dozens of major incidents, including numerous murders, although never one that had involved a police officer. The methods of investigation, however, didn't differ. The emotions did.

He spent the next ten minutes calling and texting those who needed to come to the meeting room for ten o'clock that evening, then as he was about to go in search of Tom, his mobile rang, showing a call from Harry Powell.

'Harry,' said Doug. 'How are you?'

'Yeah, I'm OK. Listen, I've just heard on the news that the man injured in the RTC this morning died.' Harry's voice caught.

Doug bit his lip and looked to the ceiling.

'I'm so sorry that you had to hear it on the telly. We've been—'

'No, no, Doug. I don't give a shit that you didn't tell me. I wanted to know if it was Milton. You've confirmed it.'

Doug listened to the sound of a bottle top being unscrewed and a large measure of liquid being poured into a glass.

'Who have you sent as FLO for Travis?' asked Harry, gulping down his brandy.

'Hazel Hamilton.'

'Good. Good choice. I like her. You picked a winner.'

'Glad you approve. Was there anything else? Are you doing OK? I can drop by later if you like.'

'No, it's OK, but thanks. And, Doug, I know that I shouldn't ask but is there anyone coming to immediate attention for Linda's death or can anyone say if it's likely to have been Milton?'

Sooner or later, Doug knew that he was going to be having this conversation with a number of people outside the investigation, and he'd guessed correctly that Harry would be the first to ask him. He'd weighed up what he should and shouldn't say, and whether telling Harry about the earlier revelation from Tom Delayhoyde would make any difference to the inquiry.

'The reason I'm asking is because I need to make sure that you're aware of something. I know it's frantic there and I'm not sure how much you've had a chance to catch up with,' said Harry. 'Linda was sure that Milton was having an affair.'

'Mmm,' said Doug.

'Did you know this anyway?'

'I've not long heard it from another source and I was aware that you already knew about it. I've read your statement.'

'I'm not sure if it's common knowledge,' said Harry, 'although I have it on good authority that it was with Sasha Jones.'

'Is there anyone else in this force who doesn't know this information? We're trying to keep it contained.'

'I've only told you and Hazel, because I had to put it in my statement. I know it's important. The young girl is going to be vilified for this, when at the end of the day Milton was the one who was cheating. She was a single girl.'

'She may be now,' said Doug, free hand stroking his temple, 'but she wasn't when she started seeing Milton. She was in a relationship with George Atkins.'

'Fucking hell,' shouted Harry. 'That headbutting lunatic. What you've got there, Doug, is a fucking Fred Karno's.'

'Yeah, I know. And I've been told that there's worse yet to come.'

Chapter 15

While the management meeting took place to discuss the next course of action for a murder-suicide of a detective inspector and his wife, Hazel sat with Travis Bowman.

She was in the unenviable position of having to explain to the teenager that he would eventually be able to see the bodies of both his parents, although they were currently at two different locations and the pathologist could only perform one post-mortem at a time.

Jenny had made herself scarce to put the kettle on for what was probably the twentieth time that day, and she had taken her son from the room with her.

Hazel had so much to tell Travis but was aware that she could easily overload him with information at the worst time of anyone's life. She had felt the personal weight of bereavement as a teenager although nothing as terrible as both of her parents at once at such a young age.

'DCI Barbara Venice will be along to see you as soon

as she can, Travis,' she said. She wanted to be sure that he was taking it in, despite her time with him being limited today. It was important to make contact, outline what she was there for and could do for him, and then let him be with family and friends.

The biggest flaw in that plan was that his family were, by and large, dead.

The door opened to reveal Jenny with a tray of refreshments as Hazel's phone began to ring. To give the others a moment to themselves, she gestured to her mobile and pointed to the hallway, and found herself alone by the front door.

'Hello, Hazel,' breathed a voice into Hazel's ear. How are things there?'

'As well as can be expected, ma'am,' she said to DCI Venice, glancing in the direction of the kitchen. She wasn't sure where Aiden had disappeared to, and no one had so far told her that the rest of the house was empty. The two uniform officers had gone to the kitchen although she couldn't hear their radios in the vast house. 'Sorry I couldn't speak to you earlier. Things have been frantic. I've told him that his dad died. I've told him that we can arrange for him to see both of his parents, with your guidance on when that's likely.'

'We've only just come out of a meeting here,' said the DCI. 'As far as both Milton and Linda's current whereabouts are concerned, nothing's changed since we briefed you earlier. How do you think Travis would respond to a visit from me this evening?'

'It's getting late, ma'am,' said Hazel. She didn't want to put the distraught young man through any more than was really necessary, especially not so that a DCI could claim to do her bit. This was about Travis. 'I'm not sure how much longer they'll want me here. Hang on, I'll ask and call you back.'

She moved down the hallway and into the lounge. Travis was sitting where she'd left him. Jenny had returned to his chair, this time stroking the young man's arm, watching his expression. He had his eyes shut, tears falling down his face.

'Sorry to interrupt,' Hazel said. 'That was the DCI. She'd like to speak to you tonight. You come first, so only if that's not going to be too late for you. I can easily tell her no.'

Her question was met with a shrug and when he opened his eyes Travis said, 'May as well. I'm not gonna get any sleep anyway.'

Only once had Hazel stayed for more than an hour on a first visit to a family, and it wasn't something she was keen to repeat. She began to explain to Travis what her role was and who was going to be able to help him. Although he made eye contact with her and nodded at several things she said, she wasn't remotely convinced that he was taking everything in. She hoped that the DCI wouldn't be long. It was clear to her when she should leave the family alone, and that time was coming.

Well aware that they could ask her to go, Hazel wanted to give them some space long before that happened. She needed to be there for them, just not to the point of intrusion at such an early stage in Travis's grief.

'When can I see my mum and dad?'

'I'll find out for you,' she answered, unsure how long that was going to take.

She took a deep breath and waited for Travis's reaction to what she had to tell him next.

'Your mum was at home for some time.'

Stunned look.

'It was a while before we were able to move her. The CSIs are still in the house. You'll be able to see your dad first, but not until the post-mortem's been carried out.'

'But I don't understand. He had a car accident.'

Travis sat bolt upright, a movement that startled Jenny on the arm of the chair, put Hazel on full alert.

'Fucking shit. You think he killed her? You think he then killed himself?'

'No, no. We're not sure what's happened at the moment. We have to look at every possibility. We'd have a post-mortem for any sudden, suspicious or unexplained death. We need to get this right, so that we can find out what's happened to both of your parents.'

Travis's face had closed down. She wasn't going to get any further and it was clear for anyone to see that he wasn't listening to her now. This wasn't unusual: people could only take so much and the full impact had finally hit him.

'I'm going to tell the DCI not to bother you tonight.' She said this to Jenny who nodded as Hazel handed her a card with her contact details.

'I'll be back tomorrow, but please call if you've any questions. I'll leave with the other officers.'

She made her way out of the room and glanced back, expecting to tell them that she'd see herself out. Neither of them was looking at her or making any move to leave each other's side.

In the kitchen, work surfaces lined two sides of the room, a fridge-freezer complete with water dispenser took up most of the third wall, and the centre of the space housed a table and chairs. The two uniform officers sat on one side and Aiden sat across from them.

'I'm about to go,' she said, coming to stand at the head of the table. Three faces looked up at her. 'I'll leave this here,' she said, placing a bereavement pack on the table. 'Can you let Travis know it's here? I've explained that I'll be back tomorrow.'

'Thank you,' said Aiden, giving her the briefest of smiles. It was an innocent enough expression.

The four of them made their way to the front door saying their goodbyes, and then the three officers walked towards the marked police car.

Hazel got in the back of the marked vehicle so they could talk in private and leaned forward.

Keeping her voice low, she asked, 'Everything OK in there?'

The two men exchanged a look. The driver spoke first.

'I'm not happy about Aiden. He asked us some odd questions.'

'Like what?' said Hazel.

'He wanted to know about viewing the bodies. He was especially interested in Mrs Bowman.'

'That's a little unusual, except something lots of people want to know is where their loved ones are and when they can see them. Just because she's not his family, doesn't mean that he's not upset.'

The next thing the police officer said gave Hazel a queasy feeling.

'Yes, but he asked if he could touch her. He wanted to know if he could kiss her goodbye.'

Chapter 16

Tuesday 6 June

The following morning started with a packed conference room. More and more civilian employees and police officers, both plain-clothes and uniform, arrived one after the other, filling the room.

Each of them felt an unusual tension in the air: tempers were often raised, behind-the-scenes intelligence taskings and manic officers demanding certain actions to be completed within record time were the norm. This, however, was different.

One of their own had either died in a traffic accident or had committed suicide. In itself, that was bad enough, except he might turn out to be a murderer. No one knew.

DCI Barbara Venice was only too aware that her staff were already having mixed feelings about the investigation. Her role was to lead and focus them; before that, she needed to get a grip of herself.

She had started the day by tracking down one of the

building's caretakers to have the police flag on the top of the building flown at half-mast. When he told her that he needed someone from Headquarters to agree it she'd begun to walk towards the emergency stairs leading to the roof. 'If you want something doing, do it yourself,' she'd muttered, before he promised her he would see to it straight away.

Worn out already, Barbara made her way to the conference room wondering just when the police had been overtaken by such a lot of bureaucratic cobblers, and steeled herself for the day ahead.

At the point where the room was stretched to capacity, the office manager poked her head around the door and gestured a thumbs-up to DCI Barbara Venice who had only seconds before taken her seat.

'Morning, everyone,' she shouted over the din of people already dissecting what they thought had occurred. 'There are more coming so we're on the move to the lecture theatre. Not the ideal place, I know, but any rooms larger than this one are booked for training days.'

She got up and left the room, flanked on one side by Doug Philbert and on the other by a senior CSI. Everyone else followed, notebooks in one hand and tea in the other.

'Ready for this?' said Barbara to Doug as they got into the corridor.

'Probably not for what's coming,' he replied out of the corner of his mouth.

*

Hazel made her way around a group of people scribbling down dates and addresses, checking facts as they made their way to the new venue.

She saw her opportunity to speak to the SIO as Doug Philbert was distracted by a young DC whom Hazel didn't know, and the CSI's phone rang.

'Ma'am,' she called as they piled outside to cross the car park to the training area.

Barbara stopped by the disabled ramp as Hazel caught up with her.

'Is everything OK?' she asked the DC.

'Firstly, sorry for cancelling on you last—'

'No need to apologize. If it was a bad time, so be it. How Travis feels is more important than me introducing myself to him. How is he?'

Hazel paused, unsure how blunt she should be.

They carried on across the car park and, being of similar height, they found it easy to walk together with their heads close and voices lowered.

'It's why I wanted to have a quick word with you before the briefing. I'm not holding anything back from the inquiry team, only there's something about Travis's relationship with his friend's mother that I find odd. I can't be sure, but it looked as though he was checking her out as she walked away from him.'

Barbara raised an eyebrow at this and looked across at the officer.

'There was a lot of cuddling to the bosom going on too. Wasn't sure what that was all about either.'

Despite the seriousness of the situation, Barbara

smiled at the word 'bosom'. She'd heard how tactful Hazel could be.

'OK,' the DCI said, 'raise it at the briefing only don't go into details. Is there anything else because I know you can't stay until the end.'

'There is actually. The senior CSI you've got is Jo Styles, isn't it?'

Barbara nodded and pointed to Jo who had stopped to speak on her phone and was now kneeling in the car park, trying to write down something in her CSI notebook. Her position resembled an amateur Pilates pose, and looked very uncomfortable.

'I need to speak to Jo,' said Hazel. 'It was something the uniform lads said last night after we left the house. They'd been talking to Aiden Bloomfield in the kitchen while I spoke to his mum and Travis.'

By now Jo had finished both her call and causing damage to her knee joints, and was walking towards the two women.

'Aiden asked if he could see Linda Bowman's body and whether he could touch her.'

Barbara's eyebrows shot up at this nugget of information.

'Even weirder than that, ma'am,' said Hazel, 'was that he wanted to know if he could kiss her goodbye.'

'Hi, Hazel,' said Jo as she stood in front of them, waving her mobile phone. 'The lab just called me. I think you're going to like this one.'

DCI Venice and DC Hamilton stared at her, waiting

for the forensic update that might have found them a murderer.

The rest of the inquiry team plus other officers and staff drafted in to help streamed past them. Close to sixty people walked either side of them, the three of them forming an island, parting their team.

'We've got saliva on Linda's cheek,' said Jo. 'All we have to do is find a DNA match and the chances are, that's our murderer.'

Chapter 17

The handling within a murder investigation of both a serving police officer and one currently on suspension for violence against a prisoner was a headache to all concerned. Once the briefing was finished, Doug Philbert decided that the best course of action was to go and speak to them both himself.

So he could gather his thoughts, Doug decided to take himself to the canteen on the top floor for a coffee. It wasn't something he did very frequently unless he needed to get away from his desk for fifteen minutes, take a seat in a quiet corner and look out towards the Channel. At least it was in the direction of the Channel: East Rise Police Station definitely couldn't afford a sea view. He used his imagination to picture the ships and French coast located the other side of bingo halls and the shopping centre.

He stepped out of the lift, head full of murder inquiry thoughts, and pushed open the double doors.

Initially, everything seemed normal. The thirty-five metre by thirty-five metre space was taken up at one end by the serving counter, food ranging from passable to edible, draughty sash windows open, allowing a breeze to sweep through the canteen, and the hum of about forty plain-clothes officers, uniform officers and their civilian counterparts taking their allocated mid-shift breaks.

As Doug went into the canteen, shoes squeaking on the lino floor, he noticed heads turn towards the television on the far wall.

The conversation began to drop off, the noise subsided, uniform patrols on duty since 6 a.m. laid down their knives and forks beside their fry-ups.

All eyes were on the mid-morning news.

Doug was mesmerized. He had never seen a group of people quieten so fast, act as one and be united under such macabre circumstances.

A local news reporter was standing in the Bowmans' street a healthy distance from the police cordon, pointing at Linda and Milton's home, explaining to the world that DI Milton Bowman of East Rise Police Station and his wife Linda had both been killed. He didn't use their names; for this audience, he didn't have to.

At the words, 'An incident room has been set up to investigate the suspicious deaths of a local man and his wife', Doug felt his feet take him back towards the lift. The double doors gave an almighty creak as he pulled them open. Not one pair of eyes broke contact with the television screen to glance in his direction.

He made his way down the stairs, not wishing to get

caught in the lift with anyone for the time it would take to travel the five floors down.

Once back in the sanctity of the incident room, he made his way to his office, all thoughts of a coffee prior to visiting Sasha Jones abandoned. Doug attempted to focus on the delicate matter of obtaining DNA samples from her and George Atkins for elimination purposes against the saliva found on Linda's face.

They already had DNA samples from Travis Bowman and Aiden Bloomfield which were on the way to forensics.

He tried to catch five minutes alone, a nigh on impossible task with everything going on around him. Slamming his office door with enough force that anyone in the incident room would get the message loud and clear, he sat down to eat a sandwich. The first thing he'd eaten since ten o'clock the night before when someone had ordered pizzas for the management meeting. The pizza had sat like ballast in his stomach all night and he could still taste the pepperoni.

He wasn't particularly popular in the Philbert household at that moment: the previous evening had meant he'd failed to get home in time for a visit from the mother-in-law, not something he was fretting about. However, his wife had still made him a packed lunch. Doug peered inside the foil wrapping to find cheese doorsteps and a Peperami as an unwanted side.

Sighing at this further misfortune, he heard his phone start to ring. He hesitated only momentarily when he saw it was Harry Powell calling.

'How are you, Harry?'

'Good, Dougie mate, good.'

He hated it when Harry called him 'Dougie', something Harry was well aware of.

'You back at work then?'

'Yeah, I couldn't stay at home. Not really sure what to do with myself as I've been sent to another incident room for today. All because it was me that found the body. Jesus, I didn't mean to say body, I meant to say Linda. Jesus, I said Jesus. Sorry, Dougie, I know that offends you.'

'My Christian beliefs aren't tested every time someone blasphemes. I've heard much worse over the years, mostly from you.'

After a second or two, Doug had to ask Harry to get to the point.

'Oh yes, sorry. I was a bit upset yesterday and I'd had a couple of drinks. I'm not sure if I put in my statement that when I found Linda, I put my hand out to stroke her face. The thing is, I definitely didn't touch her face. I felt her neck for a pulse and the side of her head, but no other part of her.'

Doug sat upright in his chair, eyes on yet not seeing his Cheddar and wholemeal lunch.

'Why are you telling me this now?'

Harry coughed, cleared his throat and said, 'Wasn't sure if I should call Hazel to come over and take another statement or whether you want me to make my own. I want to make sure I get the details right.'

'It's best if you don't call Hazel. She's the FLO and

she's probably with Travis at the moment. Write it yourself and I'll come and see you when you're done. Where are you?'

'I was told to come to North Downs nick for a day or two, to keep out of the way. I seem to be doing some sort of shite job swap with you whilst you pick up the slack left by my absence.'

Doug hung up, wondering not only how he was going to fit in a round trip of eighty miles to collect the statement but also why, with the discovery of saliva on her cheek, Harry had called now to tell him he hadn't touched Linda's face.

It was either a very big coincidence, or he had a leak in his incident room.

Chapter 18

Glad to be out of the briefing and grateful she didn't have to sit through another management one, Hazel made herself scarce. It was obvious to rank and file that the higher echelons of the incident room were rushing around behind the scenes trying to keep something under wraps. It was almost impossible to do so amongst the nosiest people on the planet – detectives. Any closed-door meeting was likely to start the whispers that the management were trying to keep something from them. Not forgetting that this murder had its own secrets.

Hazel also had something she was trying to keep to herself. It wasn't that she didn't want to share the information, except for the moment that's all it was. It might have meant nothing, yet she couldn't shake the feeling that there was more to the Bowmans' background than a bit of matrimonial disharmony.

She had tried to speak to Travis about the family's history and if there was anyone else that he wanted to get in touch with or wanted around him for support, but the only friend he had time for was Aiden. He didn't seem to know anything about his mother's side of the family and Milton had few relations, only a sister and her husband who lived locally.

There was nothing particularly odd in itself about Linda having no living family, but Travis knew nothing whatsoever about them.

When asked, his answer had been, 'Mum was an only child, her parents died young and she met dad. That was it.'

At such an early stage in his grief, Hazel knew better than to push Travis yet she still thought that it was strange he had no idea about his maternal grandparents.

Hazel made her way to the tiny exhibits store and spoke to the officer in charge of booking in the items so far seized from the Bowman household.

She found her squeezed into the stuffy eight- by fifteen-foot room, cheap racking filling the two longer sides of the area, completely packed to capacity with cardboard box after cardboard box marked up with the names of a variety of investigations. In front of the racking were rows of more boxes, stacked six or seven high. The rest of the room was taken up with two six-foot-high freezers and, on the far wall, a tiny desk with two computers and a civilian employee trying frantically to keep up with the incoming tide of work.

Hazel said, 'Hi there. Just trying to find something. I won't be long.'

She knew exactly what she was looking for as she

had already taken a couple of minutes to search on the HOLMES database for any photographs from the house and for the contents of Linda's handbag. Locating it was the problem.

She pulled out storage box after storage box piled high amongst boxes for two other incidents running from East Rise, all under the watchful eye of the exhibits officer.

'If you want the contents of Linda's bag,' the officer said as she fished new exhibits from a drop box and proceeded to book them on the system, 'I've taken a photocopy of the papers inside it. There's a travel card and receipts, bus timetable and stuff.'

She waved a plastic-gloved hand in the direction of a pile of paperwork and turned her back on Hazel, leaving her to it.

For several minutes, Hazel examined the details in front of her. Linda had bought a travel card at East Rise Station seven days ago, and if the handwritten scrawl of directions from Victoria Station via the District Line and the number 83 bus to Hanwell were anything to go by, she had at least planned to make her way towards Ealing.

Perhaps Hazel was reading too much into it and there was a simple explanation for the journey: meeting an old friend, relative or doing some sightseeing, although she very much doubted it. Something Jenny had said to her about Linda being on her way to the train station and refusing a lift struck a chord with the detective and set her mind working overtime.

One thing she had managed to get from Travis was that his mum rarely went further than Tesco's or the local gym. Milton had said he was going to sell her car because she never went anywhere in it, and besides, if it was an innocent visit to Ealing, surely she would have mentioned it to her son.

She still couldn't shake the feeling that she was on to something, although she had no idea of what it could be.

Once she had put the paperwork back where she had found it, Hazel sifted through a box until she found what she was looking for.

'OK if I open these?' she said to the exhibits officer, who was engrossed in what she was doing.

'Fine' the officer muttered, 'as long as you wear gloves, mark up the bag that you've opened, sign the seal and reseal it. You're the fifth person to be in here this morning. Oh, and fill in a form that you've taken it, leave it back in the drop box when you're done and please don't lose any of those photos. I haven't had a chance to look at them yet.'

Hazel did as she was told, all the while glad that she hadn't been given the task of keeping tabs on what would probably amount to thousands of exhibits, some of which might point them in the direction of a murderer.

She thanked her colleague and took herself off to a quiet corner of the incident room, gloves on, and cut open the police evidence bag. The small biscuit tin had been found by the CSIs at the back of Linda's wardrobe. The contents were simply marked *Various photos.*

This was what had puzzled Hazel. She sat completely absorbed in what she was doing as she sifted through a myriad of old black-and-white photos, 1970s colour ones with two tiny miniatures attached, old Polaroids and one at the very bottom of the tin, out of keeping with its ageing companions.

This was a very recent photograph of Linda, grim-faced, sitting beside an elderly woman's hospital bed. The papery white skin and sunken cheeks of the lady propped up against the pillows very much gave Hazel the impression that whenever the picture was taken, she wasn't much longer for this world.

Chapter 19

Once Hazel had made up her mind she was going to find out who Linda Bowman had visited in Ealing, she grabbed her stuff and was out of the incident room in record time. She knew that she didn't have long because she had to see Travis at some point and wavered for only a second or two in deciding to take the car. Driving was going to be quicker than a train, underground and bus.

The conversation with DCI Venice after the briefing about Linda's recent photo had been an odd one: Hazel got the impression that the SIO knew more than she was letting on and had seemed a little cagey. She had told Hazel that she was only to go to the hospital and nowhere else in Ealing. The only thing Hazel managed to draw out of her was that Linda might have had some family after all and previously had the surname McCall.

She didn't want to dwell on the fact that she was looking for a needle in a haystack. There'd been no doubt thousands of elderly women in the hospital over the last couple of months, and she couldn't even date the photograph, all she had was the travel card. Hazel was ready to put her trust in blind luck. At least now she had a name to ask for.

Cursing and swearing through the London traffic, she eventually reached the hospital, drove around the car park for several minutes until she saw someone heading for their car, waited for the space and then rushed inside the building.

She stood looking at the map of the hospital, clueless as to where to begin.

Hazel remained on the spot for a couple of moments, took the photograph of Linda and the patient from her bag, and with her warrant card in the other hand, made for the busy general enquiries desk. Her experience of hospitals was that the staff either couldn't do enough to help, or everyone was as obstructive as they could possibly be. Hoping for the former, she walked up to the counter and waited until a woman of about forty years of age, the first to become available, was free.

'Hi,' said Hazel, 'this may sound a little strange.'

The woman made no reaction, probably used to odd people in a hospital of such a size.

'I'm trying to find out who this patient is.' She pushed the photograph across the counter and saw the woman's expression change to irritation. Not wanting to be dismissed so easily, Hazel opened her warrant card and said, 'I'm a detective constable investigating a murder in East Rise. This younger woman on the right was murdered yesterday and she'd been here visiting this patient. I think it may be important. I have to find out who she is.'

Not everything she said was strictly true: it was a leap of faith that Linda had been visiting the woman at Ealing Hospital; however, she couldn't go to every hospital in the country and ask the same thing. It was as good a place as any to start.

As Hazel spoke, the woman, whose name badge read *Nora*, stood up and leaned across the counter. 'I've no idea who she is but from the view from this window behind them, I'd guess it was the third floor overlooking the car park. Try the oncology ward. Sad to say, I spent a bit of time in there with an uncle. It's the best I can think of.'

Hazel couldn't resist a relieved smile in Nora's direction.

'Thank you so much. It's a starting point at least.'

'Take the lift behind you and go to the third floor, turn left.'

She was across the entrance hall, jabbing at the call button before curiosity got the better of her and she asked after Nora's uncle's health. It might not have ended well.

A couple of minutes later, Hazel was once again at the mercy of the medical staff's assistance. She was admitted to the ward, made her way to the desk and asked to see the sister on duty.

She stood and waited in the stillness of the corridor trying not to think of all the sick and dying on the other side of the door. A petite woman, several years younger than herself, scrubs rustling, walked briskly along the corridor towards her.

'Hi,' said Hazel. 'Sorry to bother you but I'm here on a murder inquiry and the victim was here visiting one of your patients.' She held out the photograph, as much as a distraction from the lie she had told as anything else.

The sister leaned in to see the picture, looked up at Hazel and said, 'That's Linda. She visited Gladys a couple of times.' A hand went up to her throat before she realized that she was showing emotion. She forced her hand back down to her side and stood herself back up to five foot three. 'Linda was murdered?' she asked with a slow, disbelieving shake of her head.

'Yes, she was. I'm sorry. Did you know her well?'

The sister motioned for Hazel to step inside the small room behind the nurses' station as one of the patients made her way along the corridor.

With the door shut, she said, 'No, I wouldn't say that I knew her at all really. She came to visit Gladys on several occasions, and she always introduced her to me as "my Linda".'

She looked away, the effort of trying to remember something all over her face. 'The funny thing was, though, Gladys was confused from time to time. She was getting on and had very advanced cancer, but there were a number of times that she called or referred to Linda as Karen.'

Hazel watched as she pinched the bridge of her nose

and squeezed her eyes shut. 'I'm sure it was Karen because that's my niece's name. The thing was, Linda never corrected her and even answered to it. I thought that it would really annoy me if my mum kept getting my name wrong.' Her eyes snapped open.

'Sorry?' said Hazel. 'Did you say mum?'

'Well yes,' said the sister. 'Gladys was Linda's mother.'

Chapter 20

Sandwich consumed, Detective Inspector Doug Philbert took Detective Constable Sophia Ireland to one side, explained that he needed her assistance to interview Sasha Jones, and together they headed to one of the county's more remote police stations. It was something neither of them particularly wanted to do because it meant formally dealing with another police officer. They weren't going to arrest her; that would have been another thing entirely. Their task was to speak to her to find out where she had been the day of Linda's murder and Milton's death.

Sasha was being dropped off by her patrol sergeant. This was under the guise of welfare for her, and not, as some might have thought, because she might not have turned up of her own volition.

No one had told Sasha the full extent of why she was being spoken to by two officers from Major Crime. No doubt she must have guessed as to their reason. Everyone was still reeling from the shock of one their DIs dying in an accident, not to mention his wife being murdered.

Sophia and Doug sat in one of the empty admin offices on the second floor waiting for their witness to arrive. That was what Sasha was – a witness. Unless the time came for her to be declared a suspect, and then she would have to be treated like one, arrested, interviewed, her home searched, referred to on the news as 'a twenty-six-year-old woman currently in police custody'.

At midday, a light tap on the door indicated that Sasha was outside waiting to come in.

Sophia got up to open the door. She wasn't what she was expecting.

Sasha Jones was a very plain-looking woman. Sophia had expected the woman capable of breaking up the happy marriage of Linda and Milton Bowman to be someone remarkable. In fairness, her face was red and blotchy from crying and her eyes looked raw.

'Come in and have a seat,' said Sophia. 'We're sorry about Milton and understand that you were close.'

There was an uncomfortable silence while Sasha took out a tissue and wiped her nose, the nod of her head barely visible.

'It's important that you understand who we are and why you're here,' continued Doug, heart being melted by the vulnerable young girl, who wasn't the wanton marriage wrecker he had had her down as five minutes earlier.

'We need to ask you about Milton and your relationship with him. Clearly you're not under arrest or we'd now be having this conversation in custody.'

Sasha froze mid-nose wipe at the word 'custody' and gave Doug an intense stare. One that allowed him a glimpse of another side to her. There was something very telling about the look she flashed at the inspector, full of defiance and challenge.

'Tell me about your relationship with DI Milton Bowman,' said Doug.

Sasha shrugged, sighed and removing the damp tissue from her face said, 'We worked together on a fatal stabbing in Wolfram Street. We got to know each other then and he asked me out. Not much to tell.'

This simple statement got to Doug. In only three sentences, Sasha had made three mistakes: as a uniform PC with only a short time in the police when the Wolfram Street stabbing occurred, Sasha would not have worked with a DI. Her role had been to stand guard on the scene in the pouring rain and stop anyone entering the house where a young man had been stabbed in the neck over a drugs deal. Doug had been the late-turn DI that night and recognized the face of the young officer trying to shelter from a downpour.

The second error she made was saying the two of them had got to know each other during the investigation, when Milton had in fact only worked on that particular murder for a day. Something Doug was well aware of because Milton spoke to him about having to hand it over to another SIO in time to take his wife to Rome the following morning.

Thirdly, starting an affair with a married man,

especially a work colleague, was never 'Not much to tell'. That part might have been simple shame or modesty.

This was a young woman, who, when all was said and done, had been doing what hundreds of thousands of men and women the world over had been doing throughout history – having sex with someone they shouldn't.

All of these thoughts flew through Doug's brain where he put them to one side and continued with the plan he had in mind.

He left Sophia to ask about the affair, when it started and who else had known about it, feeling that the questions would be better received, not just from another woman, but from someone of Sasha's own rank.

'Where were you yesterday morning?' Sophia at last asked, feeling herself starting to get somewhere.

The question was met with a shrug and then Sasha said, 'I've been upset. I couldn't think straight. I only spoke to Milton the night before his accident.' Tears ran down her face, still she continued to talk. 'He'd locked himself in his bathroom at home to talk to me. It was very awkward to get any time to talk to one another in privacy, though I suppose that's what I get for having affairs with married men.'

Sophia took note of the plural.

'We didn't see that much of each other although we spoke every day. I'd have to wait for him to call me. I didn't like that part.'

'So where were you yesterday morning?' Sophia asked again.

'Oh yesterday. I'd stayed at a friend's overnight.'

'Who's your friend?'

'I'd rather not say. I don't want you speaking to her.'

Sophia leaned forward towards Sasha but was interrupted by Doug. He'd seen the look on his DC's face and thought he'd better step in.

'Sasha,' he said, 'this is important. It's a murder investigation. You're a police officer so you must understand that we need to speak to anyone connected with the victim. You were having an affair with her husband. We need to know where you were and who you were with at the relevant times. If we can't do that, you're no longer a witness, you're a suspect. Then the rules change.'

He watched her take a deep breath, look from his face to Sophia's and back again before she said, 'I was at my mum's. She's going to go mental when you talk to her. My dad was always having affairs. She threw him out when I was six so she brought me up alone. And she brought me up to behave better than this. I'm so ashamed.'

Then the tears were joined by racking sobs.

Chapter 21

'What I want to know,' he said, 'is why you get to use the name "Milo" and I get such a shit one.'

'Stop moaning,' said Milo. 'We're almost there and we don't get to pick the names, the boss does. If he decided that you should be referred to as "Diva", that's his choosing.'

'Are you both fucking laughing at me?' he said, eyes flicking back and forth between his two associates.

'And are you having a little tantrum, Diva?' said Milo.

'Even he gets to be called "Parker", just because he's the driver.'

Parker looked over his shoulder towards the back seat after pulling the Range Rover to a stop in front of a small children's play area. 'As you always sit in the back, we can put in a request to have it changed to "Lady Penelope".'

'You're such a pair of funny fuckers. Let's go, Milo.'

The two of them climbed out of the car leaving Parker to stay with the vehicle as was their usual plan, and made their way to the rear stairs leading to half a dozen flats positioned above a short row of local shops. When they got to the third flat along the balcony, they assumed their usual positions, Milo to the left, Diva to the right.

It took a little longer for the door to be answered than they'd have liked. The balcony was open to the road and passing traffic. The plan for premises such as these was to walk the last couple of hundred metres if need be because of shop-front CCTV. This was the sort of area prone to criminal damage, nuisance teenagers and the odd night-time ram raid of the off-licence and post office. It made Milo and Diva's job that little bit harder. Something that rankled Diva.

Without waiting for an invite, both men barged their way inside once the beginnings of a crack appeared between the door and its frame. The six-stone drug addict behind the door was knocked off her feet.

Milo peered down at her face as she lay prone looking up at him. Terror was written all over it. Her skinny body trembled from the top of her greasy hair to the soles of her feet and every needle track in between.

'He's, he's not here,' she said. 'You're wasting your time,' she called after Diva as he ran towards the bedroom door.

One kick against the cheap hollow door and Diva was inside the room, across it and had the gaunt partially clad man who had been about to climb out of the window by his throat. 'Not how I wish to start my day, Greg,' he shouted in his face.

Dragging Greg behind him like a rag doll, Diva pulled him back into the hallway where Milo still stood over the petrified woman.

'I really thought he'd gone,' she said, unblinking, dead eyes locked onto Milo's.

'You must think I'm stupid,' he said as he grabbed her arm and pulled her to her feet.

'Please, please,' she said. 'We didn't do anything, did we, Greg? Tell Tandy that we didn't do anything.'

'That's the problem, see, you didn't bloody do anything.' He sighed as he threw her to the corner of the kitchen and glanced over the small room. 'Look at the fucking state of this place. It's a disgrace. There's crap piled everywhere, doors pulled off their hinges and it's taxpayers like me and Diva here who have to pay for you to live like this. I don't know.'

As he spoke, he moved around the kitchen, picked up the kettle and filled it with water before setting it on to boil.

'What's this about?' said Greg, panicked look in the direction of the kettle. 'Business has been slow, that's all. I'll get the money.'

'We had a deal,' said Milo. 'You two haven't fulfilled it. Where's the money?'

'I'm telling the truth. We don't have it but we will by the end of the day. We were just about to go out, Sam, weren't we?'

The young woman on the floor nodded her head, although from the panic on her face it didn't seem that she really appreciated what the question had been. She was too transfixed by the steam coming from the kettle's spout.

By the time the water was at boiling point, the stench of urine was unmistakable in the small kitchen.

Without a word, Milo picked up the kettle by its handle and held it over Sam's head. Her immediate reaction was to bring her skinny bare arms up and over her skull. A frenzied sob came from her and she tried to fold herself into a ball. The only purpose it served was that when Milo poured the boiling water over her he managed to scald her left-hand side. The flesh bubbled, surface rising up in angry blisters.

There was a momentary silence before her nerve endings kicked in and she began to scream.

All it took was Milo to step towards Greg and he said, 'Please, please don't hurt me. I'll have the money by tonight.'

'It's funny, Diva, ain't it?' he said, looking past Greg. 'He didn't ask us not to hurt his girlfriend just then.' He glanced back down at the floor where Sam was taking shallower and shallower breaths, her body writhing in agony. 'You could do better than him, love. Get yourself a decent bloke.'

He peered down at Greg. 'And you, dipshit, get yourself our money by 10 p.m. tonight, or I'll do the same to your bollocks.'

The two men made their way back out of the flat, slowly strolling along the balcony until they reached the staircase.

'You're going to have to watch yourself,' Diva said as they walked down the stairs, 'word'll get around you've got a bit of a testicle fetish.'

'I've never known a threat to a bloke's nuts fail to work. So, where are we off to next?'

111

Chapter 22

Once she was back in the car, Hazel tried to put the revelation from the oncology sister out of her mind. She had come away with nothing more than the sister's number, the full name Gladys Anne McCall, and the details of who she would have to contact to gain access to Gladys's medical records.

Usually, Hazel would have waited around until she could get the paperwork herself. As she was under time pressure and had been told that Linda's mother, or whoever she was, had passed away the week before, she weighed up the importance of waiting for what could be hours for the notes of a dead woman against getting a traumatized nineteen-year-old to the mortuary to say goodbye to his mum.

She was having trouble understanding why Linda would keep her own parent a secret from her family and wondering exactly how Travis would react to knowing he had missed out on a grandparent on top of everything else. Why the DCI had been so coy was also irritating her. Clearly, Barbara knew more than she was letting on.

She waited until her phone connected to DCI Venice. It went to voicemail so she left a brief message, keeping her tone neutral.

'Ma'am, it's Hazel. I've just left Ealing Hospital. Linda's mother, Gladys McCall, died of cancer last week. It seems that Linda's real name was Karen McCall. I think you already know about the McCall part. I'd appreciate a call back.'

She hung up and made her way out of London.

Barbara Venice sat at her desk, mobile phone in front of her. She had no desire to answer it and speak to Hazel before finding out what the officer knew.

She drummed her fingers on the table, waited a couple of minutes and then played back the message.

If she was being honest, it was a relief that Hazel had found out the family name McCall. The name was the subject of a furtive phone call that Barbara had received very early after she learned of Linda's murder. The person she would normally have turned to for advice was Harry Powell, only she knew how devastated he was going to be when he found out that a very old friend wasn't who he thought she was.

Right at that moment, Barbara had slightly more pressing matters to attend to. She regained her composure and called Hazel back.

'Hazel, sorry I missed you.' Without waiting for the DC to speak again, she said, 'I'm glad you're on your way back. There's been a development and I need you to do something.'

She heard the hesitation and then a voice said, 'OK. What's that?'

'We're in the process of having a Section 8 PACE warrant sworn out via live link at the Magistrates' Court and it would be very helpful if you could find out where Travis is so we can keep him out of the way.'

'What's the search warrant for? Travis's house?'

'No,' said Barbara, 'I don't need you to keep him away from his own house. It'll be much easier for everyone if he isn't there to see his best friend get arrested and then the search team traipse all over the Bloomfields' home.'

The pitch of Hazel's voice got a lot higher. 'Why are we arresting Aiden?'

There was a pause before Barbara added, 'We had the DNA results back from the lab. Aiden Bloomfield's saliva was on Linda Bowman's cheek.'

Chapter 23

Afternoon of Tuesday 6 June

'Hello, Travis. It's Hazel. Is this a good time to call?'

'Yeah, it's fine. I'm here on my own. They went out for something to eat. I can't face food at the moment.'

'Can I come and get you and bring you to the police station in about an hour?'

There was a pause and what sounded like Travis taking a drink of something.

'There are a few things I need to go over with you. I know it was a lot to take in last night.'

'OK. I'll get ready and see you here then.'

She breathed a sigh of relief: Travis was no fool and would soon work out that if they were searching Aiden's house that afternoon with a warrant signed out that same day at a Magistrates' Court, Hazel would have known what was about to happen. The search team were to enter the house in only two hours' time. He was the son of a detective inspector and while he might not fully understand how everything worked, he would

115

eventually guess she had known that police officers were about to swarm all over his temporary residence.

She felt her skin prickle as she made a note of their conversation, before pulling out of the service station. Hazel knew the rest of the day was not going to be a pleasant one. Whatever her personal feelings about what she was doing, it was the safest option too. She didn't relish the idea of Travis trying to throttle Aiden when he listened to the arresting officer say he was suspected of murdering Linda. They already had enough dead bodies on their hands.

She also wanted to ask him some more background questions about Linda. Something clearly wasn't right about her past and the thought that there was more to Mrs Bowman than everyone knew was playing on Hazel's mind. Barbara Venice had cut their telephone conversation short, giving Hazel very much the impression that she would have to press her for further details the next time they spoke face to face.

Her phone rang, coming through on the hands-free as she indicated left at a roundabout. Harry Powell's name appeared on the screen and she surprised herself by hesitating as her hand moved from the indicator to the call accept button. There was no doubt about it, she liked Harry, although she felt a little concerned that he was calling her.

At the end of the day, he was also a DI and a witness so she answered the phone and with a clear voice announced, 'Hazel Hamilton.'

'You on your own?'

'Yes. What makes you ask that?'

'You've got my number stored in your phone. I watched you do it. Why didn't you say "Hello, Harry"?'

'Because you're a DI and I didn't want to sound too formal by saying "Hello, sir".'

'Well, saying "Hazel Hamilton" when you bloody well know it's me is fucking ridiculously formal.'

'As lovely as it is to have you ring me up and shout expletives down the line, is there a reason you're calling me?'

'Shouting? I was not f— well I suppose I am a bit loud. I just wondered how you were. How it's going ... Well, how you are more than anything.'

'I'm good, thanks. The usual type of murder-investigation tired. Anyway, how about you?'

'Yeah, I'm OK,' said Harry, but the feistiness in his voice that had been there only a second before was gone. Whether the brashness was the lie or whether it was the vulnerability, Hazel couldn't decide. Perhaps it was neither and the years of policing were working their powers and making her see negative aspects of people that didn't actually exist.

'You sure about that?' she said. 'Is anyone looking after you?'

'People don't tend to look after me. I tend to look after them. That's why I'm calling: I wanted to check you were OK.'

'I'm fine, Harry, just fine.'

'How about we go out some time for a drink or dinner or something? I'll even pay.'

'You're too good to be true,' she said. 'All right, I'll call you later. It's likely to be a long day.'

'Look after yourself,' Harry said before ending the conversation.

In those last three words, Hazel heard that the spark was well and truly back.

Chapter 24

The problem with Jenny Bloomfield was that she simply couldn't help herself. She loved her husband, and of course, her son. The problem was that she loved herself more.

And that involved taking care of her own needs first.

As much as she wanted to make sure that Travis was doing as well as he could under such terrible circumstances, his moping about was depressing. Aiden wasn't much better. At her suggestion to Travis that Aiden could do with getting out of the house, and her suggestion to Aiden that Travis could do with some time on his own, both boys had agreed to her plan. Mother and son left the house together.

She dropped her son off at the out-of-town retail park, largely because he was partial to the Italian food chain's all-day breakfast, though mostly as he had little option but to wait for her return, so the risk of her being caught was minimal.

Jenny leaned across, gave Aiden a kiss on his cheek and waited for him to unbuckle his seat belt. As he put his hand on the release, she said, 'Darling, you have to trust me. Everything will be all right.'

He opened his mouth to speak.

'Aiden,' she blurted before he had a chance to utter one word, 'I know that this is making you miserable, but you have to carry on as normal. Neither of us should ever talk about this. It's for the best. That way, there'll be no lies.'

He climbed out of the car without one word. She held a sad smile on her lips in case he looked back before he shuffled towards the diner.

She waved at his retreating back, more for effect than anything else, and drove across the retail park, pulled up out of sight and picked up her mobile phone.

A shiver of excitement ran through her as she reread the message. *See you at the Grand. Room 524. 1 p.m.*

Smoothing down her dress, she wriggled in her seat, realizing that her breathing had got that little bit heavier, her heart beating faster in her chest.

She refused to admit that her actions over the next hour or so would be wrong, Linda barely cold, Aiden not knowing what to do, Travis in turmoil. Jenny couldn't change what had happened, only make the best of the situation.

With the air conditioning turned up, she put the automatic Mercedes into drive and headed in the direction of the seafront, aware of how little time she had before she had to return to collect her teenage son from his mid-afternoon meal, although not aware of the consequences of having sex in a hotel room with a man she had only known for six months.

Ten minutes later, Jenny made her way across the vast tiled floor of the East Rise Grand Hotel. It was a beautiful building, still living up to its name in spite of the declining economy of the local area. A dark-haired receptionist glanced up and smiled at Jenny, a business-man waiting at a lobby table peered at her over the top of his newspaper. Even though she wasn't getting any younger, she knew that she still caught people's eye. That wasn't unintentional. People were easily manipu-lated, and Jenny was a master at it.

She called the lift, admired herself in the mirror posi-tioned behind a beautiful vase of white lilies and gave her hair a superfluous ruffle.

Right at that moment, she pushed all thoughts of murder, torment and grief out of her head. This was about her.

Jenny got into the lift without giving anyone or anything else a second thought. Poised, one hand on her hip, she stretched out the other hand to jab at the button for the fifth floor. A crafty smile crept across her face as the lift doors closed.

Chapter 25

As soon as Travis was in the car, Hazel drove as fast as the black box recording her speed would allow. She wanted to get him away in case Aiden or Jenny returned before she could whisk him to the police station.

If the Bloomfields did come back, she certainly couldn't stop him from asking if they could come along. It was clear for all to see that he was trying his best to hold it together, and right at that moment he still considered Aiden to be his friend.

'How did you sleep?' she asked, taking her eyes off the road for a second to look at his profile.

'Like both of my parents just died,' he said, leaning his head back against the seat rest and closing his eyes.

She bit her lip to stop herself saying that she would take him back to the Bloomfields' for a couple of hours' sleep, and then collect him later. Welfare she was good at but not at the cost of it getting in the way.

They drove along in silence, Hazel not sure if Travis was asleep.

She parked the car in the police station rear yard and

turned off the engine. He opened his eyes, silently got out of the Skoda and followed her inside.

'Been here loads of times as a kid,' he muttered as they walked towards a witness-interview room.

'Can I get you anything?' she said as they took seats either side of a cheap rectangular table, crime-prevention leaflets and dog-eared blank statement forms adorning its surface.

'No thanks.'

'One of the things we need to go over, Travis, is your family tree.'

He gave a wry smile.

'Am I auditioning for *Who Do You Think You Are?*'

'No, I need to establish who everyone is and if there are any other family members we need to speak to or be aware of.'

'OK. I'm not going to be awkward.'

He scratched the side of his face and looked as though he was giving the matter serious consideration. 'Like I told you, Mum's parents died young. Cancer, I think. She didn't really talk about them, and she didn't have any brothers or sisters. I don't ever remember her telling me about any aunts and uncles, grandparents, so I suppose that there weren't any.'

She gave him an encouraging smile and said, 'Have you any idea why she'd go to Ealing?'

'Ealing? What, like the film studios?'

'I don't necessarily know that she went there,' said Hazel, trying to remain guarded about the investigation, and also not wanting to cause the young man any more worry than he was already going through. 'She had a travel card in her handbag for London and bus times for Ealing.'

'Ealing? I don't think she'd ever been there in her life. She came from the West Country. You wouldn't know it from the way she talks.'

He caught what he had said and his eyes welled up. Hazel barely heard what he whispered next.

'I meant, from the way she used to talk.'

Realizing that the family history could wait a little longer, she asked him if he wanted a case worker.

'They work for the Home Office, Travis. I can't talk you into having one, but they really are very good. It does take a number of days, about five or so as soon as I refer you. They'll stay with you beyond any court case, and be with you for longer than I can stay in contact.'

'You said court case.'

'I did say court case. We're going to find out who killed your mum, although I'm not promising you it'll be today.'

She was aware that she might be telling him more than perhaps she should at this point. She felt herself torn as her job was to help him, all the while investigation and handling of the case management being her chief tasks. They didn't include being his friend or giving away tactics.

Her phone beeped at her with a message. It read *Aiden B in custody. Mum nearly nicked too for obstructing police. Want a hand?*

They were in an area of the police station seldom

used in the late afternoon. The patrols were out at calls and the CID office and incident room were a very long scream away. Hazel inched her chair closer to the panic button on the wall.

'Travis, I have to tell you something.'

His head snapped up.

'What's wrong? There can't be anything worse than what's already happened?'

'We've made an arrest,' she said, leaving her words hanging in the still air between them.

'There's no easy way to tell you this: even though we make an arrest, and we don't make an arrest for murder lightly, it doesn't mean he's guilty. We arrested him on *suspicion* of murder. I need you to understand that.'

She paused again, to allow Travis to catch his breath.

'A few minutes ago, we arrested Aiden on suspicion of your mother's murder.'

His face shut down as he stared at her, rapidly blinking, seeing nothing.

Then the red mist came down.

'The fucking bastard,' he screamed, jumping to his feet and grabbing the corner of the table.

'Travis, don't,' she shouted at him.

The interview-room door slammed open back against the wall, and three uniform officers and DC Tom Delayhoyde filled the room.

'Everything OK in here?' said one of the officers Hazel didn't recognize.

Travis looked down at his hands where they had the

table by its edges, two of the table legs inches from the ground. There wasn't a doubt in anyone's mind, including his own, that he had been about to upend the furniture, and possibly he wouldn't have stopped there.

That was the moment he crumbled. The tears came then and through them, Hazel heard, 'Sorry, sorry, Mum.'

She gestured towards the two men and two women who had rushed to her assistance that they could leave them alone now.

'I'm outside if you need me,' said Tom, pulling the door shut behind him.

She gave Travis a couple of minutes while he battled before her to take it all in. His ashen face gave her a glimpse of the stress he was under. Eventually Hazel said, 'I know it was probably the last name you were expecting me to give you.'

Even though he was rubbing his eyes, she worked out that he was shaking his head at her.

Travis looked up at her with bloodshot eyes and said, 'Not really, no. He liked my mum, he liked her a lot.'

He banged his elbows on the table and buried his face in his hands. He spoke through his fingers, forcing Hazel to lean forward so that she could make out his words and not miss a thing.

'It was stupid and childish. I know that now, I suppose I knew it at the age of fourteen. It was only mates messing about. You know how these things start?'

Hazel didn't know exactly what he was talking about but she had a sinking feeling that she had a good idea

where it was heading, and it wasn't going to help matters in the slightest.

Travis finally took his hands away and looked up at
the officer.

'We had a bet to sleep with each other's mum. I think
Aiden won.'

Chapter 26

Once Doug Philbert and Sophia Ireland were some distance from their interview with Sasha Jones, the DI asked his DC's opinion of the young officer.

'Difficult to say really,' she said, leafing through her investigator's notebook as Doug drove. 'Her breaking down in tears, wiping her eyes and sniffing uncontrollably certainly made it slow going. I got down everything she said in note form before you had her sign the statement. It seems she has little to lie about; we already know they were having an affair, so why not be upfront with us?'

'Perhaps she's keeping something back because she's a murderer?' said Doug.

'You really think so? She didn't strike me that way, although I've been wrong before.'

'You, Soph? You got something wrong?'

'Yeah, dealt with a bloke for attempted rape a couple of weeks ago. Had him down for a right sex case. Horrible bastard. Turns out that the victim had made the whole thing up as a cry for help, even though she picked him out on an ID parade. She was on CCTV with her mates the other side of town downing shots when she said it happened.'

'Look on the bright side – he might have enjoyed the penile swabs. Still, chances are he's done something else, only we can't prove it at the moment.'

'That's very cynical, Boss.'

'After all this time, do you know how to be any other way?'

'No, no, I don't,' said Sophia. 'And here we are at this probably completely innocent, yet suspended police officer's house, an officer who has been arrested for headbutting a prisoner in handcuffs with six witnesses looking on.'

'That's a bit harsh, Soph,' he said. 'I like to think that I'd have behaved differently towards a prisoner doing something so vile towards me, although I suspect I'd have had a hard time restraining myself.'

'Perhaps you're right. Let's see what he has to say for himself as regards the murder of his ex-girlfriend's boyfriend's wife.'

They got out of the car and walked about two hundred metres back towards George Atkins's house. It was a modest terraced house only a few streets from East Rise Police Station, the place where George had been stationed for the last two of his twelve years' service.

He had been one of those officers who had slipped under the radar often enough, always a feeling about him that something wasn't right: he'd cut corners before he had a full grasp of what he was doing, he drank in pubs with people he shouldn't have been drinking with and he got away with his unorthodox behaviour because he arrested a lot of people. He didn't only make arrests, he got prisoners charged and convicted, and so no one checked on what he was doing because he made the detected-crime figures look good. These weren't spoken about because, officially, they didn't exist.

George Atkins had been popular up to a point – he'd arrested a sixteen-year-old boy with hepatitis who spat in his face, so George headbutted him.

That wouldn't go away: he found himself on his own, no longer looked after by those in authority because of the good results he had brought in over a long period of time.

They knocked at the door and were greeted by a weary face.

'Suppose you want to come in,' he said, turning and walking away, not even bothering to wait until they were inside to shut the door behind them.

'Hello, George,' said Sophia, wiping her feet on the mat, more out of sarcasm than a need to avoid traipsing filth through the house. It didn't seem as though the floors needed any more help.

She cast an eye around the living room, which wasn't much better than the cluttered hallway they'd walked down and dirty kitchen they'd glanced into on their way to his sofa.

'How have things been then?' asked Doug.

'At least I'm still being paid,' George said, sitting on

the armchair nearest to him. It had a half-full ashtray resting on its arm. A matching one sat on the floor beside the sofa, only this one was overflowing.

'Sorry about the mess,' he said. 'I haven't felt like doing much lately.'

The room, perhaps the house, had been a neat and tidy place once, though it now had an air of despair, not to mention cigarette smoke. George certainly wasn't going to expand on his situation to the two police officers, but when he had been suspended, everyone had severed all ties with him. The only people he ever spoke to were senior officers and Professional Standards Department keeping him updated on his impending court case. His day now lacked purpose, not to mention the chance to be the one thing he had truly loved being – a police officer. It had been taken away from him in a couple of seconds as he reacted to a boy spitting in his face. He was spiralling towards depression. He knew it but was powerless to stop it and didn't know how to ask for help. So he stayed silent, knowing everyone expected him to be punished for what he did. No one expected it more than George himself.

'We need to speak to you about something important,' said Doug, sitting on the edge of the sofa. 'We're here about Milton Bowman and his wife.'

George sat looking from Doug on the sofa to Sophia where she stood in front of the television.

'What about them?' he asked.

'Have you heard what's happened to them?' Sophia asked.

'No, should I have?'

'They're dead.'

'Fuck. What happened? Did someone kill them?'

'What makes you say that?' interrupted Doug.

'You're both Major Crime,' he said. 'You'd hardly be here unless it was suspicious. No one drops by for social calls any more so I'm taking a wild stab in the dark here that – oh fuck. They weren't stabbed, were they, because this isn't a confession. It's an expression, a saying.'

'We need to know where you were and who you were with between certain times, so shall we get started?' asked Sophia.

George got out of his seat and started to clear the debris from the sofa so that the DC could sit down. Despite his bitterness over his arrest and suspension, he understood that, as serious as the whole episode had been, having his name associated with a murder investigation was a whole different matter.

'What do you need to know?' he asked when everyone was settled.

'I'd like to start with what happened between you and Sasha Jones,' said Doug, going straight to the heart of the matter.

George licked his lips and then rolled his eyes.

'Sash and I were getting on. It was going well. As far as I was concerned, we had a future. Then all of a sudden, she tells me there's someone else. I was angry, upset, and, of course, I wanted to know who it was.

'This was all before I got suspended, although I'm

not making excuses for what I did. Sasha and I were serious as far as I was concerned. Then she met Milton Bowman. I should have realized that something was different. She changed.'

'What did you do?' asked Doug.

George stared at him, unblinking.

'You said that you're not making excuses for what you did. So what did you do?'

George sighed, a deep, long sigh.

'You're going to find out, I suppose. I shouldn't have done it. I went to his house to have it out with him only he wasn't there. His wife was, though, Linda. I told her all about her husband and my girlfriend.'

Chapter 27

Feeling that for the first time that day they might finally be getting somewhere, Doug said, 'When did you go to the Bowmans'?'

'It was ages ago. Over three weeks ago and I haven't been back since. Ask the son, Tony, Troy ... Travis. Ask him. He was there too. He was interested to hear what his old man had been up to.'

'OK, George. We need to know exactly what the three of you spoke about and when this was,' said Sophia, getting her notebook ready.

'Oh for fuck's sake. How was I supposed to know what was going to happen? I can promise you that I didn't kill either of them. I certainly wouldn't have hurt her. She was an injured party, just like me, although I got the impression she could handle herself too. He was a real horrible bastard. He broke my leg once in a football match. Did you know about that? It was a so-called friendly game of five-a-side. He broke my leg, probably only because I'd scored three goals and he can't stand to lose. Bloke's a tosser.'

Sophia scribbled furiously to keep up.

George watched her write and they locked eyes as Sophia's pen came to a stop.

'I probably shouldn't even be talking to you without a solicitor or Police Fed representative,' said George.

He glanced up at Doug and then added, 'But the look on your face tells me that I'm going to get into even more trouble if I don't cooperate with you.'

'Why don't you go and put the kettle on and we can get this cleared up?' said Doug, unfolding his arms, trying his best to keep a neutral look on his face.

George nodded and went off to the kitchen.

'How do you know he won't do a bunk out of the back door?' said Sophia.

'All that rubbish piled up against it, he'll never get out. There must have been eight black sacks between him and the door handle.'

'I thought for a minute we were going to arrest him,' said Sophia.

'I considered it, then thought it was better to have his version now, so we can check out what he tells us. If need be, we can arrest him at the end if we're not happy. You OK with that?'

'When he comes back, do you want me duck out and call Hazel Hamilton? Let her know what he's said about Travis? She can check what he's saying.'

He kept his answer to himself as George came back in with three mugs. He placed them on a pile of old newspapers and magazines strewn across the table.

'Can't find the coasters,' he said as if it made any

difference to his furniture having three scald rings on its surface. He did have the decency to pull an empty carrier bag from his jeans pocket and begin stuffing the empty takeaway cartons into it.

'And it's black coffee,' he said when he'd sat back down in the armchair following his brief clear-up. 'I didn't expect guests and I'm out of milk. Let's get on with this then.'

Doug sat in the other armchair, having given the room the once-over while their host was making the drinks. It seemed clean enough to him. All of the mess appeared to be either rubbish that hadn't been taken out, or general untidiness over the last week or two. It didn't seem like he'd chosen to live in a state.

'When were you arrested and suspended, George?' he asked.

'Sixteen days ago. I haven't done much since. It was all well and good all the time I was at work, bringing prisoners in, getting TICs to make the figures look good, but as soon as there's a problem, no one wants to know me.'

There was a pause whilst the three of them considered the last comment, two of them thanking their lucky stars they weren't in George's position.

'Also,' continued the disgraced police officer, 'that's how I know it was about three weeks ago that I went to see Milton Bowman. Even I'm not stupid enough to go to a DI's house and kick off when I've just been nicked for assaulting a prisoner. I went around there a few days before I was arrested.'

He glanced down at his own hands and started to examine his remarkably clean fingernails.

'I know that I'm not supposed to talk about what I did to the prisoner, and I'm not making excuses, but I was so angry when I'd finished speaking to Linda and Travis. I stewed on what they'd told me for days. I was like a pressure cooker waiting to go off.'

'What did they tell you?' said Doug, aware from the sound of her pen against the page that Sophia was busy writing away.

'His wife said that over the last few years twice Milton had given her a sexually transmitted disease from different affairs he'd had. Twice she'd threatened to leave him until he begged her to stay. Sasha was simply someone else he was shagging. He used her. That's what made it even worse.

'I really loved Sash, and he took her from me, and now it looks as though I'm losing my job. I've hit rock bottom but I'm not a murderer. You're looking in the wrong place here.'

He paused, looked from Doug to Sophia and back again before he added, 'You haven't told me how they died. My money's on Milton done her in, and then topped himself. You thought of that?'

'Any idea why Milton would kill his wife?' said Doug. 'From what you just said, he begged her to stay, so why kill her?'

George sat in silence for a couple of seconds, ran his tongue over his front teeth and seemed to give what he was about to say serious consideration.

'I'll level with you,' he began, staring intently at Doug Philbert. 'I didn't like the bloke, thought he was a twat, and whatever you think of me for assaulting a prisoner, Milton was in a whole other league of dodgy copper.

'There was something not right about him. He was always operating under the radar. That stabbing in Wolfram Street, the drugs one when he met Sasha, there was something not right about that. I heard a whisper those dealing on the periphery got away with it. They were given the nod by someone.'

He sat back in his chair.

'No one would ever take my word for it, especially not now. For what my opinion's worth, I'd say Milton was behind it and his wife found out.'

Chapter 28

'Why has my son been arrested?' said Jenny Bloomfield, fists clenching and unclenching on the tabletop where she'd been pounding them. 'And why am I here in the police station?'

'I've told you, Mrs Bloomfield,' said DC Tom Delayhoyde, 'your son's been arrested on suspicion of the murder of Linda Bowman. You can't stay at home because we have a warrant to search it and it'll take some time. We've had to bring you here to allow the CSIs and search team to do their jobs without interruption.'

'So can I leave?'

He'd known this was coming.

'You're not under arrest at the—'

'Then you can't stop me from going.' She stood up, her fitted red dress a stark contrast to the grey and beige of the witness-interview room that Hazel Hamilton and Travis Bowman had occupied only a couple of hours beforehand.

'This afternoon at your home, you came very close

to being arrested for obstructing a police officer in the execution of their duty. It's going to do Aiden no favours if you walk out of here without telling me what you know.'

She flashed him a winning smile, smoothed down her dress and said, 'Forgive me, Tom, was it? The last couple of days have been very trying for all of us.'

'I've also got a DNA kit here,' he said, picking up a plastic-wrapped pack and holding it out briefly. He didn't take his eyes off her and thought he saw a flash of panic streak across her face.

'You have Aiden in custody, so I don't see why you want mine too, but of course I'll let you have it.'

'It's for elimination purposes,' he said. 'The officers haven't taken yours yet. Before we do that, tell me about Aiden and where he was yesterday morning.'

Jenny opened her mouth to say something but Tom put his hand up and continued. 'Whatever you tell me must be the truth. Don't try to help Aiden by leaving anything out or, even worse, making anything up. OK?'

She nodded slowly and wiggled back in her chair, crossing her legs.

'You're probably too young to have children,' she said, 'but when you do have them, you worry about them night and day. Where they are, what they're up to. We have a daughter too, but she married an Australian and she never comes home. I didn't like him, he wasn't good enough as far as I was concerned, although that's probably a natural thing for a parent to think. It's mostly me and Aiden, as his father's away most of the time. I know where Aiden is almost every minute of the day.'

Tom gave a tight smile and was pleased to break eye contact with her when his phone bleeped at him. The text message read *Aiden wants a solicitor. No interview yet.*

'So where was he yesterday morning?' Tom asked again.

'He was at home in bed. He wanted to go out Sunday evening with Travis. They were going to see a band at the Three Blackbirds. An old schoolfriend of theirs is the lead singer and they wanted to go along and support her. Neither Aiden nor Travis drink very often. They're both very much into their fitness, they're always at the gym together if they're not at one another's houses. It's been that way for years.

'Anyway, it was decided that Travis would stay over so they could walk to the pub from our house and both have a couple of beers. I was in bed when they came in about midnight, you know what people are like after they've had a couple of drinks, crashing and banging. It's especially true of young men like them. I could hear them talking and then they both went to bed. When I woke up about six o'clock, they were still in their own rooms. I know because Aiden left his door open and I could hear Travis snoring away.'

She gave a happy little nod at this.

'And what time did they get up?' Tom asked.

'Neither of them came downstairs until after nine. I

know it was after nine because the news had finished on the radio and I was thinking about going out. The main reason I didn't was the local news said that the dual carriageway was blocked because of an accident and something about the air ambulance. I didn't know the significance of it at the time.'

She cast her eyes down at her hands, now folded in her lap. 'Of course, it was Milton. Poor Travis had no idea of what the rest of the day was going to bring. And now you've got my son in here, arrested for the murder of his best friend's mum. It's clear to me that you've got the wrong person. I know my son and he's not capable of killing someone. You should be looking for someone else. Why would he kill her?'

'That's one thing we'd like to find out, although first we have to establish whether he did or he didn't kill her. Shall we start with how well you knew Linda?'

'I had no time for her lately, no time at all. The last time I had a proper conversation with her ended in quite a row. It was about a month ago when I went to pick Aiden up for lunch with his grandmother.'

'What was the row about?'

She paused and picked invisible thread from her dress.

For the first time, Jenny seemed reluctant to answer. Up until that point, even when she was trying to stop the arresting officers from taking her son away, she'd argued and shouted, even tried to be pleasant when that wasn't working. There hadn't been a time when she had nothing to say.

Until now.

Jenny hadn't so far said anything to alert Tom to the fact that she might be lying, but now it was the parts she was leaving out that rang alarm bells.

'It wasn't about anything in particular. I think I was late getting to her. Travis had already gone out and she wanted to go out. It was merely one of those silly things that old friends sometimes fall out over. Aiden isn't a child; she could have left him in her house to shut the door behind him. She seemed to overreact at being on her own with him.'

Tom had one of those rare chill-down-the-spine moments in policing when he knew he was on to something. There was definitely more to the argument than she was letting on, and it just might take him much closer to finding Linda Bowman's killer.

Chapter 29

Hazel left Travis with a DC from Major Crime and gave him instructions to go to the canteen for a cup of tea, having made sure the television was switched off, and wait for her. She didn't want her witness wandering off and she needed to speak to Barbara Venice.

'Just got the preliminary post-mortem results back for Linda Bowman,' said the DCI. 'You won't be surprised to hear that, subject to toxicology results and so on, the cause of death was extensive skull fracturing.'

'I'm about ready to set off with Travis so he can see her and formally identify the body. I've checked that he didn't want anyone else to do it. We all know that this is going to break his heart but he wants to see her anyway.'

'Hazel, I don't want to teach you to suck eggs but—'

'Don't let him touch the body, I know. Well, she's got head injuries so I'll have that uncomfortable conversation with him when we get nearer. He's been through so much that surely, if he gets the chance, he can at least hold her hand?'

'At least keep an eye on him; just don't go soft on us.'

'Never, ma'am. Far too tough for that.'

She backed towards the door, itching to get back to Travis and at the same time wanting to ask more about the McCalls.

'And, Hazel, thanks for going to the hospital today. I know you've got enough to do. I'll let you know more about Linda's family as soon as I can, and to be honest, I haven't got the complete picture myself just yet.'

Hazel looked at the detective chief inspector, decided to smile at her, and said, 'I'll catch up with you later. I only dropped in to let you know that I'm taking Travis to see his mum. Did you need me to ask him anything in particular?'

'No. Make sure you look after yourself and limit your hours. I'll see you tomorrow and call if you need anything.'

'I could do with a life,' she called as she made her way towards the security door leading from the Major Crime Department.

'Then make sure you get one,' the DCI called back.

Thoughts of all the things she should be doing over the next few days vied for space in Hazel's mind as she walked towards the lift to take her to the canteen on the fifth floor. She jabbed at the buttons, willing one of the lifts to arrive so she could put her personal life aside and get on with something that she was much better at, more at home with – her job.

She pulled her phone from her trouser pocket as it started to ring. As she answered it, the doors opened and she caught her reflection from the mirror at the back of the lift. She stood where she was and watched her own face break into a smile as she said to the caller, 'Hello, Harry.'

'Hello, Hazel.'

She heard a pause before he said, 'You're probably too frantic with work to talk to the likes of me.'

'No, I've got time,' was all she said, automatic doors closing again, taking the lift off somewhere without her.

'I was wondering how it was going.'

'I can't really—'

'No, no, of course you can't. Let's be honest, although I'm desperate to know how it's going and how far you've got, the real reason I'm ringing you is to see if you fancy that drink some time.'

'I'd love to,' she said.

'How about this evening?' said Harry.

Hazel hesitated. She was trying to estimate how long it would take to get to the hospital, see Linda's body, speak to Travis and get him dropped off at a relative's house, fill in all the necessary paperwork, update all those who needed updating and then fit in shaving her legs and washing her hair.

'If you can't do tonight, we can make it another day,' said Harry. 'Only if you've got time.'

'Today might be a little awkward. I've got to contact the charity and postpone picking up a dog, and most importantly, I've got to take Travis somewhere.'

'Ah,' said Harry.

'Precisely,' she said. 'That's why I can't commit to how long I'm going to be. Saying goodbye to your mum can take time.'

'OK. Well call me when you're off duty. It doesn't matter what time of day or night. I could do with someone to talk to. I can't think of anyone else I'd rather have ring me.'

As she put her phone away and made her way up the five flights of stairs, all thoughts of taking the lift banished from her mind, she wondered how much this was affecting Harry. He'd been friends with Linda for years, and hadn't merely lost her to a murderer, but had found her bloodied, damaged body. She wasn't even sure if he knew her real name.

Hazel liked Harry a lot. She'd always had a bit of a soft spot for him, although strictly in a professional working capacity. She could see through the bravado and bluster to the thing that really made him tick: he was decent and couldn't abide anything or anyone who wasn't.

The only thing that bothered her about going out with him was whether he was thinking clearly; perhaps when the dust settled, he'd come to his senses and realize that he'd made a terrible mistake. She didn't want to be someone else's burden. Hazel wasn't comfortable dating someone who was on the rebound, and this seemed to be taking being on the rebound to a new level: finding the murdered body of someone you'd adored for decades was bad enough. Add a wife who had walked out, and Hazel couldn't fathom what was going on in Harry's mind.

One thing was for sure, Harry rarely uttered a single sentence without a liberal sprinkling of profanity. Their conversation had lasted for one minute and four seconds according to her mobile, and he hadn't sworn once.

There was definitely something wrong with Harry Powell.

Chapter 30

As Hazel was driving Travis to the viewing room at the mortuary, Aiden Bloomfield was being given his legal rights and being booked into custody.

He'd been searched, his clothing seized, his photograph and fingerprints taken, another DNA sample taken, not to mention so many other forensic samples, cuttings and scrapings, he'd lost track of what was happening. When asked if he would like to speak to a solicitor, he'd not known what to do.

The custody sergeant's attitude hadn't been what he was expecting either. He was slow and patient with Aiden. He'd explained what was happening and told him it was a very serious matter and that he should think very carefully about having a solicitor. He'd gone with the custody sergeant's offer of calling him one from 'the scheme'. Aiden had no idea what the scheme was, but it was billed as a good thing. He took it to be some sort of call-out rota which might have been explained to him too. He couldn't fully grasp what was going on in this previously unknown world.

Eventually, he was walked down corridors smelling of body odour, past large blue metal doors leading to cells, some of the doors open and some closed. Angry voices and banging came from behind two of the closed ones as Aiden made his way to number 14.

His was the only cell with a chair outside it.

'I'm going to leave the door open and sit out here,' said the officer in uniform who had escorted Aiden to his designated cell. 'You need a drink?'

Aiden didn't know at that moment what he needed, except to be out of the police station and at home, wishing that the last forty-eight hours hadn't happened. How he had come to end up here, he couldn't begin to work out. He wanted to scream at them that it was all a terrible mistake, they had the wrong person, but wasn't that what everyone said?

Instead, he simply shook his head at the young man in front of him.

'You may as well get your head down,' said the officer. 'Your brief will be here soon. And that's about all I know.'

The police officer knew better than to get into a conversation with a prisoner whose custody record was headed 'Murder'. He'd sat and watched prisoners on constant supervision many times in his eight years as a uniform officer. Normally they settled down and went to sleep. Only once had he had to go in the cell when a woman arrested for trying to kill her own daughter had started to eat the foam linings from her custody-issue disposable feet coverings. He got the impression that the teenager in front of him was far too startled by the day's events to give him any problems.

He held the heavy cell door open and motioned for Aiden to go inside.

It was empty except for a bench built into the far wall, thin blue mattress and pillow on top of it, and a metal toilet with no seat or toilet paper.

The officer saw him looking at the meagre facilities.

'You need to use it, let me know and I'll push the door to, give you some privacy. Toilet paper's out here too.'

Something about Aiden's demeanour made the officer feel sorry for him. He'd clearly never found himself in custody before, and certainly not for something that might lead to him spending decades in prison.

'Some of the ones we get in here think it's funny to block the toilets with the whole roll,' he explained.

Aiden walked over to the bench, sat on the edge and put his head in his hands.

How had his life gone so wrong that he was now having his toilet-paper sheets monitored?

Right then, he hated Linda Bowman with all his heart and he was glad she was dead.

Chapter 31

The drive to the hospital's chapel of rest was about the tensest part of being a family liaison officer. Hazel's job was to be a police officer and investigate; it would take the truly inhuman to remain unaffected by the atmosphere in the car. She knew what they were about to do and Travis had a good idea of the hideous task in front of him. Many people lived their entire lives without seeing a dead body. A great number of those who had dealings with corpses did it in a professional capacity. Few nineteen-year-old students stood in the same room with death, and not when the cadaver used to be their mother.

She parked the car in the police bay close to the entrance. She had tried to keep the conversation going as much as she could, and checked with Travis that his aunt Una, Milton's sister, was going to meet them after he had seen his mum. Travis seemed reluctant to allow his aunt to see Linda and Hazel wasn't able to establish why. She decided to work on it throughout the rest of the day, but for now, she had something a little more pressing to tell him.

'Travis,' she said, turning off the engine, 'I haven't been to this chapel of rest before. They vary.'

She stared at his profile. His jaw was clenched and she saw him swallow and nod at her, looking straight ahead.

'Because they vary, until I get in there, I won't know if your mum will be in the same room as us or behind glass.'

'Behind glass? I can't touch her?'

'If she's in a separate viewing room and you want to touch her, I can ask for you.'

She took a deep, silent breath. 'The thing is, if you are allowed to hold her hand, she'll be covered by a sheet. It's important that you don't move anything that's covering her.'

Without moving the back of his skull from the head-rest he slowly turned his head in her direction.

'Is she ... Will she ...?'

'Do you remember me telling you that the pathologist had to carry out a post-mortem?'

'Mmm.'

'And your mum has head injuries. It's important for you that you don't try to move her.'

Hazel really didn't want to spell it out, but she needed him to understand that the parts of his mum that weren't exposed were covered for a reason. The staff had to preserve the dignity of everyone, whether they were alive or dead, and to cause as little anguish as possible.

Years before, she'd learned the hard way when one of

the first families she was assigned to was taken in to see their twenty-two-year-old daughter. The young woman had been stabbed in the heart on her way home from a party when a fight had broken out on the night bus she was on, and she took her last breath on the top deck, despite the best efforts of the attending paramedics. The hospital staff at the chapel of rest hadn't pulled the sheet up fully to the girl's neck. The huge ugly stitches of the opening up of her chest cavity were on display when the parents rushed into the room before Hazel could stop them.

As if they hadn't had enough to deal with.

Janine Casey.

That was her name. Hazel had never forgotten the sight of her stretched out, resewn body, nor the scream from her mother, yet she couldn't always remember the girl's name.

That had been one of the worst days in her twenty years as a police officer. Others had surpassed it, but they were few in number.

'I also need to warn you,' said Hazel, eyes remaining on his face, 'what you see may not be pleasant. I haven't seen your mum, so I don't know how she is.'

She gave him a second to attempt to gather himself, and then added, 'Once you've seen her, I'll need a short statement from you, if you're up to it. We can't release your mum's name to the press until she's formally identified. That's important because we want people to come forward and help us, tell us what they know.'

He nodded at her again, trying to stop the tide of tears that wanted to come.

'When you're ready,' she said.

The hospital staff were expecting them.

After several minutes of Travis chewing the inside of his mouth, and crossing and uncrossing his arms over his chest, they were taken through a door to where his mum lay.

Within seconds of opening the door, Travis held his mum's cold dead fingers within his own.

His shoulders shook as the stark reality of death took hold of him, tearing his world into pieces. Minutes went by and eventually he said, 'It's my mum.'

Throughout the time they were with Linda Bowman's body, Hazel remained to the side of Travis, out of his eyeline whilst he was fully in hers. Even though they had a suspect in custody, it didn't mean they had the correct person yet, or that there was only one killer.

Both Travis's and Aiden's behaviour had always struck Hazel as a little odd, and now that the formal identification and viewing of Linda was underway, she was about to turn to her main business – that of investigating a murder.

Chapter 32

Finishing work on time wasn't an option for Hazel. She had known when she'd got out of bed that morning that her working day was going to last much longer than her rostered eight hours.

It was twelve hours since she'd begun her tour of duty when she signed out in the incident-room office diary and headed home. As she neared her car parked outside the police station, she took out her mobile phone and called Harry.

It wasn't a deeply considered decision, although she had been thinking about him all day. It struck her that she really needed some company and Harry had told her to call him, no matter what the time of night.

'Hey,' she said when he answered.

'Hey,' he replied. 'Are you calling to tell me that you're finished for the day?'

'I'm by my car, about to drive home.'

'Have you eaten?' said Harry, phone in one hand, the

156

other on the door of the oven as he checked to see how his home-made lasagne was coming along.

'No. I'm starving too. Still fancy a drink? We could go for something to eat as well.'

Harry shut the oven door.

'That sounds like a bloody good idea,' he said, turning the oven off. 'I don't have any plans at all.'

'How about we meet in an hour?' said Hazel, getting into her car.

'Do you know the Lazy Bullock in Steep Street?' said Harry.

He smiled as the sound of her laugh trilled in his ear.

'I know where it is although I've never been there,' she said. 'It sounds intriguing. I'll see you in there at nine o'clock.'

She drove home, smiling to herself that Harry had sworn down the phone, and also chosen a public house with a name as close to an obscenity as he could manage. Clearly he was feeling a little more like his old self.

The best thing about meeting him there was that it meant she didn't need too long to get ready: if she drove herself, there was clearly no chance of her regretting a lack of depilatory action in a few hours' time, and she definitely didn't have time for more than a shower and running her disposable razor up and down her legs.

What she needed right now was good company, a beer and food cooked by someone else. She'd see how tonight went and not rush into anything.

Harry meanwhile took the lasagne out of the oven to

cool, ran upstairs for his second shower of the evening, put on fresh clothes and even used aftershave for the first time since his wife left him.

Hazel knew that she wouldn't be having sex that evening; Harry wasn't going to risk it.

Chapter 33

Feeling more miserable than she thought she deserved to, Jenny Bloomfield slammed the door of Tom Delayhoyde's unmarked Ford Focus as he dropped her off at the town centre Premier Inn. He had offered to come inside with her, his suggestion met with a look of disdain.

It was something that had never crossed Jenny's mind, and why would it? The police were searching every inch of her home and her car, all because they had a Magistrates' Court search warrant, and had told her she couldn't come back or enter her home for at least a day. The realization that she had effectively been thrown out of her own house was the ultimate insult. She was sure they couldn't do this, even though according to the law it appeared that they could.

It was all she could do to concentrate on putting one three and a half inch designer heel in front of another, retain her composure and walk away, head held high.

How different this lobby felt beneath her feet from

the one she had sashayed herself across just a few hours earlier. This short promenade didn't even hold the promise of sex at the end of it.

She glanced towards the open-plan bar area visible just beyond reception and knew that she had made a mistake. She should have gone to the Grand. He would still have been there, waiting for her in the bar with a glass of champagne, ready as ever to make her forget she was a wife and mother. Make her feel how she hadn't felt in years.

Jenny gave an involuntary shudder.

The cheerful receptionist was saying something to her about a booking.

'Of course,' muttered Jenny as she pulled a credit card from her purse and slid it across the counter. Once again she wondered if she could get a cab and escape out of there. The only thing stopping her was that the police might think her behaviour was suspicious now she had been dropped off, and she definitely didn't want to alert them to anything.

Even so, she watched her fingers as they punched in her credit card pin number, filled out a form with her details on, and waited for her plastic room key.

'Will you be dining with us this evening?' asked the helpful young man.

'I hardly think so,' she said, before turning towards the corridor leading to the rooms. 'I take it you don't have a lift.'

'No, we don't,' he said, flat tone to his voice.

'It's just as well I only have a small amount of

luggage then,' she said to herself as she glanced down at the handbag over her shoulder.

First thing in the morning, she planned on walking to East Rise's only department store and purchasing herself a change of clothes. Just at that particular moment, she had never been more grateful for her clandestine meetings. Basic toiletries and a change of underwear weren't something she used to carry around with her.

Once inside the room, she closed the door, leaned her back against it and tried to evoke the feelings she had experienced in the last hotel room she found herself in.

A darkened room, two glasses of Buck's Fizz on a silver tray, a virtual stranger approaching her as she walked in. The feeling of her mouth being kissed by a man who wasn't her husband, something so illicit but so pleasurable.

A small gasp escaping from her as he ran his hands down her back, unzipping her dress, letting it fall to the floor.

Being kissed all over.

She opened her eyes. They focused on the purple soft furnishings hanging at a window with a view of a brick wall.

Jenny told herself that this was only temporary. Everything would be fine.

Chapter 34

'Don't know about you two,' said Milo, 'but this is my least favourite place of work in this shithole town.'

He glanced out of the window as Parker pulled the Range Rover to a stop at the end of the cul-de-sac.

'Fucking nasty place to do business,' agreed Diva, slow shake of his head as he glanced at the properties laid out in front of him.

'It really gives me no pleasure to be here, doing this,' said Milo, indicating the semi-circle of twelve bungalows, some with outdoor grab rails leading up to the front doors, a mobility scooter parked in one of the small front gardens.

Parker turned his head and spoke to his two associates in the back seat. 'Which one of you wants to tell Tandy that you didn't fancy it today?'

'No need to be fucking funny,' said Milo. 'We'll do our job, it just pisses me off that some dickhead at the council thought, I know what's a great idea. Let's have bungalows for the elderly, design them in a nice fan shape, give them all a little garden, and then we'll stick the ugly sisters and their drug-dealing old slag mother in there with them. My old mum lives somewhere like this. It gets me down, that's all.'

'Well fortunately,' said Diva, 'we're not here to find out if the social housing experiment is working, we're here to make sure this trio of dogs are doing as they're told. Come on.'

The two drug dealers got out of the car and made their way to the second property in the crescent. They hadn't walked more than about five feet when the front door started to open and a haggard face appeared in the gap before the door began to close again.

Both men broke into a run, Milo beating Diva to it. One swift kick with his boot and the wooden door crashed open, rebounded off the wall and came back on his foot. Unperturbed, he smoothed down his jacket, pushed the door so it was fully open and stepped inside.

Only when he heard Diva behind him and the latch closing did he move forward down the dingy corridor towards the only other opening off the hallway and the sounds of an evening television game show.

'Come out, come out, wherever you are.'

He took another step towards the retreating occupant, no doubt cowering in the living room or in one of the two disgusting bedrooms leading off it.

'Come on, Cynthia,' Milo called out. 'Be a good girl. I won't even hold it against you that your front door's scuffed my new boots. Fortunately, they're steel toe-capped so no harm done. Not yet anyway.'

He pushed the door open, careful where he put his

hand on the frame. A number of brown and black marks were visible along the paintwork, once white but now, like most of the place, covered in a yellow nicotine stain.

'It really is vile in here, Cynth,' he said as he looked down at the grey-haired widow, perched on the edge of the floral two-seater settee, trembling beneath her nylon housecoat.

'Evening, Cynth,' said Diva as he stood beside Milo, his own steel toe-capped boots coming to a stop at the edge of the petrified woman's slippers. 'It's like 19-fucking-75 in here. You might have got dressed, instead of sitting there in your nightie and curlers.'

'The, the girls aren't here,' she said. 'You've missed them.'

'Not to worry,' said Diva as he reached down and grabbed her chin, tipping her face up towards his. 'If the ugly sisters aren't here, we can make do with the wicked witch. Now where do you want to start?'

'Start?' she whispered.

'I'm feeling generous today. Fingers or toes?'

As he said the word 'toes', Diva inched his left foot forward, sole of his boot coming into contact with her big toe through the thin material of her cheap slippers.

She gave a gasp and her eyes widened.

'Please,' she said, 'I've got your money.'

He instantly let go of her face and straightened up.

'Well, why didn't you say so,' said Milo.

'Exactly,' said Diva. 'Making me go and touch you and everything. Where is it then?'

Still shaking, Cynthia got up from the settee and managed to make the six feet or so to the open-plan kitchen. She took a tea caddy down from the dusty shelf beside the kettle and tried to concentrate on undoing the lid.

Milo blew the air out of his cheeks, Diva looked at his watch and, just as both were losing their temper, she undid the tin and handed them a two-inch-thick wad of banknotes.

'Nice doing business with you,' said Diva as he counted and pocketed the money.

'See you same time next week,' said Milo as they made their way back to the front door. 'And try and clear up. This place is a fucking pigsty.'

'Don't know about you,' said Diva when they were both back inside the Range Rover, 'I feel a little hard done by now. I didn't expect them to have the money.'

His comment was met with a look of total disgust from his colleague.

'She's an old lady. Have some respect.'

Chapter 35

A few lucky detectives, such as Hazel, were allowed to go off duty. She still had to remain on the end of the phone, mainly for Travis, whilst most of the team were about to work long into the night.

Detective Constable Pierre Rainer had broken the happy news to Sophia as she got back from her already long day speaking to Sasha Jones and then George Atkins that she was earmarked for an even longer night of interviewing with the recently arrested Aiden Bloomfield.

'Did you murder Linda Bowman?' asked Pierre.

'No, of course I didn't,' said Aiden. 'I was crazy about her. I didn't murder her and I certainly wouldn't hurt her in any way.'

He looked across the interview-room table to where the two detectives sat, his brief on the same side of the table as him. He guessed it was supposed to be a show of solidarity that his solicitor had chosen to position herself shoulder to shoulder with him. He probably smelled, so she might well come to regret that as the night wore on.

'I had a bit of a thing for her,' he said, hands raised in front of him to stress his point. 'When we were kids, me and Travis used to mess around and say how nice-looking each other's mums were. You know how kids do.'

Neither Sophia nor Pierre could relate to what he was saying, but their job wasn't to judge. Not outwardly anyway.

'Well, it went a bit too far,' said Aiden, giving a small laugh. 'It'd probably be fairly funny if Linda wasn't dead. That's the thing though, she is dead 'cept I swear to you, I didn't kill her.'

'When did you last see her?' asked Pierre.

Aiden leaned forward and put his head in his hands.

'That morning.' He looked up at Pierre whose face was impossible to read. 'I saw her that morning. She told me the night before that Milton was going out early and if I wanted to see her, if I was serious about her, I needed to get over as soon as I could.'

Aiden picked up the paper cup next to him and took a sip of water.

'I don't think she had any intention of taking it further, you know. I'm not totally stupid. I realize that not only is she – was she – much older than me, but married and my best friend's mum. It doesn't get messier than that, well at least not until someone killed her.'

'What happened when you got to her house?' said Pierre.

'I got up early, walked over there, knocked on the front door and she let me in. It was a bit awkward really but we started kissing and ... Will Travis get to find out about this?'

'Don't worry about that. What happened?'

Aiden rubbed both hands across his face. 'We were in the kitchen. We kissed, and then she said it was wrong, she'd never been unfaithful to her husband in all the years they'd been together, despite the things he'd got up to. She started saying that two wrongs didn't make a right. She was messing with my head.'

He stopped speaking and after a few seconds, Pierre said, 'So how did you feel?'

'Yeah, good one. You want me to say how angry I was. Of course I felt stupid. She'd told me to come to her house at six in the morning when she knew she'd be alone. Her husband was on his way to work and her only son sleeping off a big night out at my house. I'm a nineteen-year-old fella, for Christ's sake. I thought my luck was well in. I'd even bought condoms the night before from the bogs in the Three Blackbirds. That's how much I thought things were going to happen.

'Now, in the cold light of day, I can see that she was leading me on. And before you try to make out that I lost my temper with her and bashed her on the head, when I left her, she was still very much alive. She told me to go because someone else knocked at the front door. We were in the kitchen and you can't see the street from that room. She panicked and thought that it might be Milton come home for something without his keys to let himself in. Who else was going to knock on the door at 6.30 in the morning? Even the milkman doesn't make a noise at that time.'

'Who was it?' asked Pierre.

'I don't know. I went out the back gate once I heard the front door shut. I didn't see anyone and there were no other cars parked outside. Milton's definitely wasn't there. It made me start to think that she'd asked some other bloke over to make a mug of me, so I went home, got back into bed and waited until I heard Travis get up and crash about in the shower. Then I did the same and had a cup of tea with my mum.'

It could have been a plausible story. Only problem was, no one had told Aiden or his solicitor what the cause of death was, and certainly no one had mentioned Linda had died from head injuries.

Chapter 36

When Hazel pulled into the Lazy Bullock's car park, she made a point of looking for Harry's car and choosing a space as far from it as she could manage. If he decided at the end of the night he wanted to kiss her goodbye, she wanted to give him as much distance across the tarmac as possible for him to pluck up the courage.

He'd got there before her which was a good sign, and she was five minutes early. Hazel didn't want to appear too keen so she sat for three minutes checking her messages on her phone before walking across to the door.

At one minute to nine, she made her entrance.

Harry sat at a table laid for dinner, close enough to the bar that they wouldn't have to go too far for their order, yet far enough away from other customers that they wouldn't be overheard. It was the same table she'd have chosen, had she got there first.

He stood up and pulled out another chair for her.

'Hello,' he said. 'You look nice. I'm glad you could make it.'

'Thanks,' she said, 'it's exactly what I need at the moment.'

'How do you know?' he said. 'I might be getting on your tits by the end of the night. Oh, good God. I didn't mean – I wasn't ...'

She felt herself start to laugh. The only time in the last couple of days she had managed to find anything funny was when she was talking to Harry.

'You're quite the tonic,' she said.

'Talking of drinks, what can I get you?'

'Half a lager. I'm taking no chances in case I get called back to work. And, sorry, but I'll have to keep my phone next to me on the table in case I'm needed. I took a risk leaving when I did.'

She watched Harry walk up to the almost empty bar, chat briefly to the barmaid, get their drinks and menus, and walk back over.

'I've not eaten in this pub for a while,' he said, putting the drinks down and handing her a menu. 'It's like a bloody morgue in here tonight.' He shook his head. 'I've done it again, haven't I? I can guess where you were today. I don't want to talk job all night, but how's Travis bearing up?'

'Under the circumstances, he's OK,' she said, noisily peeling the plastic pages of her menu apart.

Harry sat watching her. He took a sip of his pint.

'The beer's good,' he said, 'so good it looks like they glued the menu pages together with it. Are you happy to eat here? It used to be a really busy boozer until the landlord ran off with the takings a while back and it's never been the same since.'

'We're here now,' she said, pulling her fingers off the tacky surface of the menu, and laying her hand on top of Harry's.

He sat up a little straighter in his chair, smoothed his jacket and said, 'Starters?'

'You can't go wrong with vegetable soup.'

Twenty minutes later, they were both working their way through bowls of soup that neither of them was enjoying.

'How's your starter?' Harry asked.

'I didn't think it was possible to burn soup.'

'Yeah, it's a bit shit, isn't it? You want me to send them back?'

'No, it's fine. It's an improvement on driving whilst trying to eat a sandwich. How was your day?'

He shrugged and buttered his bread roll. 'It was all right except I'd rather be back in our incident room. Completely understand why I'm not, being a friend of Linda's and all that, but a murder investigation can take months. One of the reasons I tried so hard for promotion was because I wanted to work at East Rise Major Crime, now I've been sent away with my tail between my legs. As if everything else wasn't bad enough.'

'Do you mind if I ask you something?' said Hazel.

She paused and took a sip of her lager while the waitress cleared their bowls.

They both said a polite British 'Thank you', even

though the food had been passable and nothing more, and waited until she was out of earshot.

'Why are you now single?'

'The promotion I mentioned earlier?'

She nodded a 'Go on' at him.

'I took my eye off the ball. For a long time, I thought that the two of us were fine, we'd been through the grief of the early years, struggling financially, having kids, sleepless nights, all that bollocks. As far as I was concerned, we were steady and we were about to reap the rewards, despite the usual bickering all couples do. I thought if I got promoted to DI, with only five years left to go until I could retire, we'd have our future mapped out and it'd all be rosy.'

He took a long pull on his drink and finished it off.

'Turned out, she'd had enough of me and never paying her enough attention. Fate intervened, her dad died, leaving her mum alone in a huge house in Dorset. She took the kids and left six months ago. They're not coming back.'

'I'm sorry.'

'Don't be. She was a miserable fucker.'

The waitress returned with their main courses and got them more drinks, Hazel opting for lemonade.

'How's your chicken?' asked Harry. 'And be truthful. Mine's awful, so I doubt yours is any better.'

'It's OK,' she said. 'Anyway, I came out more for the company than the food and drink.'

'This steak's a disgrace. I hope this hasn't put you off coming out again with me.'

'Can I choose the location next time?'

'Next time? Certainly.'

He smiled at her, and then followed it with a frown aimed at his dinner.

'You know I'd like to tell you more about Linda and how things are going,' said Hazel.

'I know, and I'm not asking, though I'd love to know. That's not why I asked you to come to dinner with me.'

They halted their conversation as the waitress returned to clear the table.

'Was everything OK with your meal?' she asked, picking up Harry's plate.

'Tell the chef it's a draw,' said Harry. 'He couldn't cook it and I couldn't eat it.'

Without another word, the rest of the dirty plates were cleared away and they were alone once more.

'Perhaps I'll be able to tell you more over the weekend,' Hazel said.

'The weekend?'

'It's my weekend off. I won't get two days off now but if I can get an evening off perhaps we could go somewhere else.'

'You're on,' he said, pulling out her chair for her as she got up to leave.

Harry held the door open for her and said, 'Where's your car?'

She pointed to the farthest, darkest part of the car park, and felt Harry fall in step beside her.

As she opened her car door, Harry bent down to kiss her on the cheek and wish her goodnight.

Even though she'd enjoyed the evening, and liked the feel of the warmth of Harry's lips as they brushed her face, it conjured up images of Linda Bowman's last kiss.

Something she couldn't get out of her head the entire journey home.

Chapter 37

Doug Philbert waited until most of the staff in the incident room had either gone home for the evening or back out on enquiries before he made his way to Barbara Venice's office.

She looked up at him as he stood in the doorway, smiled and gestured for him to come in.

'You look as concerned as I feel, Doug,' she said. Something was weighing heavy on his mind and it was time to share it with her.

'I need to speak to you about a couple of things.' He sat down, cleared his throat, crossed his legs.

She waited a few seconds before she said, 'If this is about Linda's past, you don't need to look so worried. Since you called me on Monday morning, I've not been sitting idle. Things are in motion, not to mention what Hazel found out at Ealing Hospital.'

Doug could tell that Barbara was giving him her most winning smile, being everything he could hope for in a detective chief inspector. He was determined not to get up and leave the room before he unburdened his mind with his confession.

'It's, er, it's not only about her identity, you see.' He shifted in his seat, loosened his tie. Took a deep breath. 'There were other things I was aware of, and I did nothing.'

From Barbara's posture, he could tell he had her full attention.

'When I called you the other morning to tell you that I knew Linda Bowman wasn't in fact Linda Bowman, but was Karen McCall, what I didn't fully explain was how I knew her real identity.'

When he paused and saw Barbara open her mouth to comment, he gave a small shake of his head and held his palm out to stop her. He knew if he didn't get this off his chest, he never would.

'Whatever you think of me, please believe me, Barbara, when I say I did it for the right reasons.'

He watched her shift her expression to neutral, non-judgemental, and lean back in her chair, elbows resting on the chair's arms.

'Several years ago, I was working here late one night. I can't remember what for, and that's not important. I was the last one here and when I went downstairs to my car, I saw a woman wandering around the car park. As you know, the outer part of the car park nearest to the road is accessible by foot so I went to find out why a member of the public was walking about between the staff cars.'

He pushed his glasses back up his nose, a nervous gesture he was well aware of, before he continued.

'It was Linda. I could see she'd been crying and wanted to know where Milton was. He'd told her he was working late and was somewhere at East Rise. Of course, I hadn't seen him and knowing that despicable man – I know I shouldn't speak ill of the dead – he was probably off somewhere with a woman. We all know what he was like.'

The sound of an 'Mmm' came from Barbara but there was no stopping Doug now.

'I didn't have the heart to tell her what I suspected he was up to, although she was never a stupid woman. I made up something about him probably being at North Downs or Riverstone Police Station. I didn't fool her for one minute. Regardless of all that, she'd been drinking and was starting to get hysterical. I did the only decent thing I could think of; I took her home.'

He watched Barbara's jaw drop before he hastily added, 'This isn't me confessing to an affair: I took her home with the intention of dropping her at the door but she got more and more morose as the journey went on. I took her inside to sober her up.'

Doug massaged his temples, took another deep breath and said, 'Linda wanted another drink when we got inside the house. She'd gone out and left Travis in bed. He could only have been about eight or nine at the time and I went and checked on him, firstly to make sure he hadn't woken up and walked out into the night looking for his mum, and secondly, I was worried she might have hurt him.'

'What makes you think she'd have hurt him?' said Barbara.

'The things she was saying unnerved me. At one point, she said, "You think you know me, Milton thinks he knows me, no one actually knows me and what I'm capable of." Wouldn't you have checked on the boy?'

'Was Travis OK?' Barbara asked.

'He was fine, slept through the whole thing, fortunately. I went back downstairs and Linda had poured herself a drink, vodka or something. I knew that I couldn't stay all night and got the impression that this wasn't the first time something like this had happened. I wouldn't be able to keep an eye on her indefinitely. This was when she told me that her name was really Karen McCall and her family were put in Witness Protection in 1987.'

When Doug stopped rubbing the sides of his head, Barbara said, 'Since we spoke about this a couple of days ago, I've been in contact with Witness Protection. As you already know, Karen, her brother and her parents were all moved from the East End overnight and relocated to Plymouth, told never to come back.'

'Except she did come back,' said Doug. 'She met Milton when he was on holiday, moved back here. She told me that she didn't see the harm in it, after all, her mother Gladys hated it in Plymouth, missed the East End and went back, bold as brass. The extended McCall family all knew that she was back but never touched a hair on her head. I think that was one of the things that irritated Linda. She'd done what she was told whilst her mother went back home. The old man, Alec, he died some years ago too. I'm sure that by now you know as much as I do about the whys and wherefores of her midnight flit with her family several decades ago. The stuff I need to tell you is something different.'

Barbara waited. Doug confessed.

'Linda lifted her jumper up. She had bruises to her stomach. More on her arms. She told me Milton did it.'

'What did you do?' said Barbara. It was a straight-forward question asked without judgement.

'Nothing. I did absolutely nothing.'

'You—'

'No, no,' he said. 'There's no excuse for standing by and allowing anyone to suffer at the hands of a domestic abuser. I went one step further than ignoring it, I was a DI at the time and Milton was a DC. I decided to take him under my wing and keep an eye on him. I did it because I thought if I got to know him, understand what he was about, perhaps I could find out if Linda was telling the truth. You see, the problem was, I didn't actually believe her. Or perhaps if I'm honest with myself, I didn't want to believe her. Things were different then, attitudes were different. Partly, I suppose, I didn't want to do anything because I didn't want to take action against one of our own. Shameful.'

'You're not to blame for any of this,' said Barbara. 'Too true that you should have done something about her abuse if she was being beaten by Milton. Even so, you're not responsible for her death. We really don't think Milton killed her.'

For the first time since the news on Monday morning, Doug felt the pressure lifting from his shoulders. 'Why do you say that?'

'It took a while to get Milton's clothes back from the hospital and then off to the lab. The blood pattern distribution expert's taken a look at them, she can't find any traces of Linda's blood, no blood splatters consistent with her injuries, and as luck would have it, it was a new suit. Milton hadn't even got around to cutting the tags out. From his bank account, he only bought it on Saturday.'

'I know that this isn't about me,' said Doug as he allowed his shoulders to drop, 'except I'm very relieved to hear that. I've not been sleeping and it's weighed so heavily on my mind. I've been thinking over and over, if only I'd have reported it to someone, got Milton arrested. I don't know . . .'

'Doug,' she said, 'let's keep this to ourselves, shall we? There's no point in telling anyone else.'

Those were the words that Doug had longed to hear.

Chapter 38

Wednesday 7 June

'Morning, Haze. Briefing at eight o'clock,' called Pierre Rainer as he disappeared in the direction of the incident room's tiny kitchen, burdened with a tray of empty mugs no one had bothered to wash up from the previous day.

She had had a fitful night's sleep and wasn't looking forward to picking up Travis from his aunt's house and taking him to view his father's body, any more than she'd been keen to take him to see his mum's. It was, of course, necessary, and her feelings didn't enter into it. Travis wanted to say goodbye, even though she had explained that he didn't have to do it today; he was able to cut himself some slack and no one would expect him to have to contend with another hideous task so soon. It didn't make the work ahead any easier for Hazel, even though it was her job and not her dead family they were visiting. Trying to put such thoughts aside for now, she went and took a seat for the briefing.

Everyone piled into the conference room, sat and prepared to listen for the next couple of hours to what their colleagues had to say about the investigation and any developments overnight.

'Morning, everyone,' said DCI Barbara Venice from the top of the table. 'You're stuck with me at the moment because the out-of-county SIO, who was coming to take this over, got called to a rape and won't be coming for now. Not ideal, but we've had worse staffing situations so we'll crack on.

'Now, we're going to start the briefing with Pierre and Sophia because they've got to get back to interview the suspect as soon as possible. Tell us what he's been saying.'

Detective Constable Pierre Rainer had the full attention of the room.

'Aiden Bloomfield has told us that he liked Linda Bowman, although it hadn't developed into a sexual relationship. They'd flirted a bit and had exchanged mobile numbers. The only time he made any effort to see her was the morning of her murder.'

'Convenient,' murmured someone from the back of the room.

Pierre glanced around the room. 'His phone records would seem to show that they arranged to meet on numerous occasions and she cancelled him every time. Even now, he thinks that she was stringing him along. In all fairness, I think he's right. Hazel may be able to get some more from Travis about his parents' relationship, although for the moment, everything seems to show that Linda was a devoted wife and mum up until the point she started to lead Aiden on. What set that in motion, we currently don't know. Sophia's updated me on her enquiry with George Atkins, so if I had to guess, I'd say that his visit and what he said to her possibly triggered it.'

He went on to summarize the interviews of the previous evening and caught everyone's attention when he told them about the mystery visitor to the Bowman house at 6.30 in the morning.

'I don't need to tell you that this leaves us having to know who this person is,' said the DCI. 'That's, of course, if there actually was a visitor. What time did Milton leave his home address?'

Tom Delayhoyde cleared his throat. 'I can help with that, ma'am. My first task was to look at Mr Bowman's movements for the twenty-four hours before his accident. The call from Luke Morgan, the witness who saw the car crash, came in on the three nines system at 7.29 a.m. The Bowman house is about three miles from East Rise nick where he was due to start work at 8 a.m. Clearly that's plenty of time, even in traffic, to get there.'

He cleared his throat and looked down again at his notes.

'Serious collision investigation has looked at Mr Bowman's car. They haven't given us all of the information yet, this is just a preliminary report cos they know what we're dealing with. The car had an onboard computer. The start of his journey that morning at six o'clock shows that he did eight miles before impact. He was approximately two miles from his home address, so he clearly went somewhere else. I've looked at the Automatic Number Plate Reader, although I've not had time to track him properly. It looks as though he went in the direction of Roseville.'

'That's very interesting,' joined in Sophia. 'That's where Sasha Jones lives.'

In case anyone in the room wasn't sure of the significance of the name, she added, 'One of our PCs who's been having an affair with Milton Bowman.'

The room erupted into murmurings from all sides of the table.

'OK, everyone,' said the DCI. 'Not only are we getting a little distracted here from the agenda, but also I don't think I need to tell anyone in this room that it goes no further until we've got to the bottom of this. If Milton was at Sasha's house the whole time, depending on the time of death, it eliminates them both. Until that moment, she hears none of it. If it gets out of this room, I'll find out who couldn't keep their mouth shut and you can forget any idea of Major Crime for the rest of your career. What career you'll have left anyway. Got it?'

She surveyed the room, stony-faced.

Most nodded, a few looked the other way. The general consensus had been that Sasha Jones might have been the next witness to be propelled to suspect status and get herself arrested. That had all changed now.

'Right, everyone,' said the DCI, taking charge of the room. 'For now, we complete the Trace, Interview and Eliminate enquiry with Sasha Jones. This time, we get the truth from her about where she was. Make it abundantly clear to her what's going to happen if we don't get the complete picture.'

The DCI peered across at Sophia, who nodded in agreement.

'I'll go back and see her,' said DI Philbert. 'The reason we didn't finish the enquiry to the point of eliminating her from the murder was because she kept crying and there was snot everywhere.

'I've got something else I need to put to her anyway,' were his final words on it.

Doug sat and stewed over whether he should speak to Barbara after the briefing about George Atkins's unfounded allegations that Milton had been involved in something untoward around the time of the Wolfram Street stabbing. His boss seemed to have enough to contend with, and raising the idea that Milton might have been a corrupt officer on top of everything else could probably wait.

Hazel was the next to speak and gave a recap on Travis and how his behaviour had been.

'He's clearly distraught, which will surprise no one. Whether Milton killed himself or it was an accident, it doesn't take away from the fact that he's dead and Travis's mother has been murdered. Understandably, he didn't take it very well that his best friend had been arrested on suspicion of her murder. Interestingly, he didn't ask why we'd arrested Aiden. That could simply be shock or he's intelligent enough to know that we won't tell him. I've not read too much into it, just I've made a note of it.'

She tapped her investigator's notebook.

'I'm not meeting him until much later today as he's bound to have had enough of me by now. He also needs some time with his aunt, and we've still got his father's body to see at some stage, hopefully later today. At some point, possibly not today, I'm going to ask him if he knew his dad was having an affair, what George Atkins said to him and his mum when he visited, plus a few other things that aren't sitting right with me at the moment.'

She left it there, unable to hold Barbara Venice's gaze. She had pulled her aside prior to the briefing and told her not to mention Ealing Hospital or the names Karen McCall or Gladys McCall. It wasn't something that made her feel in the slightest bit comfortable.

'Thank you, Hazel,' said the DCI, giving nothing else away.

Hazel sat and listened to the rest of the briefing. She made notes and chipped in where she could assist. She even managed to pay attention to the administrative part of the briefing at the end where the DCI thanked everyone for their hard work, then told them it wasn't about to get any easier. There were staff coming from neighbouring counties' police forces to help them, there was more funding currently available and everyone's working day was to be a minimum of ten hours, plus at least one of their days off worked through, and staff weren't to be released to other investigations without the strict permission of the DCI.

Although the detective constable had managed to stay focused, the instant the first chair scraped across the floor, signalling a stampede for toilets, tea and telephone calls, her mind flew to Harry.

She'd fought all morning against calling him as she didn't want to seem too keen. She also didn't want to find herself telling him anything regarding the investigation that she ought not to share with him. He hadn't tried to get information out of her but if she steeled herself to speak to him she was less likely to let slip.

As Hazel left the room, she took her phone out of her pocket to call him. She sidestepped Tom Delayhoyde who seemed lost in thought, mind, she assumed, on the murder inquiry.

Tom made his way to another part of East Rise Police Station to gather his thoughts about something that didn't form a part of the senior investigating officer's priorities.

His head was full of the thought of his former relationship with Sasha Jones, and whether his own reputation would now be dragged through the mud.

Something he was desperate to avoid.

Chapter 39

Empty rooms were few and far between but Tom Delayhoyde managed to find himself alone in the space that used to be the officers' bar back in the day when East Rise was still the regional headquarters. He had heard from his dad that this one had been heavily subsidised by the other bar and the beer was better. It was decades before a woman had set foot in there, according to his dad, unless she was there to pull the pints or clean the ashtrays and hoover.

Nowadays it was the gym and golf where they all met and plotted who would go where and do what. Even without a smoky bar and sodden beer mats to linger over, the world hadn't changed; it had merely moved venues.

At least those in charge were getting some exercise and improving their longevity.

Tom, in the meantime, didn't want anything to get in the way of his career and blight the future with his new wife.

He took out his phone and called her.

'Hello, love,' Debbie said after only two rings. 'I've got some great news when you get home.'

'What's that?'

'It'll have to wait, but all I will say is that I didn't expect it to happen this quickly. Try to get off on time tonight. I'm looking forward to seeing you later.'

'If you're saying what I think you are, I'm absolutely blown away with it.'

Tom sat smiling to himself, excited wife on the other end of the line, even more determined now that nothing was going to get in the way of their happiness. Even so, he felt a tinge of despair that his wife's unsubtle hint at the announcement of a baby, his parents' first grandchild, meant she was expecting him home before midnight to celebrate.

Debbie was the most important person in the world: they had met, fallen in love, moved in together, planned and dreamed a future and now here it was taking shape.

Sasha was a dim and distant memory.

He ran his hands across his face, phone on the table in front of him, wishing he had never got involved with her in the first place. The ringing of his mobile snapped him out of it.

The screen showed *Sasha*.

He stared at the mobile, unsure if he should answer it. Even talking to her seemed to be betraying his wife. He dismissed the idea: Sasha was a long time before he'd got married, and the feelings he had for Debbie put anything he'd ever had for Sasha in the shade.

Tom hesitated, unsure if he should be talking to her. He knew the drill with a witness or anyone contacting the incident room – record anything they said in a notebook and then transfer that information to a message form so it could be registered on the HOLMES system. He had to make it known they'd talked. It wasn't worth losing his job over. If she told anyone they'd spoken and he didn't get in there first, he could be in trouble. He didn't relish that prospect, especially as he was one of the department's new additions. No one else was likely to put their neck on the line defending his actions. Now he had not only a wife, but probably a baby to look after. Nothing was worth the risk.

'Look after yourself, son,' his dad had always told him. 'They'll fuck you over soon as look at you. Don't give anyone the chance to do your legs. There's no honour amongst thieves and certainly not amongst those looking to save their own skin.'

He answered the phone, opening his notebook with his other hand to make a note of everything she said to him.

'Hello, Sasha,' he said. 'How are you keeping?'

A sob preceded her reply.

Tom tried not to verbalize his impatience down the line.

'What's up, Sash? I'm at work and probably shouldn't be talking to you. I'll have to pass on that we've spoken, and make a note of whatever you tell me.'

'Thing is, Tom,' she started and then paused, holding it together for as long as she could. 'Thing is, I don't know who else to talk to. Milton told me that he had a terrible row with his wife that morning before he left home. I know I should have passed all this on but I panicked. I was worried he really had killed her. I don't know what to do.'

He took a deep breath. 'Look, you're telling the wrong person about this. You need the DI to come back and talk to you again.'

He listened and heard a sniff, what sounded like Sasha blowing her nose and then she said, 'It's not only that. I met Milton at the Wolfram Street stabbing and—'

'You really shouldn't be telling me—'

'No, listen, please, Tom. I, I overheard some things, some things I probably shouldn't have, and it's to do with Milton and some stuff that he might have been mixed up with. I really am so worried and have no idea where to turn.'

Tom closed his eyes, slowly shook his head and, wishing he had never got mixed up with Sasha Jones, said the only thing he could to keep his job, a roof over his family's head: 'Leave it with me, I'll speak to Doug Philbert and get him to come back and see you again.'

Chapter 40

Following endless questioning, spanning hours, Aiden had been given a ready meal of slops that a dog would have turned its nose up at, and had settled down in his cell. He had struggled to sleep on the thin mattress, covered by an itchy blanket, and the door open so that he could hear the violent drunks being brought in overnight. Eventually, he had drifted off to sleep, only to be woken by someone screaming in a nearby cell. He dropped back off to sleep again, already growing used to a life inside.

He woke up at some point the next day, a fact he realized due to sounds of life that only a new day can bring, plus a cleaner mopping the corridor outside his cell and a woman police officer sitting outside the door.

He turned over and looked at her.

'Morning, Aiden,' she said. 'I've got toothpaste, shower gel and a towel here if you want it. I'll get a male officer to take you to the shower. Want a tea?'

Once again, he had no idea what he wanted, but it

wasn't going to be solved with yet another cup of tea in a polystyrene cup with powdered milk.

'I'm not cut out for prison,' he said, still prostrate and arm over his face.

When he removed his arm and looked away, the police officer was scribbling on his custody record. He came to the conclusion that she was writing down what he had just said to her.

Everything he said and did was documented. It was more pitiful in police custody than he could ever have expected.

One thing he did know was that he would need to keep a lid on things the whole time he was in the police station. He couldn't afford to lose his temper. He had only done that a few times in his life and it had never ended well. If they saw what he could really be like, it might alter their view of him. At that moment in time, he had no idea what they knew and whether it would be enough to charge him with murder. The very thought of it made him shudder despite the warmth of the cell block. He couldn't face the thought of being sent to prison to wait for the start of a trial. Aiden had little idea of how these things worked but he'd heard of people being on remand for months before they got anywhere near a judge and jury.

He was facing things on his own for now with only the assistance of a legal representative he had known a few hours. He wasn't even allowed to call his mum just to hear her voice. The detectives who had been interviewing him told him he wasn't to speak to her. He couldn't afford to let anyone know he was desperate to talk to his mum. It was something that probably wouldn't go down very well in prison.

His brief had called it 'delaying intimation'. He hadn't understood what that meant either at the time, except he couldn't talk to anyone in case he spoke about why he was in the police station in the first place. As if he'd be stupid enough to talk about Linda and the whole sorry state of affairs.

He followed a male uniform officer along the corridor towards the shower, towel over one arm and his meagre squeeze of shower gel in a tube, as if this was how he normally started every day.

There was nothing normal about this day, even if it hadn't begun with a strange man watching him strip naked and get into a shower tray barely bigger than he was.

Aiden took his time, enjoying the feeling of the water on his skin. It was hardly freedom but at least the water came from somewhere else other than a custody block. He hadn't tasted or smelled fresh air for twenty hours now, and he wasn't too sure when he would again. His solicitor had given him the worst case scenario by telling him that the police could, under certain circumstances, keep him there for up to thirty-six hours but before then could go to a Magistrates' Court and ask for more time. She hadn't answered his question of exactly how long. She had given him a vague and wafty answer that the police didn't usually ask for the full amount but were likely to ask for another twenty-four to thirty-six hours.

It hadn't made him feel any better, but he guessed that she was trying her best under the circumstances.

While Aiden attempted to scrub the grime of the last day from his skin, under a temperamental shower head placed so far up the wall its water pressure was all but useless, he made his mind up about one thing.

Today, he was going to tell the police the truth about Linda.

Chapter 41

'We need to speak to you again, Sasha,' said Doug Philbert. 'Sophia is busy interviewing at the moment so DCI Venice is with me instead.'

Sasha Jones's face peered from behind the door at the detective inspector and Barbara Venice. She looked as though she had only got out of bed when Doug rapped on the door.

'I'm not dressed,' said Sasha, 'but come in.'

She opened the door to reveal herself wearing only a T-shirt that was attempting to cover her backside as she turned to go up the stairs.

Neither Doug nor Barbara could fail to notice, as she took the steps two at a time, Sasha's remarkably long shapely legs, leading to a very pert bottom.

'Go on through to the kitchen,' she called over her shoulder, just as her naked derrière made an appearance.

Barbara smacked Doug's arm to get his attention, and shook her head at him when he mouthed, 'What?' at her.

Still shaking her head, she made her way to the kitchen and gave it the once-over.

'This is an impressive kitchen,' she said to Doug as he pulled out a chair at the wooden table in the centre of the room. 'Wouldn't mind one like this myself. Wonder how she can afford this?'

Keeping his voice down, Doug said, 'Remember what we agreed on in the car: less Jack Regan and more Jack Frost. She's a young girl.'

'You've changed your tune now you've seen her killer pins. Bloody men.'

'She was in bed. How is she supposed to dress?'

'Don't try and steer this away from you gawking at her.'

Barbara got the last word on the matter as they both became aware of the sounds of Sasha coming back down the stairs.

She appeared in the kitchen doorway barefoot and dressed in sky-blue leggings and a long white sweat-shirt. Her long dark hair was draped forward over her shoulders, making her appear demure. Barbara wasn't sure if it was deliberate and this was part of the act, or if the young pale-faced woman in front of them really had simply been caught up with the wrong man. No one could help who they fell in love with.

Barbara introduced herself, stressing the *Detective Chief Inspector* part.

'How are you feeling today?' asked Doug.

'I'm OK, thanks.' She smiled at him, head cocked to one side.

Sasha padded across the tiled floor, took the lid off the kettle and filled it from the tap. She turned and waggled the kettle at them. 'Tea? We wouldn't get far in our job without a cuppa, would we?'

'Thanks,' said Doug.

After she pressed the switch on the kettle, she took a seat opposite Barbara and placed her hands on the table.

'Listen. Thank you for coming back to see me. I've been very stupid. I lied to you about where I was that morning. The morning that ...'

She broke eye contact with Barbara, glanced towards the kettle on the worktop where it was quietly performing its sole function.

'I think I'm over the tears and they just keep on coming.' She laughed at her own attempt at a joke. No one else joined in.

She took a deep breath and said, 'The morning that Milton died, he'd been here with me. On Mondays, he used to go into the office early to catch up on weekend crime and so on, get ahead of the game. He told his wife that due to pressure and cutbacks, he had to go in earlier and earlier. The truth was, he used to come over here for about five-thirty, six a.m. and we would at least get an hour or two together.

'I panicked when you asked me where I was when Milton was injured and his wife was found. As a police officer, I really should know better. You've got to see it from my point of view – if you're having a relationship with a married man, you get used to lying. It doesn't make anything go away or justify it, but it becomes habit sooner than you'd think.

'We got used to lying, and I didn't want anyone, especially his son, to know that I'd been the last person he was with. When you came to see me, I already knew that his wife was dead. It was all over the nick and impossible not to know. Anyway, I knew that she'd been found and it was being investigated. I was hoping it was a sudden death rather than a suspicious one. You know, like a heart attack or she'd fallen down the stairs or something. I simply wasn't thinking straight.'

She chose that moment to get up and make the tea, sniffing into a tissue she plucked from a box next to the tea caddy, boiling water sloshing into the mugs lined up beside the draining board.

'You didn't tell me her injuries when we last spoke, sir,' she said. 'You did tell me it was a murder investigation and I said the first thing I thought of. I haven't spoken to my mum, yet I know only too well that she would have been on the phone the second you'd walked out of the door if you had been to see her.'

Sasha turned to the drinks, her back to the two detectives at her kitchen table. Barbara glanced at Doug and raised an eyebrow at him; he gave a tiny shrug.

They waited until she got the milk from the fridge, added a little to each mug, returned the carton to its place inside the door, and sat back down opposite Barbara.

Sasha pulled her drink towards her and placed her hands around the blue stoneware mug, peeking out at Barbara from under the safety of her fringe.

Doug watched Barbara leaning forward in her seat,

about to strike. He wanted to get in first with some more details about the morning of Linda's murder before the DCI said something that was likely to jeopardize communication.

'What we need to know,' said Doug, leaning forward himself, 'is exactly what time Milton got here, how long he was here and at what time he left. Don't leave any detail out, no matter how small or insignificant you may think it is. We also know that you called Tom Delayhoyde and we need you to explain what you told him too.'

'OK,' said Sasha, smiling at him, showing on her face some sense of relief that she could at last get this off her chest.

'There is, however, one more thing,' said Barbara. 'Making accusations – possibly criminally related accusations – about officers, especially those who are deceased, is a very serious matter. I want you to think very carefully in relation to what you know, or think you know, about the Wolfram Street murder and Milton's involvement in it.

'Mr Bowman was at the forefront of a campaign to reduce drug dealing in East Rise, with, may I add, considerable success. The operations he organized and trialled have been taken up county-wide and mean that there are fewer dealers on the streets, there's a massive drop in anti-social behaviour and the community feels safer. So, Sasha, don't leave anything out of your statement, just be mindful of what you tell us you *think* you saw and heard at Wolfram Street.'

Chapter 42

'So, Aiden,' began DC Pierre Rainer, everyone seated in the same places in the interview room, 'that's the introductions and caution explained. We've got more questions for you. I'd like to start with—'

'I need to tell you something,' said Aiden.

His solicitor shot forward in her seat, abandoning the pad she had been preparing to make notes on for the next hour or so.

'I think this is a good time for me to speak to my client without—' she began but Aiden interrupted her once again.

'No, I need to tell you something and I thought about it all last night when I couldn't get to sleep and when I did some bloke was wailing and moaning, someone else was banging, and was still at it when I got in the shower first thing. I need to tell you this. It won't go away.'

He paused, unsure how he was going to backtrack on what he'd told them the day before, the hours they had spent going over and over the detail of his visit to Linda that morning.

He had no idea, of course, that they hadn't believed him anyway. Pierre and Sophia weren't the only two working on Linda's murder. A team of over fifty were working away behind the scenes, taking statements, examining crime scenes, downloading electronic equipment, talking to people.

Aiden was clueless that the officers listening to him knew his story didn't add up; they had been paying attention but hadn't once hinted at disbelief. He couldn't possibly know that because this was a murder investigation and nothing was left to chance. Add to that the thing detectives excelled at in such circumstances – biding their time.

What they hadn't expected was for him to start telling the truth – that didn't usually happen halfway through an interview.

Everyone waited for Aiden to speak.

He took a sip of water, hand grabbing the thin disposable cup too hard and wrinkling the sides of it. He put it back down.

'I went to see Linda, but Milton's car was still on the drive. She'd told me beforehand that she'd leave the side gate unlocked and I should go to the kitchen door. She was going to get up and leave it open as soon as Milton left. She didn't want the neighbours to see me on the doorstep at that time in the morning, you see.'

His comment was met with a nod from Pierre.

'Well, I wasn't expecting him to be there, so I didn't know what to do. I thought if I left and waited around the corner, at that time in the morning, I'd stick out like a sore thumb if he then drove past me. I knew their kitchen didn't look out onto the pathway to the side of the house, and I'm embarrassed to tell you this, but I was trying to overhear their conversation.

'I knew that they weren't getting on from what Travis had told me, as much as hearing it from Linda. She may have been leading me on, getting me to feel a bit sorry for her, only Travis had nothing to gain from it. It was just two mates talking about stuff.'

The mention of Travis seemed to make him sink in his seat, shoulders rounded, head hanging a little lower.

Aiden shuffled forward in his wooden chair and said, 'I opened the gate and walked along the side of the house. There's only the side of the garage along that wall, so I knew no one would see me until I got to the back of the house at the edge of the garden. The top window above the sink was open and I could hear them talking. They weren't exactly shouting but Linda said that she was disgusted with him and his behaviour. How everything he did was for appearances and their life together was a miserable one, all based on a lie anyway. She sounded so angry, but it was that kind of measured angry. Do you know what I mean? When someone is so annoyed, they're calm. I don't know how else to describe it. She didn't sound like herself at all, it was like a different Linda.'

He looked from Pierre to Sophia and back again before continuing.

'I heard a noise like someone slamming a cup down or something like that, and Milton said to her, "If you don't like your life here, you know what you can do. Don't let me stop you leaving, but you'll find out exactly how unpleasant I can make life for you." He didn't exactly threaten her, just got really nasty.'

Aiden put his head in his hands and said, 'I didn't tell you this before because if Linda was fine before Milton left, I was the last person to see her before she was killed. And I know how that looks.'

Chapter 43

As soon as Jenny Bloomfield woke up alone, miserable and mother to a murder suspect, she recognized that the best way to feel better was to tend to her own needs. Only momentarily did she pause to wonder how her own sexual gratification could improve the situation in any way. Nonetheless, she certainly didn't envisage it making things any worse.

She showered, changed into what clean clothes she had, put yesterday's dress back on, and left the hotel for the most expensive boutique she could find. Most of her shopping was done miles away, usually in London, but today East Rise would have to do. Jenny didn't want to dwell too much on the implications of her impending actions when her son was in police custody for murder and her husband flying home from Dubai on the next flight that had an available first-class seat. Her friend Linda was after all dead. Having sex wouldn't make her any less murdered, so she might as well try to forget her own anguish.

Within an hour of leaving the Premier Inn, Jenny

stood in the lobby of the Grand, lift on its way to her, about to take her to the fifth floor. The fifth floor would undoubtedly take her much higher.

That delightful thought on her mind, she stepped into the lift and made her way to her lover's hotel room, smoothing down her new silk dress as she went.

It hadn't entered her head that he would have anyone else with him. They had never discussed exclusivity; she was married at the end of the day. Neither had a claim on the other, although it still took her a second to recover from the look of hesitation on his face as he opened the door.

'Were you expecting someone?' she said as she leaned a hip against the door frame.

A sly smile tugged at his mouth and he said, 'No one else I'd rather have knock on my door,' before he pulled her inside and kicked the door shut without releasing his grip on her.

Despite Jenny's desire to see him, feel his body on top of hers, she was clear-headed enough to glance around the room and notice that there were no obvious signs of another woman. As he threw her onto the bed, pushing the scatter cushions to one side, the last thought she had for the next hour other than of what he was doing to her was that the made bed was surely a good sign.

Jenny lay on her side, flushed face towards her lover. He ran his hand down her cheek. A caress that made her shudder.

'Sorry I dropped by unannounced,' she said.

'Well, it worked out very well for me that you did.' He smiled at her, beautiful green eyes staring into hers. 'I do have to go out soon. I've got a lunchtime meeting I was about to leave for.'

'I didn't mean to stop you.'

'Stop apologizing, although I am going to have to get back in the shower and leave before very long.'

She closed her eyes and said, 'I get that you're busy. I just wanted some company, your company.'

'Everything OK?' he said.

'It's my friend, well sort of my friend, who I told you about. You remember that I mentioned I knew a woman whose son is best friends with my son?'

'Yeah, I remember,' he said as he stroked her hair. 'She'd been a bit crappy to you over time and you've not seen much of her lately. Is that the one? Lisa or Lindsay or something?'

'Linda, Linda airs and graces Bowman.' She touched the corners of her eyes with her thumb and forefinger. 'I shouldn't have said that. It's wrong to speak ill of the dead, especially those taken so violently.'

'Bloody hell,' he said, leaning up on his elbow, hand now moving to her chin. 'She's dead? What happened?'

Jenny allowed a tear to escape and said, 'Someone murdered her in her house. My son's been arrested for it.'

'Your son?'

The tone of his voice made her snap open her eyes. She didn't like the expression he was showing her.

He threw himself back on the pillow. 'Your son. Fucking hell.'

'Don't think bad of me being here, please.'

She stretched out to grab his wrist just as he pushed himself to a sitting position on the edge of the bed. Jenny left her hand in the air, unsure whether to caress his back. The last thing she needed right now was someone else to turn away from her and abandon her.

'I'm getting in the shower,' he said. 'See yourself out.'

For a minute or so, until she heard the sound of water running, Jenny remained motionless.

She refused to lie on the bed and cry. The scorn of another man wouldn't destroy her. She would do what she had always done: get herself dressed, muster her dignity and harvest anything she could for her own survival.

By the time she was dressed, earrings picked up from the floor and her shoes back on, the only things she needed were her abandoned handbag and her holdall containing yesterday's clothing. As she bent to pick them up, paperwork on the desktop caught her attention.

In her present state of mind, the content of the paperwork didn't alarm her as it should have done.

She gave little thought to the name 'Sean Turner' printed at the top of a Visiting Order for prison inmate TD1548 Jack McCall.

Chapter 44

'How long have you been standing there?' asked Doug, catching sight of Barbara Venice in the doorway.

'Only for a few seconds. I didn't want to interrupt you – you looked so lost in thought. Is this a good time to run some things by you?'

Inside the office with the door closed, Barbara made herself comfortable in the chair next to her DI's desk.

'What's the matter, Barb?' he said.

'I'm getting a real battering over this one: the press are particularly interested, unsurprisingly. Witness Protection stuff aside, I'm already worried. Perhaps I should have dealt with Sasha Jones differently. It's not as if I don't want to find out that Milton might have murdered his own wife.

'And I've got to go and ask for more funding and get an update together for the chief. That aside, I wanted to go through who we're looking at for Linda's death. Hazel was right to be concerned that she had no history or family; the McCalls were one of London's biggest criminal families and changed their identities. It hasn't passed me by that we could be looking at someone settling an old score so we need to make sure the inquiry team aren't walking into anything dangerous. And let's not forget that this could be down to a completely unrelated passing stranger killing her. I'd appreciate you lending me your ear for few minutes.'

Doug sat back in his chair, arms crossed over his chest, ready to listen to the woman he'd tutored when she'd joined the police three years after him. He'd shown her the ropes and then watched her get promoted faster, and seemingly with less work, than himself. The truth was he was content with his role as detective inspector. He had thought about pushing for the next rank up. He had worked hard to get where he was, and was, quite frankly, fed up with jumping through hoops.

Completing projects for the sake of it had never appealed to him, and he realized he was never going to go any further in his career without carrying out meaningless tasks that didn't improve policing in any way. Reinventing the wheel, the rank and file called it, with good reason too. Most of it was nonsense. No one said this though, they wanted promotion and telling the truth wasn't the way to go about it.

'Is there anything further coming from Aiden Bloomfield's interviews?' Doug asked.

'Not so far. I'm not sure about him. There's something not right – trying to sleep with his best friend's mum, for a start. Why didn't he just masturbate and buy computer games like normal teenage boys?'

'I've got teenage sons. I think, from now on, I'll give the Wii Fit a miss.'

'OK, Doug. Apart from Aiden, there's his mother, Jenny.'

He raised an eyebrow at this suggestion.

'Really?' he asked. 'It's not normally something a woman would do, is it? Smash another woman's head in.'

'I don't know,' she wondered, playing with the locket on the chain around her neck. 'People never fail to surprise me, even after all these years in this job. I've lost my temper a few times over the years, and whilst I'd never do it, if you were really angry with someone and they turned their back on you, you just might do it.'

'What reason would she have for going over there at that time of day and having any kind of conversation with Linda, let alone a row? It doesn't make sense.'

Barbara let out a sigh and rubbed the bridge of her nose.

'I suppose you're right, but who else do we have? Travis?'

'No, not Travis,' said Doug. 'He loved his mum. He wouldn't hurt a hair on her head. He loved her.'

They both sat in silence, thinking over the possibility of Travis killing his own mother before Barbara said, 'It wouldn't be the first time someone killed one of their parents although I can't think of any reason he'd have. Not unless he thought his mum really was sleeping with his best friend.'

'Now you've said that out loud,' he said, 'it sounds

even more unlikely. Surely he'd attack his friend rather than his mum. We know Travis and Aiden were out drinking together on Sunday and both at the Bloomfields' overnight. Travis would've had every opportunity to attack Aiden if he knew what they were up to and was that angry with them both.'

'I suppose you're right,' she said. 'One other thing that's been bothering me, Doug. Was I right to get Sasha to reconsider about Wolfram Street? If there's one thing I know for sure, it's that Milton would never have got himself involved in unscrupulous activity with drug dealers.'

He smiled at her. 'If there's one thing I'm certain of, it's that Milton played no part in anything underhand or corrupt.'

Chapter 45

'All right, boy? It's Jack,' Sean heard the voice say as he pressed his mobile phone to his ear.

Sean had been relieved to come out of the shower and find Jenny gone, the feeling only fleeting as it was replaced with wondering what he'd done so wrong that it warranted a direct line to Jack McCall.

That concern didn't give way to lethargy when it came to saving his own skin. 'What number are you calling me from?' he asked.

A chuckle sounded in Sean's ear.

'Don't shit a brick,' he said. 'It's easier to get a mobile phone in here than in a fucking branch of Carphone Warehouse. Relax, they won't have your number on record or know what we've spoken about. I nicked this off some nonce. He's not likely to breathe a word.'

'I'm all set to visit you,' said Sean. 'We were supposed to talk then.'

'Well, there's been a development.'

Sean sat on the edge of his hotel bed, scent of Jenny still on the sheets. He listened to the sounds of prisoners shouting, their hollers and laughter echoing along corridors, metal doors slamming shut, and thanked his good luck that he wasn't there too. Life was definitely better for him than for most of his family. A few were dead, a few were inside, those who were alive were criminals.

'What's happened?' asked Sean, not knowing whether to panic just yet as he ran an eye over his few possessions scattered around the room and worked out how long it would take him to pack, check out and disappear from East Rise.

'Just been told I should expect some visitors on Friday morning.'

'Friday morning?' said Sean. 'I'm supposed to be seeing you in a couple of hours' time.'

'Let's forget about that, shall we?' Jack's voice wasn't giving much away by its tone, then it rarely did. Even and measured was how he had always been, no more so than when it came to business.

'Who's coming to see you?' Sean closed his eyes as he asked the question, guessing the answer before he heard it.

'If I was a gambling man, I'd put a couple of quid on it being coppers. You brought them to my door, boy?'

'No, no, I haven't. We've been careful, very careful. Business is going as we agreed with the right client base. I told you about the contact I made at Wolfram Street. He's had his uses, and although sadly he's not around any more, it was a clean break, no loose ends to tie up.'

'That's very comforting to know. Man of my

215

age with only eighteen months left to go in here. If everything goes well, they'll probably move me to an open prison. We can have a get-together. You, me and the boys. How about that?'

'Sounds great.' By the time Sean had finished his last word, Jack had hung up.

Chapter 46

As soon as DC Pierre Rainer and DC Sophia Ireland had halted Aiden Bloomfield's interview for a break, they made their way to Doug Philbert. The DI was in his office with Barbara Venice writing up her file for Linda Bowman's murder.

'Hi. What did he say?' said Doug.

They updated him on the last hour and a half of interview and gave him a second to digest the information.

'We've got no blood, tissue or other obvious contact trace on Milton's clothes or skin from Linda,' said Doug. 'Helpfully, he was wearing a brand-new suit that day, tags still on it, so any blood would have been recent. Apart from his own blood, and there was a lot of that, we have no one else's on him or his clothing, so it would support Aiden's version that Linda was still alive when Milton walked out of the house.'

'The results from ANPR show that he didn't go back there either,' said the DCI.

'Unless,' said Pierre, 'he didn't use his own car to go back there.'

'You missed the rest of the briefing,' said Doug. 'We went back to cover everything with Sasha Jones and get a complete picture from her, whereabouts she was, timings etc. Her car was in a local garage all weekend. That's been checked out and she hasn't got access to any other vehicle. It's several miles from Sasha's house to the Bowmans', so she couldn't have got there and back on foot.'

'There may be a car, taxi or motorbike we don't know about,' said Sophia, who up to this point had stood and listened, trying her best to keep an open mind.

Doug and Barbara exchanged a look. She sensed something new was coming.

'Good point and I like your way of thinking,' said Barbara, 'except there's nothing else to indicate that Sasha or Milton left her house much before the accident just before half seven that morning. Plus, the neighbours have been spoken to about the noise.'

'Noise?' asked Sophia.

'Yeah, noise,' said Barbara.

'Oh noise,' said Sophia again. 'You mean Sasha and Milton were banging—'

'Oh yes and it was definitely two of them,' said Doug, scratching at the side of his neck. 'The neighbour remembers what day and time because he does shift work and only got into bed a little after six. He knocked on the wall several times between six and around seven until it stopped. He said it happens most Monday mornings but usually he's on his way to work, rather than trying to get some shut-eye.'

'Bearing in mind the estimated time of death from the post-mortem, it does help us rule out either Milton or Sasha as being responsible, providing Aiden is telling us the truth,' said Pierre, closing his eyes and in his head running through everything they had spoken to their suspect about so far. 'It would still be easier for Aiden to make up a story to explain away his DNA on Linda's cheek which could only have got there on the morning of her death.'

'That's true,' said Barbara, 'and not forgetting Aiden had been out the night before with Travis so he couldn't have seen Linda that evening. Travis has told Hazel in detail how his mother never went to bed without using cleanser, toner and night cream on her face, moisturizer in the morning. He didn't realize the significance, and according to Hazel, shot her a look of utter bewilderment at being asked such a seemingly absurd question.'

'There was a fair amount of saliva, according to the CSI,' said Doug. 'It's unlikely so much of it would have remained on her face after so many beauty products had been rubbed around her skin. I can't see that she would fail to wash a teenager's drool from her cheek in any case, whatever toiletries she used.'

'What's next?' asked Sophia. 'We've covered most things, a few loose ends to tie up. The only thing he hasn't told us is who it was at the door, and he's claiming he doesn't know. If, of course, anyone did knock on the door.'

'That and who hit Linda Bowman on the back of the

219

skull,' added Pierre. 'Talking of which, have we had confirmation of what the weapon could have been?'

'It's funny you should ask,' said Doug. 'Jo Styles, the senior CSI, went out earlier to a house in the next street to the Bowmans' road. The couple had been away on holiday and only came home this morning. They hadn't been seen on the house-to-house enquiries, but read the note put through their door, looked in their front garden and found what they thought was a hammer thrown into the rose bushes.

'Jo went out herself to be on the safe side and she's on her way back in with a hammer covered in what looks like blood and hair. It looks like we have our murder weapon.'

Chapter 47

Afternoon of Wednesday 7 June

Glad of a couple of hours to catch up on her paperwork, Hazel left East Rise Police Station and drove to a nearby coffee shop where she bought a takeaway latte, then headed for the coast.

She sat in her unmarked car at White Sands Bay looking out to sea, trying to clear her mind. Most days were fine; she could cope. All she had to do was keep a lid on her feelings, not let on that everything petrified her. Some days, she doubted she was in the right job. How she envied those who felt threatened, had problems with their neighbours, saw a fight and instead of running towards it to break it up made scarce and called the police.

Except she was the police. Didn't she have to deal with all these problems so that everyone else could go about their lives unmolested and in relative safety?

Coffee cooling in her hands as she leaned against the steering wheel, she tried to recall what had made her want to join the police in the first place. It always came back to her dad's death. She might have only been a teenager at the time, numbed by the shock of what the police told her, except what stuck in her mind so vividly about that evening was the stifled yawns of one of the officers and the lack of information from the other one. He didn't seem to have a clue as to how the accident had happened, so all she was able to understand was that one of the two most important people in her world was now dead.

It left her with no doubt that she could do a better job. So she tried to.

Unwilling to slip into a state of depression, she gulped her coffee and started the car to make her way to Travis. Whatever she was feeling, it couldn't hold a candle to his mental anguish.

There were so many things she needed to speak to him about, but she had never before been a family liaison officer for an only child who had lost both of his parents on the same day in separate incidents. She doubted if any other teenager anywhere on the planet could be that unlucky. That made her think about famine and war zones, where whole families or even villages were wiped out in a day.

She banished these thoughts, recognizing that she would have to keep a check on herself: Hazel could feel a gloom creeping into her working day and that would end with it bleeding into her private life. She glanced down at her file on the passenger seat where she had tucked her welfare questionnaire. She fully intended to be truthful when she completed it, but only in case she lost her mind and needed counselling, or even worse, wasn't doing the best job she could for Travis.

He had done his best to put on a brave face. Having got to know him a little over the last couple of days, Hazel saw beneath the mask he tried to pull down. He wasn't fooling anyone so full credit to him for giving it a go. He had called Hazel the night before for seemingly no apparent reason, although she got the impression it was to chat to someone who understood. He had few people he could talk to, and as much as his aunt Una was trying her best, she was also in mourning for her sister-in-law and brother.

Travis had ended the call when he choked up, and instantly sent her a text message that brought a lump to her throat.

It simply said, *Alone and petrified. See you tomorrow. Thank you. xx*

She parked the car a couple of houses up from where Travis was staying and took out her phone. He'd asked her to call or text him when she got there, rather than come in. Hazel knew that, sooner or later, she would have to see where he was staying but for now, the checks had been carried out on his aunt and uncle and their home, and there was no objection to it being a safe place for him to stay. In fact, it was the only place for him to stay, barring a hotel.

In her peripheral vision, she caught a figure walking towards the car and looked up.

Travis got into the Mondeo and sat staring straight ahead in the direction of where he had just come from.

'She's doing my fucking head in,' he said.

The last thing Hazel needed on top of everything else was her witness disappearing. He was legally entitled to go wherever he wanted, but his absence would seem highly suspicious, and there were so many things she needed him to tell her.

'Can I help?'

He shook his head. 'No, I don't think so. She means well. We've always got on OK and Uncle John's decent enough. They keep on about my bloody feelings all the time. "You will tell us if we can do anything", or "Let us know if you want to talk", or "Please don't think you can't speak about them to us". It's fucking getting me down; people keep being so nice to me.

'Trouble is, what I want to say is that my dad was a total prick most of the time. He cheated on my mum, at least three times I know of. The last one was a bloody copper. What a cliché. Do you willingly shag each other or is it in your contract?'

Hazel thought of Harry: very inappropriate under the circumstances.

'Sorry, Hazel,' he said through the hands that were now covering his face. 'I don't mean to give you a hard time, just there aren't many people left I can talk to.'

'Tell me how you knew about the affairs.'

He shifted in his seat so he was side on to her.

'The first one, I didn't exactly know, just I guessed that something was up. You know, rows, late nights, my mum crying, dad acting a bit odd. Then things seemed to pick up and at the time, I was only fifteen, I thought no more of it. About two years after that, I snuck out to the pub with a couple of older mates. Because of my age, we sat at the back of the boozer, keeping out of the way with our pints of Hürlimann's. It's mental strong stuff and I wasn't used to it, especially as I'd never really drunk alcohol. It was busy in there so we thought we stood little chance of them realizing I was only seventeen. There was a big group of people standing in front of us, so when they all suddenly left, it emptied out. I was on my second pint and when I thought I saw my dad, I put it down to beer goggles.'

He gave a small laugh and said, 'Thing was, I was feeling a bit brave after a couple of drinks, so I got up to speak to him and say "You look just like my dad". Only trouble was, as I got to the other side of the high-backed wooden seat, I realized that not only was it my dad, hiding at the back of the pub, but he had his arm around a woman who wasn't my mum.'

She could see the hatred hardening his face as he told her his tale, which up until this week had probably been about the worst thing he'd had to deal with.

'Yep, there was my dad, one hand on her shoulder, the other stroking her thigh. I've got to hand it to him, she was a looker. If I'd have seen her somewhere else, I might have tried to chat her up. If she wasn't being groped by my old man, that is. I don't know how my mum put up with him. He was quite a miserable sod as well. You know who she always liked, had a good word for?'

It was Hazel's turn to shake her head, with a gnawing feeling of where this was going.

'Harry, Harry Powell. Do you know him?'

'Yeah, I do.'

'He's a decent bloke. I like him. When I was still at school, he took me out a couple of times with his own kids. He used to take his sons to rugby every week, and even went and watched his daughter's dance competitions. I've got better memories being at his house, arsing around in the garden with his boys and Harry, than I have with my own dad.'

'Your dad must have been busy at work some of the time,' said Hazel, trying both to say something favourable about Milton, whose body they were about to view, and to deflect away from Harry.

'I suppose he was, but so was Harry. If you see him, would you let him know that I was asking after him?'

'I probably won't be talking to him for some time now,' said Hazel, about to turn the engine over, 'but if I do, I'll pass your message on. You ready?'

'As ready as I'll ever be. Let's get this over with.'

Chapter 48

Evening of Wednesday 7 June

Completely worn out by the day's events, Hazel went home, kicked her shoes off at the door and went straight upstairs to run herself a bath. She stood watching the water pour from the taps, added bubble bath and watched the foam rise up.

Despite the warmth of the day, she needed to soak in water as hot as she could stand it. It was less about rinsing the day off, more a case of needing to be still and do nothing for as long as she could make herself.

Submerged in the bath a few minutes later, Hazel thought back over the day and how Travis had held it together viewing his dad's body. At one point, she even got an uneasy feeling that he wasn't as distressed as he should have been, which forced her to consider once more the possibility that he was in some way responsible for his father's death. She immediately dismissed such a notion: Milton's death had either been an accident or suicide. No one else was in the car at the time and the witness, Luke Morgan, said he heard the car and saw it drive straight at the concrete flowerbed. Travis couldn't have had anything to do with that.

The bath water was now turning chilly, so Hazel guessed that she had suitably relaxed. Her mind was still on Travis though and as she towelled herself dry she reminded herself to ask him about the third affair he'd been aware of his dad having. She knew to pick her moment carefully for that one but she wasn't going to concentrate on it now.

She had made the mistake of going down that route before, and overthinking and worrying about something didn't usually resolve it, merely made her mental health suffer. She had learned the hard way and liked to think that she was now adept at making whatever remained of the day her own.

She tied her dressing gown cord around her waist, and was making her way downstairs, thoughts of hot chocolate with marshmallows and whipped cream forming in her mind, when her mobile phone rang.

In her haste to get upstairs and take a bath, she had left her phone in her bag at the bottom of the stairs, next to her discarded shoes. Fumbling through her bag, she found her mobile and her heart leaped when she saw Harry's name on the screen. Then she hesitated.

She had already told him as much as she could when they'd spoken some hours ago. If she spoke to him now, it would overlap with work and she wanted this time to herself. Also it would mean that she would have to face up to what Travis had told her about his mother being particularly fond of Harry. It was a conversation the two of them should have face to face, and not over the phone, she sitting at the bottom of the stairs in her dressing gown, wet hair dripping onto her shoulders.

By the time she had thought all of this, the call had, of course, gone to voicemail.

Hazel took the phone to the kitchen and made herself wait until the kettle boiled and her drink was made before she allowed herself to play back his message.

'Hi, Haze. You OK? Call me back, can you? I fucking hate leaving messages.'

There had been a pause at the end as though he was going to say something more, then she heard him clear his throat and end the call.

She took her time calling him back. She still didn't know what to say.

'Hi, Harry,' she said. 'How are things?'

'It could be worse, I suppose. I've decided to take a couple of weeks off, give myself some time to sort things out.'

'That's good. Are you going away?'

She heard him take a drink of something, and from the glug guessed it was beer straight from the bottle.

'Are you trying to get rid of me?' he asked.

'Not at all. It seems a shame to use up so much holiday and spend it at home.'

'No, I've always been partial to a week or two at windowsill bay. And besides, I was thinking of growing a moustache.'

'You need a fortnight off work for that? That's impressive facial furniture.'

'You've gotta have a hobby. Er, I was wondering if you'd be able to get a day or two off. We could have a trip somewhere. Day trip, I mean day trip, not like a weekend or anything.'

Hazel paused, torn between not wanting to interrupt her role as FLO and not wanting Harry to think she was having second thoughts. The problem wasn't so much second thoughts, more concern that Harry was getting into a relationship for all the wrong reasons.

'Can I let you know in a day or two? We've already got plans to meet one evening over the weekend, plus my elderly neighbour's left me a note with a polite reminder that I've promised to take her to her son's in the next few days. It's been really hectic and today was another of those days with Travis. He may need me around.'

'Oh, yeah, certainly. I know it's busy. I'm sorry if I'm making this awkward at all. I'm not trying to do that.'

There was a hesitation in Harry's voice.

'We all need someone around from time to time. Tell Travis I'm thinking of him.'

'Harry,' she said. 'There is one other thing you could help me with.'

'Oh yeah? Anything at all. What do you need?'

'Remember I mentioned how I foster dogs for a charity? It's for women fleeing from domestic violence who have nowhere else to go.'

'Yeah ...'

'I've had a call and I've provisionally agreed. I probably shouldn't, only I hate to turn them down. It's a woman with three kids and a Dalmatian. The dog's currently in kennels but they're desperate. Is there any chance that you'd pop in and walk the dog if I take it?'

'What?'

'If you're on holiday, you'd have a bit more time than me. I'd really appreciate it. That's as long as you're not scared of dogs.'

'Scared? Of dogs? I've been bitten by dogs bigger than a Dalmatian.'

'Thank you so much.'

'Not a problem, Haze. I can't wait.'

Then Harry hung up.

Chapter 49

'Here we go again,' said Milo as Parker brought the Range Rover to a stop in the town centre car park. 'Sometimes, I simply don't get enough variety in my working day.'

As he leaned through the gap between the front passenger's seat and the driver's seat, Diva said, 'Perhaps you should mention it at your next staff appraisal.'

'What's the plan with this next loser?' said Parker.

'He's living in the homeless hostel about fifty metres around that corner,' said Diva. 'We can't go in there. They've got all sorts of cameras, number-plate readers and very astute staff who'll ask questions. He'll be wandering around this corner in the next half-hour. We take him for a little ride and then I'm going to break his fingers with a hammer.'

Parker spun around in his seat. 'You're going to use a hammer? Are you insane?'

'What's your problem?'

'You'd better not get blood on my upholstery.'

'I'm not going to do it in here,' said Diva.

'Stop arguing, you two,' interrupted Milo. 'Here's Stevie now and he's nice and early. Good lad.'

He jumped out of the car and made a move towards the slight young man, jeans and T-shirt hanging off his frame. The scowl on his face gave way to pure terror as he realized who had called his name.

Chapter 50

Thursday 8 June

Once again, DI Doug Philbert sat in DCI Barbara Venice's office, discussing the names of those connected to the murder.

'OK,' she said, 'if we go through all the names we have, the first is Milton Bowman himself, even though we've ruled him out.'

'Yep,' he agreed, 'and Sasha Jones along with him.'

'At the moment, that leaves us with George Atkins, currently suspended for assaulting a prisoner, Travis Bowman, my least favourite, Aiden Bloomfield, Jenny Bloomfield, and always the worry is the passing and unconnected stranger.'

'And now, of course,' said Doug, 'we've the McCall Witness Protection issue to deal with.'

They sat for a couple of seconds, each considering the options. Neither of them wanted to think that Travis could have done such a thing to his own mother. Besides, according to Jenny Bloomfield, he was in bed asleep some distance away. It hadn't escaped them that up until recently that was what Aiden had also claimed.

Something had been bothering Doug and he needed to voice it, just say the words out loud, never mind anyone else hearing them.

'Jenny Bloomfield has already lied to us,' he said. 'She is a bit of a strange character, and she's got a son to protect.'

'Being a mother doesn't make you a killer either,' said Barbara. 'I do think there's something odd about the whole thing, including their trying to sleep with each other's mother.'

'I'm really not sure what to make of her. At least her DNA has now gone to the lab so we'll see if there's any match to the hammer Jo brought in.'

'What time did you ask Hazel to get here?' asked the DCI, looking at her watch.

'She's due here any time. Before she arrives, I need to speak to you about something,' said Doug, getting up and shutting the door. 'In case anyone in the corridor overhears this.'

He sat back down and looked at his superior officer. 'I think that Harry Powell is keen on Hazel. Yeah, I know what you're thinking, only they are both single.'

'Apart from the issues further down the line of them working together, it's not a problem as long as he's not a suspect or likely to be. It would be better if they didn't see each other at the moment, although we can't stop them.'

'I know, I know. Hazel knows better than to talk to

him about the investigation but we should give her a bit of guidance, just in case.'

'When you say guidance, Doug, I think what you mean is you want me to speak to her.'

Doug glanced up at Hazel's face peering through the glass panel in the door and he broke into a smile.

'Seeing as you offered, that would be a great idea.'

He was up and out of his seat before his DCI had a chance to react.

Opening the door, he almost pulled Hazel into the room and said, 'Have a seat. I'll go and get us some teas.'

He closed the door behind him and watched Barbara Venice's face through the glass as she narrowed her eyes at him. He winked back and hurried off to the kitchen.

'How have things been, Hazel?' she asked the officer.

'Not so bad, ma'am. Are we getting anywhere? I heard about the hammer that's been found.'

Barbara paused and thought about how she should answer this question. She knew the importance of keeping Hazel updated: because of her role within the deceased's family, she needed to be aware of what she was looking out for, and she also had to be aware of any danger she was in herself. At the moment, the only real danger the DCI knew of was one of the detective inspectors trying to sleep with her.

'Things are hopefully moving on. Can I ask you about something a little delicate?'

She saw Hazel's facial muscles freeze as she gave a measured nod.

'Who you choose to spend time with out of work is nothing whatsoever to do with me, or anyone else in this job, not unless it conflicts with you being a police officer.'

Hazel opened her mouth to say something, shut it again and fiddled with her watch.

'I've known Harry Powell a long time,' said Barbara, 'and a more decent man you'd be hard put to find. I'm not going to be as patronizing as to tell you to be careful what you say to him about Linda's murder, but if he does start to ask you too many questions, would you do me a favour?'

She waited until Hazel looked up at her from examining her watch and said, 'What's that?'

'Tell him if he wants to know anything, not to bother you. He should call me direct. I'll tell him everything I'm allowed to.'

'And what exactly will that be?' asked Hazel.

'Absolutely sod all. Leave me to deal with Harry.'

As if he'd been listening in the corridor until the awkward part was over, Doug appeared back at the door with three mugs of tea, managed to manoeuvre the door open and said, 'So that's all sorted then. Let's talk about our suspects and the McCall family.'

Chapter 51

When Jenny Bloomfield thought that her day could not possibly get any worse, she was proved wrong. She had left the Grand the day before and made her way back to the Premier Inn, not knowing where else to go as the police were still searching her home. She hadn't liked the fact that the young detective with the boy-band hair had dropped her off at the Premier Inn in the first place. She didn't want the police to know where she was staying, in fact, she didn't want anyone to know where she was staying. The whole thing was a huge embarrassment, not to mention Sean recoiling from her when he learned about Aiden's arrest. Being stuck in the budget hotel wasn't a pleasing prospect, yet she had little choice. Until her husband was back from Dubai, she was facing her son's arrest for murder all on her own.

The room wasn't making her feel any better with its soulless air.

She went to stand by the window and wondered yet again if she should call Sean, explain to him that she had needed him, that was why she'd come to his hotel room whilst her son was in a police cell. Up till now the time they'd spent together had always been sensational, yet her memory of those stolen couple of hours was simply that now – a memory. The thought that she had lost him for good panicked her. She longed to have him undress her, caress her, make her forget what was going on around her. That was another reason for longing for his company. Since the day they had met six months ago, Jenny on her way out of the Grand's restaurant from her fortnightly lunch, Sean about to check in, he had never asked her a great deal about herself.

She told him a little bit about her family, her friends, why she always ate at the Grand twice a month, alone.

Unlike most men, Sean didn't seem to want to talk about himself much and she didn't even know what he did for a living, yet he seemed to fund his lifestyle somehow.

She had even mentioned Linda to him. Of course, she was sorry that Linda was dead, although when she thought about it, she had never liked her with her smugness and better-than-everyone-else way about her. All the while Linda had been showing a pious façade she'd been flirting with Aiden. Jenny had witnessed it on a number of occasions and hadn't liked what she'd seen. Every mother would scrutinize their offspring's choice of partner, but Linda Bowman was old, three years older than Jenny, and as far as Jenny was concerned, looked and acted much older. It would have been easier if Milton hadn't made a pass at her one day when his wife's back was turned. Jenny had laughed it off at the time, making light of the situation. Nevertheless, she had heard the stories about him trying it on with a number of women, some attempts more successful than others. She had heard Travis talk about his father's attitude to his work colleagues and it sounded as though he was ruthless when it came to getting himself promoted as well.

Milton used anyone he could get his hands on. How was she to know that Linda wasn't the same? Perhaps it was what had made their marriage work.

Many times Jenny had sat at home at her kitchen table, listening to Travis telling her how his dad worked longer and longer hours and Monday mornings were particularly tough as he had to leave so early. According to Travis, the Bowman family had started to eat their Sunday meal earlier and earlier as Milton needed to get up at 5 a.m. to get ahead of the week. Jenny had listened to Travis talking about his home life and felt a genuine pity for him. She had always liked him and welcomed him to her home whenever he needed to get away from the rows at his own house. When he wasn't at university, he stayed more and more often and she had got to know him almost as well as her own son.

Jenny looked out of the window through the grimy once-white net to the even grimier street below. She watched two women stop and greet each other and saw them exchange pleasantries, laugh and listen intently to one another for a minute or two. They seemed not to have a care in the world. If only she could feel that same way. At that moment, it felt as if her entire future was about to be snatched out of her hands. She hadn't manipulated events as successfully as she'd thought.

If she was being honest with herself, she was amazed that the police had made an arrest, especially of her own son. Surely the entire unfortunate episode would be put down to a random attack, a passing opportunist villain trying his luck. Possibly they would even blame Milton.

When the police officers had tracked down Travis to her house and delivered their terrible news about Linda, 'found in suspicious circumstances', they had said, a death that 'definitely wasn't down to natural causes', Jenny could not possibly have known that the police would never get an opportunity to question Milton about his involvement. The news that he was dead, in what was looking like a suicide, should have put an end to their investigation.

It would have been the best solution for everyone, particularly bearing in mind Linda's past. Jenny wasn't clear on most of the details, only enough to know that something about Linda wasn't right. Her guarded answers about her family and childhood always seemed stilted and forced. More than once Jenny had seen her on her way to the train station and stopped to give her a lift, failing every time to elicit from her where she was going. There had been more to her than met the eye, that much she was positive of.

The investigation into her death was bound to unearth a few buried secrets.

Once more Jenny was lost in thought, staring out of the window. Her mind was burdened with the practicalities of what she would do next.

She chewed on a fingernail, an action she hated but which she found herself doing nonetheless.

A noise in the corridor immediately outside her hotel room snapped her back to attention.

It was the unmistakable sound of a number of people trying to keep quiet.

It was now her turn.

She heard a key in the door and waited for it to open.

Above all else, she had to admit, she was worried about her son. What mother wouldn't be worried about her boy having been in a police station for over two days now, especially when he was under arrest for murder?

She would have been scared witless, were it not for one thing and one thing alone: she was going to get him out of custody by telling the police that she was responsible for Linda's death. It seemed the obvious solution.

Chapter 52

Three of them huddled in Barbara Venice's office wasn't doing much to lower the already uncomfortable temperature, despite the open window. The noise of seagulls filled the room as Doug closed the door behind him.

'Sorry about that,' said Barbara, 'I'm going to have to shut the window. There seems to be a nest on the next windowsill up. I'll have to shout otherwise and this matter is a little sensitive.'

When the three of them were settled again, Barbara said, 'Doug and I want you to do some work which won't yet be common knowledge.'

'OK,' said Hazel and glanced at the DI and then the DCI. 'What's it relate to?'

'Well . . .' said Barbara as she folded her hands on the desk in front of her, 'it's more to do with Linda than Milton. You're security cleared, same as the rest of us, but I have to trust you that this won't go any further. There are only a handful of us who know about this so assume that everyone else should be told nothing except for myself and Doug.'

'You've got me interested,' said Hazel. 'I admit that much.'

Doug shifted in his seat, adjusted his glasses and said, 'We've been aware since Monday that Linda and her family were sent into Witness Protection in 1987.'

He paused, expecting Hazel to speak. He had correctly guessed at her expression of incredulity and so continued uninterrupted. 'The woman you made enquiries about at Ealing Hospital, Gladys McCall, wasn't only Linda's mother, she and her late husband Alec McCall were East End villains, along with most of their extended family.'

'We're telling you this because you need to know,' said Barbara. 'The McCall family was a very violent criminal family in the 1970s and early 1980s. It was a time when armed robberies were on the increase and firearms were a common occurrence. Alec McCall, Linda's father, was one of the most violent of the entire clan.'

'Bloody hell,' said Hazel. 'Oh, excuse me, ma'am.'

Her apology was waved away.

'Anyway, Alec, Gladys and their two children, Kelvin and Karen, or Linda as we knew her, disappeared. Alec gave evidence against the rest of the family: brothers, uncles, nieces, nephews and the others were arrested and sent to prison.'

'Bloody hell,' said Hazel again. 'So what brought her to East Rise?'

'It would seem the Bowman family,' said Doug. 'What we do know is that she was married to Milton in 1995 and Travis was born in 1998. Exactly how they met and whether Milton really knew who she was is something we're going to have to piece together.'

'Where am I going to start?' said Hazel, feeling a little out of her depth. 'All Travis knew was that his mum was from the West Country, met Milton and moved here. Why would she be stupid enough to do that? It was a very risky move.'

'We can't help who we fall in love with,' said Barbara.

'Point taken,' answered Hazel with more of a miserable twang to her voice than she intended. 'Is it likely to be another member of the family who found out she was visiting her mother in hospital and followed her?'

She watched the other two exchange a wary look.

'We can't rule it out,' said Barbara. 'We've got the intelligence bureau working on it, the informant handlers are tasking their sources and you're to go and meet with Witness Protection to find out what they know.'

'Witness Protection?' said Hazel. 'Not a department I ever thought I'd work with. Are you sure I'm security cleared for this?'

'Definitely,' said Barbara, 'and above all, I, we, trust you to do a good job. I'll email you the contact details and let you take it from there.'

Hazel took this as her dismissal and left the office, a touch bedraggled for the entire experience.

Tom Delayhoyde stopped to talk to her as he made

his way towards the stationery cupboard. 'You all right, Haze?'

'Never been better. You?'

'Fantastic. I'm off to interview Jenny Bloomfield. She just got arrested for murder.'

Chapter 53

Jenny Bloomfield found herself in an interview room at Riverstone Police Station. She hadn't been given a reason why she'd been taken so far away from East Rise, but being level-headed, decided for herself that the police didn't want her bumping into her own son in the custody area. She guessed their reason was to stop them communicating. If she had managed to speak to Aiden, she would have told him not to worry and that everything would soon be cleared up. Even though she maintained a cool outward appearance as if she was taking everything in her stride, she was petrified.

If she had seen Aiden, she would have broken down and told the police anything they wanted to know, confessed to any crime to get him out of there. Jenny was grateful that she at least didn't have to worry about cracking under the strain of being fixed with a look that told her how much her only son hated her for allowing him to be in that position and doing nothing to free him.

What she had decided, however, was that she was

going to cooperate and tell them everything. Well, she was going to tell them almost everything. She wasn't completely stupid and had done her homework.

Jenny liked to manipulate people and she knew that police officers weren't particularly intelligent. Those escorting her to custody and dealing with her so far hadn't done much to change her opinion. The majority of people who committed crime got caught because they were stupid or lazy, or sometimes they were even both. It was the only reason the prisons were so crowded and the police caught anyone. Add someone with brains to a crime, they became untouchable.

That was what Jenny was thinking when Detective Constable Tom Delayhoyde and Detective Constable Pete Clements walked into the interview room to begin their first interview with her.

Jenny's solicitor sat beside her. She got the impression that he hadn't taken much of a liking to her and despite his advice being to make no comment to the questions put to her, she had said that she wanted to tell the truth, to clear her son's name if nothing else.

'Did you murder Linda Bowman?' asked Tom.

'I wouldn't say "murder", officer,' she said, voice even. 'I did hit her on the head with a hammer. I think I hit her a few times, although I simply lashed out and can't recall it all. Definitely on her head somewhere, I think to the back, possibly the side.'

'Why did you hit her?'

'I'd gone to her house when I knew that her son and husband would be out so that I could talk some sense into her. I knew that she was toying with my son's affections. He's only nineteen years old. He doesn't know any better. I wouldn't dream of doing the same thing with her boy, Travis. What an unpleasant woman she was.'

Jenny sat forward in the chair and placed her hands on the desk. Long, delicate manicured fingers still on the tabletop.

'I didn't intend to kill her. I went to talk to her. That's all.'

'Where did you get the hammer from?' asked Tom.

'It was on the side in the kitchen. She wound me up so much.'

Jenny squeezed a tear from her eye and dabbed it away with her little finger.

'You wouldn't believe the things she was saying to me. At one point she slapped me too. I was scared of her. She was taller than me, and a couple of dress sizes bigger.'

She brushed her hands down the front of her sweatshirt. 'I'm tiny by comparison. I thought she was going for the hammer, so I grabbed it first.'

'Whereabouts was the hammer?'

'On the work surface, next to her.'

'When did she slap you?'

'Does it matter?' Jenny said, voice rising. 'She slapped my face. Isn't that enough?'

She had made the error of talking too much and too fast. Something she realized as soon as she opened her mouth and uttered the last sentence.

Jenny paused, cast her eyes down and said, 'She slapped me hard around the side of my face. No one had ever hit me before. I was so shocked; I was out of control. I reached across to the hammer at the same time as Linda went for it. If I hadn't got there first, she would have used it on me and I'd have been the one who was dead, and all through no fault of my own.'

Tom nodded at her, allowed her to talk. She didn't need much encouragement.

An hour went by, filled with Tom asking questions and Jenny only too happy to answer them.

As far as she was concerned, she was talking her son out of getting charged with murder.

The rest of the murder inquiry team had different ideas.

Chapter 54

Afternoon of Thursday 8 June

Before too long, still reeling from the Witness Protection revelation, Hazel found herself back with Travis. At her suggestion, she went to see him at his aunt and uncle's house, unsure of the welcome she would find but prepared to deal with it anyhow.

Once Una had made them cups of tea and left them to it, Hazel began to explain to Travis about the force's latest arrest. She really wanted to get him talking about other matters first, for a split second weighed up whether she should ask him questions before explaining that Jenny Bloomfield was now in custody. It was a risky strategy not to tell him, and besides, he deserved to know. Hazel always put herself in the place of the bereaved and knew how badly she would react to having such news kept from her. After all, from when her father was killed, she had first-hand experience of how the handling of such news shouldn't be done.

'Something else has happened,' she said, waiting

until Travis had put down the mug of near-boiling liquid.

'It can't be any bloody worse than what's gone on so far.'

She gave an empty smile and had the good grace to look embarrassed.

'Again, Travis, this won't be easy for you to take in. Today we arrested Jenny for your mum's murder.'

The only indication of the rage inside him was the clenching of his jaw and his mouth as it fought for something to say.

'For fuck's sake,' he said, spitting the words at her. 'What else are you going to throw at me? This is beyond a joke. What's happened to Aiden?'

'He's still in custody. We haven't finished talking to him yet.'

In an attempt to get him to look at her again, Hazel moved forward on her chair in the dining room and lowered her face towards his bowed head. Eventually it worked and he looked straight at her, features hardened by the last three days.

Not expecting the news about Jenny to cause him as much angst as the news that his best friend had been arrested, Hazel nevertheless pushed her scalding-hot drink out of his reach; though he was less likely to cause a problem at his only remaining family's home.

'Do you want me to get your aunt in here to explain to her too?' asked Hazel. 'It's a lot for you to take in and she'll want to know what's happening as well.'

A minuscule nod was her only reply.

Seconds later, as if Una had been standing feet from the closed door, she came in and joined them, taking the seat beside Travis and slipping her hand into his.

From the corner of her eye, Hazel saw Travis cling to his aunt's fingers, dwarfed by his own. She wasn't sure how much more one person could take. There were so many who wanted to help him but up to now he had taken little notice of anything Hazel had tried to tell him. Leaflets she had brought him only gave him the miserable news that one in twenty-five children and young people had experienced bereavement of a parent or sibling, all the while aiming to and wanting to help. The problem was that Travis seemed to be stuck in the well of misery and had no energy or inclination to get himself out. And why should he at such an early stage?

Every time Hazel spoke to him, she brought him more grief and bad news, and it was rubbing off on her.

'Why did you arrest this woman?' asked Una. Travis's aunt was short, petite and, so far, had showed nothing less than a robust demeanour and was holding herself together very well under the circumstances.

'All I can say at the moment is that we have DNA evidence that would suggest she had something to do with it,' said Hazel. Forcing herself to avoid biting her lip, something she often did when she knew that she was talking utter nonsense, Hazel continued to explain what little she could.

'Please understand that we now have two suspects in custody, so there's only so much I can tell you. Feel free to ask me questions, absolutely anything. Some of them I can't answer or I just don't have the answer right now.'

'The obvious one is did one of them do it?' said Travis, face now ashen. 'I'm not sleeping, I'm not eating, I can't do anything. All I'm focused on now is knowing what happened and why. Then, I want them to go to prison.'

He put his hands up to his face, taking his aunt's slender hands with him, crying fistfuls of tears.

From a very early age, Hazel had been good at keeping secrets. Passively she sat there, watching the torment before her, keeping to herself all that she knew and knowing exactly how devastated Travis was going to be by the end of all this.

Chapter 55

Sean had secrets of his own, and not only his affair with Jenny. He had done his homework and knew East Rise as if he had lived there himself. Mostly, he thought it was a shithole, sprawls of depressing run-down areas, now and again a small pocket of hope in the guise of people who took some pride in where they lived and didn't feel it necessary to dump sofas and electrical equipment in their front garden.

For many weeks prior to bumping into Jenny Bloomfield in the Grand, Sean had found himself wandering the streets, perching on benches on the seafront, pretending to read a newspaper in a coffee shop. All the while he was running an eye over the town to weigh up whether it was right for his next business venture.

The day he saw Jenny striding out of the hotel's restaurant was the day his luck really changed. He was about to check himself in for a two-night stay to see to some business and the sight of her almost took his breath away.

From top to toe, smooth bobbed haircut down to

her black leather boots, red wool coat in between, Sean was smitten.

He smiled to himself when he remembered how he stepped in front of her and said, 'Excuse me.' She stopped walking, one eyebrow raised at him. 'I'm new here and I just wondered if you could recommend somewhere to eat?'

'The restaurant here is really very good,' she said, smiled and made to step around him.

'Please,' he said, 'give me a moment.' He looked over her shoulder towards the dining area, gave her his best smile and added, 'I know this is very forward of me, but is there any chance you'll join me.'

He saw the hesitation in her eyes, a flicker towards the exit. 'I'm sorry,' he said. 'It was wrong of me to ask you. I saw you come out of the restaurant and hated that you were alone. And I craved some company. Forgive me.'

He moved aside, hand gesture to indicate that she should pass by.

Five minutes later they were occupying the same table Jenny had just vacated, she with a large glass of Sauvignon Blanc, he with a large measure of Scotch.

Once again Sean smiled as he thought about that very first drink with Jenny. Like he did with most parts of his life, he had taken a gamble. Under different circumstances, it might have turned into something more long-term. They both understood that couldn't happen. Now he came to think about it, it possibly wasn't a conversation that they had ever had: she was married and made no mention of leaving her husband, and Sean couldn't see a future in it. Definitely not in his line of work.

Work was what he was now getting himself involved in. He leaned back against the wooden bench, flaky paint sticking to his jacket, one hand over his eyes to shield them from the glare of the afternoon sun, and he waited until he heard the sound of a three litre diesel Range Rover pull to a stop behind him. The noise of the passenger door opening propelled him from his seat towards the car. A similarly suit-clad business associate of his stood holding the door for him.

Sean jumped in the back, put his seat belt on, and once the door was pushed shut for him and he had the full attention of the other three, he said, 'Best we get to work then, gentlemen. Who are we going to kick seven shades of shit out of first?'

Chapter 56

An hour after she'd arrived, Hazel left Una and John's house, closing the front door behind her. Travis had cried so much that after six tear-filled breakdowns she had lost count. It was heartbreaking to see. A couple of times, she had felt her own eyes misting over and used rapid blinking to make it stop. Clearly, he was a young man who had adored his mum, and despite his anger towards his dad's philandering, he still had loved him and wanted nothing more than his parents alive and well.

That was never going to happen. Hazel's job allowed her more of a practical than a wishful approach. Not an altogether unrealistic outcome to all of this was someone being charged with Linda Bowman's murder. This was something she was thrilled to be a part of: being actively engaged and utilized in a plan, not sitting on the sidelines watching the action as others took charge. She really got a kick from her job, she thought now, all her concerns about maybe having chosen the wrong career path faded from her mind.

The whole team was working as hard as it could, and now it had two PACE clocks racing against the prisoners' time in custody. Most of what she had been told she wasn't going to share with Travis or any other member of his family for the time being, yet it warmed her soul to realize that people were doing everything possible to work out who the killer really was. That included finding out about Gladys McCall and Linda's past.

Someone else she wasn't going to be sharing it with was Harry Powell.

Not giving away too much to members of the public, even if they were the family of the murdered, was easy enough: deny everything up until the point of looking unhelpful, and then apologize for not being able to tell them anything further. Police officers were an entirely different beast. They were nosy and it wasn't so much that they knew the answers, as no one had that much foresight, it was that they knew the system. Few knew it better than Harry.

As she walked back to her car, Hazel watched his name appear on her phone's screen.

Despite her reservations about giving too much away, she was desperate to speak to him again. He'd not been far from her thoughts since she'd sat in his kitchen watching him cry over his friend, followed by a clumsy hand-hold at the front door as they both grabbed for the handle. She'd loved talking to him and had even enjoyed their terrible dining experience. Her life could hardly be described as lacking or sad; still she thought and clung to the idea that Harry might become someone important to her in the months to come, despite the awkwardness of an office romance with the boss.

'Hello, Harry,' she said as she answered the phone with one hand, and opened the car door with the other.

'How are you getting on?' he asked.

'Not so bad. I'm a bit tired. I don't need to tell you that goes with the job.'

Once she was in the car, doors shut, Hazel said, 'I know you're not going to ask me how close we are to charging anyone for Linda's murder and I appreciate that.'

She listened for the awkward pause. It didn't come.

'Oh no, fuck that. I know I can't ask and you won't tell me anyway. No, I was calling to ask if you've had any luck with getting a day off. I know I only asked you yesterday, but if I'm honest, I want something to look forward to. What do you reckon? A day out in London? Brighton? Walmer?'

'Walmer?'

'It's got a castle. The Queen Mum used to stay there.'

'I'll think about it.'

'The day out or Walmer?'

'You know I want to spend the day with you but I'll let you know about Walmer Castle. I'll look into it. I like to do my research and make sure I'm not getting involved with anything I'm not happy with.'

'That's me fucked then.'

Hazel heard the start of a laugh and then Harry

chasing to add, 'I don't mean me fucked. I mean – oh fuckety fuck.'

'Harry, you're either the biggest buffoon I've ever met, or you're a real lady-killer.'

No sooner were the words out of her mouth, then Hazel realized what a mistake she had made.

'S-sorry,' she stammered. 'It's been a tough few days and I'm managing to think straight when I'm with Travis or working. Only as soon as I'm alone, I'm losing the plot a little. Tiredness, that's all it is.'

Sitting in the driver's seat of her unmarked car, she pulled the visor down and looked at her reflection. The dark circles under her eyes were the first thing she saw, followed by the paleness of her skin.

'As long as you're looking after yourself, darling,' said Harry. 'I'm always happy to help out if you're in need of a decent meal, Dalmatian walking or someone to talk through all this bollocks with. And before you tell me off or report me, I know that you can't discuss some of it with me. I'm not asking, you know.'

'I know, I know. I have some sleep to catch up on and then I'm due a day off soon, so can I get back to you about the day out?'

'Course you can.'

'How about Friday night?' said Hazel. 'I'm not usually so forward but for you I'll make an exception.'

'Dinner at mine? I'm not the best chef in the world but it'll be an improvement on the pub.'

She let out a slow breath and said, 'I'll text you when I finish work.'

They said goodbye and Hazel sat with the phone in her hand, thoughts of a day with Harry making her feel better than she had in a while. She really wasn't sure what was causing her heart to beat just that little bit faster at the prospect of spending more time with him. She'd known the buzz of excitement at the thought of a new relationship and taking a leap forward towards the unknown, only this time Hazel thought she might have found herself someone to share her hopes and dreams with. Someone to come home to at the end of the day and unburden her heart and mind without the fear of leaving herself vulnerable. Harry was someone she could trust with her fragile feelings.

Perhaps, they just might have a chance.

Chapter 57

Friday 9 June

Enquiries were ongoing all over the county. Anyone with anything sensible to suggest was listened to and officers sent to every possible location in an attempt to capture anything and everything that would prove the guilt of those in custody, or to point towards someone else, including someone from Linda's past.

Unfortunately for Aiden and his mother Jenny, it wasn't looking favourable for either of them.

After being woken in the early hours by the sounds of a drunk being carted off to a cell, Aiden had found it difficult to get back to sleep. The officer watching him had allowed him to poke his head around the cell door and watch the abusive and violent individual being bedded down for the night. The murder suspect had observed with total fascination as the officers, one guarding the man's head, had placed him face down on the floor of the cell, searched him and then, one by one, checked out of the tiny room to leave him to sleep it off.

The last police officer had slammed the metal door shut on the latest addition to the cell block when Aiden heard hammering on the door, and a voice shout out, 'Come back here, you bastards! Come back here and I'll shit in your hat and punch it!'

Wondering what kind of hell the rest of his life might consist of if he went to prison, Aiden made his way back to his mattress that had probably housed hundreds of thieves, rapists and wife-beaters, and waited for the morning.

It came around quicker than he had hoped, but at least it gave him something to do and someone to talk to.

The time Aiden had now spent in custody meant that he had adapted to the daily timetable: seeing his solicitor, then the interview with the detectives, then more time with the solicitor, followed by being put back into his cell. He waited patiently for the jailer to collect him from his cell and take him to see his solicitor, although everyone else called her his 'brief'. It crossed his mind that he might have to learn another language if things went very badly for him. Prison was bound to have its own lingo.

This morning's jailer turned out to be a young blonde woman he took to be Polish from her name badge and accent. As she led him to where his brief was waiting, he startled himself with the realization that he seemed to be accepting what was happening to him.

No sooner than he thought that things couldn't go any lower, his solicitor gave him the news that the police had made another arrest.

'That's good news then?' he said, saliva collecting in the sides of his mouth as the full impact of this information dawned on him. He locked on to her next words, holding his breath.

'It depends how you look at it, Aiden,' she said. 'The police have told me who they've arrested. Brace yourself for what I'm about to say to you – it's your mother.'

He sat staring at her, looking at her but not really seeing. He didn't know whether to believe what she was telling him, yet she had no reason to lie to him. He felt he'd been locked up for so long, he'd change places with anyone, no matter who they were. In fact he had felt over the last day or so that he literally would have sold his own mother if it would have saved his miserable skin.

Now he had the opportunity to find out how low he would stoop.

It took Aiden some time to fully grasp what his solicitor was telling him. Even though she couldn't give him too many facts about his mother's arrest, he was intelligent enough to understand that if he had been arrested because his saliva was on Linda's cheek, the police had something tying his mother to the murder.

Back in the interview room with the same two detectives, Aiden wasn't really sure what he was going to say. He had spent some time convincing his solicitor that he should continue to answer the questions, although she didn't want him to. She tried everything she could to convince him that he had cooperated with the police and now they had his version, he could exercise his right to make no comment. He simply couldn't bring himself to.

Things had seemed bad enough for him when Linda, a woman he idolized, had been murdered and he'd been arrested for it, but now his mum was in a police cell accused of the same killing.

Once the DVDs were recording and everyone had gone through their introductions, which Aiden was already conditioned to, DC Pierre Rainer asked the first important question of the day.

'Your mother, Jenny Bloomfield, has been arrested on suspicion of Linda Bowman's murder. Did your mum tell you she killed Linda?'

'Of course she didn't, or I would have told you. I wouldn't have sat here denying it if I'd known who was responsible, would I?'

Pierre gave him a quizzical look and said, 'Perhaps you would have for your own mother? After all, she let you sit in a cell for over two days.'

As the meaning of his words hit home, Aiden began to say, 'She's—' before being cut off by his solicitor.

'Are you saying, officer, that she's confessed?' said the brief. 'I haven't been given this information.'

'When your mother was interviewed,' continued Pierre, 'she said that she went to the Bowmans' house to talk to Linda and she struck her on the head with a hammer.'

The detective let the words sit there. Pierre's adrenalin was off the starting block. This was the best part of interviewing and it was where hours of biding his time now came into its own. He had set a trap and he knew full well that Aiden was about to get caught in it.

'There you go then,' said Aiden, right on cue, voice wobbling. 'My mum hit her on the head with a hammer. I didn't hit her with anything, especially not with a hammer, for fuck's sake.'

'Then, Aiden,' continued Pierre, calm and composed on the outside, heart racing, 'how do you explain your DNA being on the handle of the hammer?'

A split second of silence was shattered by the solicitor who said, 'This is information that wasn't disclosed to me. I'm advising my client to answer no comment to all further questions at this time. We need a consultation.'

Without anything further being asked, Pierre ended the interview and the four of them sat in a tense silence for several minutes while the DVDs finalized and the machine whirred to a stop, ejecting the discs. Pierre and Sophia then set about completing the labels to seal up the recordings and everyone present signed the relevant paperwork.

The procedure had given Sophia and Pierre time to gauge Aiden's reaction. He seemed on the brink of hyperventilating, eyes darting from left to right, not focusing on anything at all.

Once the officers had left him and his solicitor to speak in private, Pierre couldn't resist whispering in Sophia's ear, 'He looked bad enough at that news, wait until we hit him with the really good stuff.'

Chapter 58

Even though DI Doug Philbert was deeply involved in the Bowman murder, he had been called to two other incidents over the last two days: one was a drugs over-dose and the other was the body of an illegal immigrant found in a shipping container. Despite not leading the investigation into either of them, he was on call for the county and still had to attend, make decisions and set the wheels in motion for handing over to other members of staff. He was now trying to get the rest of the week covered, although under the circumstances, he wasn't at all comfortable asking for a favour from his very last option.

According to the duty roster, there were only a couple of people free, and one of them was Harry Powell. He picked up the phone.

'Dougie, my old son. How are things?'

'They're busy, Harry. It's the usual. How are things with you?'

'Not so bad. I've booked a couple of weeks' leave and thought I'd go and visit the kids, not that they're exactly kids any more, more like sulky teenagers. Thought I'd take them out a few times. I've got some other plans too.'

'Would they happen to include Hazel by any chance?'

He heard Harry laugh before he said, 'I'm trying my best. I like her.'

'I'm not going to poke my nose into someone else's business, especially not yours, but don't you think it's a bit soon after your wife leaving you?'

A lengthy pause filled the air.

'She left six months ago.'

'Oh, I didn't think it was so long ago and it's really none of my business. I'm sorry.'

'Don't be. I just didn't advertise the fact that my life was such a fuck-up. I miss the kids, but her moaning got me down. Some days, without her here, I feel as though I've gone deaf. Anyway, what are you ringing me for?'

'I was wondering if you could do me a favour and cover the rest of my on-call until your annual leave starts? I'm flat out here with Linda's and Milton's deaths and could do without any more interruptions.'

'As it's you, Dougie, of course I can. Is there any update on Milton? I feel I'm on sturdier ground asking you about him rather than about Linda. It was either an accident or suicide, I'm guessing.'

Even though Doug had telephoned Harry for a favour, he had foreseen that he wouldn't pass up an opportunity to ask about the investigation.

'Coroner's Report is being done. There's nothing

back from serious collision investigation to suggest there was any defect with the car, there were no road hazards, driving conditions were all good, and there was no drink or drugs in Milton's blood or urine.'

He heard Harry sigh and then comment, 'I hate to think it was suicide, especially if you've now made a second arrest. It'd make everything that little bit worse, for some reason. All I got from the news was that you'd nicked a thirty-nine-year-old woman. I'm going to guess it was the mother of the young lad you've already got in custody.'

This time, Doug had no doubt that this hadn't come from anyone within the incident room: Harry would have worked this one out by himself somehow.

'There's something else, Harry. Something about Linda.'

'Go on.'

'She wasn't who we all thought she was.'

'I'm not following.' There was a sharp edge to Harry's voice.

'I can't say too much at this stage. When I can, I'll let you know.'

It had been a cruel trick to pull on an old friend simply to find out if Harry knew the truth. From his reaction, it was safe to assume that Harry knew nothing of the woman for whom he had held a candle for over twenty years.

The trouble seemed to be that it wasn't panning out to be the most straightforward murder investigation. Doug had worked on hundreds over the years as a constable in uniform, as a detective doing the enquiries and interviewing, and later as a sergeant and now as an inspector. Still he failed to recall one single murder he had investigated where he had had two suspects in custody, both with their DNA on the murder weapon and at the scene with the body, where one was claiming sole responsibility, the other denying it, and the evidence suggesting a different set of circumstances.

It crossed his mind, not for the first time, that Jenny was taking the blame for something she thought her son had done, whilst all along he was a completely innocent party.

Perhaps they didn't even have the right people in custody.

Chapter 59

'OK then, boys,' said Sean, 'last port of call before the weekend. This one should be easy. Just some skank and her fella. Are you ready?'

The driver waited with the car whilst the other three decamped and made their way to the entrance of the four-storey property. In its heyday, it had probably been an impressive building, except now it had fallen into ruin, not unlike the kind of people who lived there.

Not one for standing idle, Sean rang every one of the eight buzzers even though it was the property at the front on the ground floor he wanted to get to.

Someone within the building released the catch and the three men stepped inside.

Suit jackets buttoned, fists clenched, all three were soon standing shoulder to shoulder outside Trixie Maitland's flat. A noise from the other side of the thin plywood door was unmistakably of someone pretending to be out.

'Trixie,' said Sean. 'I think it would be much better if I didn't have to boot the lock in, don't you?'

272

'Oh, er, just a minute,' called a woman's voice. She sounded out of it, but then she usually was. Trixie was one of hundreds Sean had seen over the years getting through life rather than living it. Within a couple of seconds, she opened the door on her pitiful existence.

He ran an eye over the kitchen area a couple of feet behind where she stood. She'd washed up since he was last there. Perhaps she was trying to give up the gear. He couldn't have that. He needed her.

'Jimmy not here?' said Sean as he stepped over the threshold and looked around the place. Off the kitchen was an open-plan living and sleeping area, no cupboards, no wardrobes, or in fact space for them. The only part that could have housed another person was the shower and toilet area to the left of the kitchen and the door to that was wide open.

'No, no, he went out,' she said as she pulled the sleeves of her jumper down to her knuckles and backed away, backside pressed against the front of the cooker.

'Don't look so nervous,' said Sean. He pointed to the toilet and Danny went inside and shut the door.

'Everything as we spoke about?' said Sean as he moved towards her. His black leather shoes touching the end of her bare feet.

'Yeah, yeah,' she said, turning her head from left to right, avoiding looking up into his eyes. 'It's all been fine. We've got everything set up, you see. It's just as you said, just as you said, Tandy.'

'Well that's good then,' he murmured in her ear, leaning down seven or eight inches until he was level with her face. 'I don't want anything going wrong now. A few things have gone wrong lately and it's really fucked me off, Trixie.'

He watched her screw her eyes up and swallow as he ran a hand along the length of her face. She started as he raised his voice and added, 'But don't worry your gorgeous head about it right now, we've got a present for you.'

Danny had emerged from the toilet, something that Sean thought his hostess was unaware of in her petrified state. He looked round at his young apprentice who held out a bag of heroin to him.

This was met with a look of disgust. Sean knew where the drugs had been stashed and wasn't about to handle them under any circumstances. He pointed to the worktop behind Trixie.

'Look what we've left for you,' said Sean as he waited for her to open her eyes.

Momentary indecision ran across her features until the screaming desire for Class A drugs became too much and she lunged for them.

He put his arm across to stop her before she could reach them.

'And we'd appreciate your feedback about the quality. If you enjoy them, tell your friends, if you don't, tell us.'

All three of them laughed and got ready to turn towards the door.

'We'll be in touch,' said Sean. 'After all, we know where you live.'

Chapter 60

'I've never known a prison visit take place so quickly,' said Hazel as she sat with DI Philbert in the visiting area of the Category A prison.

'He's got to agree to speak to us yet,' said Doug as he glanced around the room.

They were in a large open area, dozens of low soft seats and twenty or so tables, bars at the windows and a high counter at one end with two prison officers keeping watch. Their attention was mainly drawn to the far corner, where six inmates stood at a shelf four feet from the ground, folding hundreds of pairs of jeans.

Hazel nodded in their direction. 'Those jeans look designer. Imagine paying two hundred quid for a pair and later on finding out that they'd been packaged up by a terrorist.'

'It's no worse than the eight-year-old kids who made them in the first place.'

'Look,' said Hazel, someone at the security door to the left of the workers catching her eye. 'Do you think that's him?'

'That's him,' answered Doug. 'First hurdle over is he came out of his cell. Now we need to get him to talk about Linda.'

He thudded towards them, prison guard a couple of feet behind him.

'Here are your visitors,' said the guard. 'Let me know when you're done.'

Hazel couldn't help but notice that all activity had ceased as soon as Jack McCall had come into view.

'Jack,' said Doug, 'we're police officers. Thank you for seeing us.'

He gave a snort of laughter. 'I knew what you were as soon as I walked in.'

He sat down on the sofa opposite Hazel. He looked at her. 'He's in charge then?'

'He's a higher rank than me, but I only let him think he's in charge.'

This time he gave what sounded like a genuine laugh.

'All right then, what do you want?'

'We want to ask you about your brother, Alec—'

'Dead.'

Hazel persevered. 'We know he's dead but something recently happened to do with his family.'

Jack McCall raised an eyebrow, shifted in his seat, stretched his arms along the back of the sofa. 'Go on.'

'When did you last see Gladys?' said Hazel, holding his stare.

'Now, Gladys, I liked,' he said. 'When Alec decided that he was going to grass on the rest of his kin, she was the one I was most surprised by. You'll know all this, cos you'll have done your homework, but it was before your time. Probably not his.'

He jerked his head in Doug's direction without taking his eyes off Hazel. 'We were quite some family, mostly me and Alec. We did a bit of protection stuff, security work you could call it. We were the G4S of our time. Lot smaller scale but much more effective. Anyway, we started to make it big, take over and get a name for ourselves. Just as it all looked as though it was going really well, Alec decided that he didn't want to be the enforcer no more.

'His kids were getting older. Right little pair of sods, always arguing. Kelvin was showing potential, Karen probably more so, come to think of it, and then one day, they all disappeared. All four of them. Turned out that bastard had turned against his own and was going to bubble us all at court. So the last time I saw Gladys was right before they all done a moonlight flit in 1987. I saw Alec the next year at court. He got sent down too of course, but I never understood why he done it, and now he's dead, I can't say that I really give a crap. Water under the bridge.'

Hazel thought fast about what she was going to ask him next. He had given her a lot more than she had expected, so now she needed to keep him talking.

'And Karen and Kelvin?'

This was met with an indifferent shrug.

'I'm in here. I don't get out much.'

'Have you any idea where they are?'

'No, darling, that's the thing about Witness

Protection, the witnesses get protected. Unless they're stupid enough to go and do something that draws them to people's attention, they could be anywhere in the world.'

Jack McCall folded his arms across his chest.

She wanted to see his reaction to her next question.

'Did you know that Karen is dead?'

A look that she interpreted as mild interest.

'Is that a surprise to you, Jack?' she asked.

'Well, I didn't kill her.'

'I didn't say she was murdered,' Hazel replied.

He smiled, unfolded his arms and palms outstretched to her said, 'You wouldn't have bothered coming all this way to tell me that she died peacefully in her sleep of natural causes, so come on, let's not waste any more time. What exactly do you want?'

'Karen McCall was given a new identity in 1987. She was given a new name, got married in 1995. They lived an hour's drive from here until last Monday when someone murdered her. What do you know about her death?'

'As much as you do. Anyway, if you'll excuse me, I've got arts and crafts in twenty minutes. I'm making a cigarette box out of matchsticks. It's highly combustible, of course, but you have to get your kicks somehow in here.'

Jack held one hand in the air for the briefest of times, not a gesture that would have been out of place in a restaurant, only in this instance it wasn't a waiter he was summoning but a prison guard.

He stood up, smoothed down his sweatshirt and said, 'Fancy Karen marrying a copper. What was she thinking?'

'I never said that Karen married a police officer,' said Hazel, also now on her feet.

'I must have seen it on the news,' he said, gave her a wink and turned back towards the security door.

'Hang on,' said Doug, 'how did you know?'

The officers tried to follow him until a second prison guard barred their way.

'I'm afraid I can't let you on the wing,' he said.

Hazel and Doug stood and watched as Jack McCall slowly turned towards them, arms outstretched whilst he was patted down and searched as he awaited his return to his cell.

'We can't stop him from leaving,' said Doug to Hazel.

'Do you think he was behind the murder in any way?' said Hazel with a defeated air.

'He clearly knows something,' said Doug, 'and he's making utter mugs of us.'

They stood in the visiting area as Jack McCall waved his fingers at them in a parting gesture, and then for good measure, as the metal gate was slammed shut, the prisoner on the far side of it blew them a kiss.

Chapter 61

The atmosphere in the interview at Riverstone Police Station was unusual in that both the suspect and the police officers thought that everything was going well. The solicitor had considered walking out on Jenny Bloomfield as she was proving to be a very difficult client. He was far too much of a professional for that, but the woman had infuriated him. The officers were trying their best to handle her in spite of her repeated attempts to gain the upper hand every time they asked her a question.

Sometimes, it was a wiggle in her chair, and sometimes she appeared to flirt with them.

What was foremost in Jenny's mind was that she had nothing to worry about as far as her son was concerned. Granted that, yes, his infatuation with Linda now meant that she had had to tell the police that she hit Linda on the head with a hammer, except she was careful to point out that it had been a temporary act of madness and none of it premeditated. All of this was for Aiden anyway, so the hope she'd held on to the entire time she'd been under arrest was that it would help him. She hadn't ever expected to be in a police station explaining her actions that morning in the Bowmans' kitchen. She had intended to go there early that day, on foot so that no one heard her drive away or wondered where her car was. She had even left her mobile phone at home on silent. Even now, the police would have a hard time proving she was there without her current explanation. Quite what it was the police were capable of finding out with mobile phones and electronic devices, she wasn't entirely sure. What she did know was that many a criminal was caught through using one. She knew that she wasn't a common criminal, simply a mother who loved her son and was pouring out her heart explaining that she had merely lashed out when taunted by Linda Bowman.

Linda Bowman was someone who had laughed at her. She had thrown her head back and laughed when Jenny begged her to leave Aiden alone. She had tried to appeal to her, one mother to another, but couldn't bear to hear her mocking her. She definitely couldn't stand to hear her ridicule Aiden and say what a stupid lovesick child he was.

She was tired of telling the police over and over again that both she and Linda had gone for the weapon simultaneously. She happened to get there first or it would have been her lying dead and Linda answering their questions. That was the moment she found the hammer in her grip and watched her own hand as it whipped out in front of her, straight towards Linda.

She told them that she hadn't intended to kill her; they were bound to show her some leniency. The worst was bound to be manslaughter and after only a few years she'd be allowed to go home and be with her family once more.

For now, all she had to do was keep up the repetition of her story.

'OK, Jenny,' said DC Tom Delayhoyde, 'I want to talk about the hammer. Tell me where you got it from.'

She rolled her eyes at him and said, 'I've told you this already. It was on the work surface next to Linda where we were standing in the kitchen.'

'Yes, you did tell me. You drew me a diagram, didn't you?' Tom pushed towards her the piece of paper, complete with matchstick figures in biro, depicting the murder drama in Linda Bowman's kitchen.

'This is you here, and this is Linda here,' said Tom, tapping the end of his pen on the drawing.

'That's right,' said Jenny.

'You've told me that the hammer was here?' asked Tom.

'Yes.'

'And when was the very first time you touched that hammer?'

It was now Tom's turn to allow his pulse to race a little as he waited for his suspect's reply.

'I've told you that the first time I picked that hammer up was in the kitchen. I hadn't touched it up until then, and that's why it's now got my DNA on it.'

'Your DNA,' echoed Tom, pausing to enjoy the moment. 'How did Aiden's DNA end up on it?'

'What?' Jenny whispered. 'What?'

'My opinion counts for nothing, Jenny,' said Tom, 'although I think you've told us you hit Linda when it was Aiden who really did it. You've already explained how angry you were when she laughed about Aiden. You'd do anything to protect your son. Even if that meant confessing to murder.'

She began to make a moaning noise. It started small like a sigh and then it grew louder and louder before she wrapped her arms up over her head and began to rock backwards and forwards in her seat.

All eyes were on her for a couple of seconds before the solicitor collected himself and said, 'My client can't be held to account for how someone else's DNA ended up somewhere. I wasn't told of this earlier and I think that this will be a good time for a break.'

'Yes,' said Tom, 'I think you're right about that. Jenny, I'm going to turn the DVDs off. Is there anything else you want to say before I do that?'

She continued to make incomprehensible sounds and sway in her seat, all composure gone.

Chapter 62

Afternoon of Friday 9 June

Even though Hazel hadn't wanted to go back and bother Travis so soon, there was still a lot she had to ask him. He had spoken to her at great length over the last few days, mostly about how he was feeling and coping, but she needed more detail about the last week or so of his parents' lives.

One of the most pressing matters now, of course, was what had occurred at the Bloomfields' house the weekend before his mother's murder. The late grandmother he knew nothing about, not to mention his mother's clandestine identity, were other contentious subjects she didn't relish the idea of raising. One thing at a time.

When Hazel had left Travis at his aunt's house, she had promised to return in a couple of hours to give him time to compose himself. In truth, she needed to go back over her paperwork and grab herself something to eat. She could hardly tell the grieving youngster that she was so hungry she couldn't concentrate, so she made a discreet exit and took herself off to the nearest coffee shop with her notebooks and sat down to read through her pages of scribble to find what it was that was niggling her.

Forty minutes later, half-eaten BLT sandwich, mug of tea and notebooks in front of her, Hazel scanned page after page until she found what she was looking for.

In her neat black writing, she read the words she had written days beforehand that might make all the difference to Aiden Bloomfield's future. If she was correct about her feelings, it would not only point towards his innocence, but highlight his own mother's cold-blooded planning in a murder.

The coffee shop was far too busy for her to dial the number she was desperate to call. In a couple of seconds, she downed the mug of tea, wrapped the rest of her lunch in a paper serviette and rushed from the shop. As fast as she could manage with the food balanced on the top of her handbag, her notebooks under one arm and her car keys in her free hand, she hurried to the privacy of her unmarked police car to call Doug Philbert.

'Come on, come on,' she muttered as the sound of his mobile ringing came through on her phone.

'Hello, Hazel,' he said at last.

'Sir, I've just gone over my notes and there's something you should know.'

'Go on.'

'I made notes of everything Travis, Aiden and Jenny

told me in the early hours of the investigation.' She took a deep breath.

'I think this is important: at the briefing, CSI Jo Styles told us about the mixed DNA profile on the hammer showing a match to Aiden and Jenny Bloomfield. So by that, Jo is saying that they both handled the hammer at some point. It doesn't necessarily mean that they both used the hammer to smash Linda's skull to pieces.'

'Go on,' said the DI.

'Well, I appreciate that Jenny could have handled it innocently before the murder, meaning her DNA was also on it. Don't forget though, Aiden could have used the hammer at another time, couldn't he?' Without giving the detective inspector time to comment, she carried on. 'There's been so much going on, it only just dawned on me that when I very first went to the Bloomfields' house, there were lots of photographs hanging on the wall. One of them was of Aiden and it was hung out of line with the others. You see where I'm going with this?'

'I think so, Hazel, but go on.'

'It was just a line, a comment that didn't seem important at the time. Jenny asked Travis to hang a photo in the hallway when he was staying there. Aiden took the hammer and did it himself, then rowed with Jenny because she said that he didn't hang it at the right level. It's not unreasonable to assume it was the same hammer.'

There was a silence on the end of the phone before Doug said, 'Are you on your own at the moment? I've got Barbara here with me and I don't want anyone else to hear what I'm about to tell you.'

'Yes, I'm alone in my car.'

'Up until being told that Aiden's DNA was on the hammer, Jenny repeatedly told Tom Delayhoyde in interview that the first time she had seen or touched that hammer was when she picked it up from the work-top in Linda's kitchen. That's obviously very convenient for her if she didn't take the murder weapon to the scene. She's making every attempt to distance herself from the planning aspect of killing her.'

Hazel rubbed her forehead and concentrated on what she was being told.

'The thing is though, sir, that doesn't add up if it's got Aiden's DNA on it. If the first time that hammer really was in her hand was when she picked it up and hit Linda with it, it could have Aiden's DNA on it if either he handled it way before the murder, he took it with him for some reason, or this is a mother protecting her son. That could only mean he was there and used the hammer too.'

'We know Aiden was there, and might well have inflicted some of the blows, even taken the hammer from his mother. We've had something else come back from the lab too.'

When Hazel had made her call to the DI, she intended to show him an innocent explanation of how Aiden's DNA was on the murder weapon. Now she seemed to be adding to his guilt. It wasn't that she had any problem with the guilty going to prison for taking another life, far from it. Her concerns lay with Travis. She preferred the scenario whereby Travis at least had his best friend on his side, if never by his side again. He had lost so much and this was proving a test too far for him.

With a certain amount of trepidation, she said, 'What else has happened?'

'There can be no innocent explanation for this one – we found traces of Aiden's DNA in Linda's bedroom. This time, it was semen.'

Chapter 63

Huddled in a corner of the incident room at East Rise, the interview team consisting of Pierre and Sophia made a call to their counterparts, Tom and Pete at Riverstone Police Station. The four of them wanted to get their heads together to discuss what their prisoners had said so far.

'Have you heard the news?' said Sophia into the telephone on loudspeaker. Without waiting for a reply, she said, 'There was semen on the bed sheets and a couple of other places in Linda and Milton's bedroom. It was no great surprise as Milton was sleeping there with his own wife. Samples went to the lab, and we've been told that they matched to Aiden's DNA.'

'Bloody hell,' said Tom, leaning closer to the speaker. 'One possibility is that Aiden was in bed with Linda when Jenny got there.'

'Apparently,' said Sophia with a grimace that only Pierre could see, 'the CSI thought it looked like old semen.'

Tom and Pete made noises of displeasure and Pierre's

contribution was, 'Don't fancy a crime scene investigator's job much.'

'Anyway,' said Tom, 'our plan is to get back into interview when Jenny's calmed down and see what else she's got to say about the hammer. It'll be interesting to see where she goes with this. Now she'll either have to say that Aiden was there and touched the hammer, he brought it with him, or that she took it with her from home.'

'Personally,' added Pete, 'I'll find it very interesting whether she's prepared to distance her son from murder by saying that she took the hammer with her from her own house, or whether she's prepared to take him down with her and deny that she planned to go to Linda's house with it in her own hand.'

All four of them mulled over the possibility of whether a mother's love would stop her from admitting that she had lied about finding the hammer in the kitchen.

'What enquiries are we doing around the origins of the murder weapon itself?' asked Pete.

'Pierre can update you on that,' said Sophia.

'I got some time to run out and find out where the hammer came from,' said Pierre. 'What I can tell you is that it matches the set in the garage at the Bowmans', plus there's one missing that's the right size and shape.'

'How do we know this?' said Pete.

'Haven't you looked at the scene photos on the Photoshare Drive?' asked Sophia. 'Or looked at the three hundred and sixty degree video footage that the CSIs took?'

'Er, no,' said Pete.

A tutting noise came down the line at Pete.

'Which one of you did that?' said Pete.

'It was me,' said Pierre, 'but Soph's shaking her head at you. Barbara Venice will have your guts for garters if she finds out that you haven't even looked at the scene photos and made yourself familiar with the layout of the house.'

'First off,' said Pete, 'just don't tell her. Secondly, what's that got to do with the hammer?'

'If you'd have looked,' said Sophia, 'you would have seen that the garage was one of the most obsessively tidy places ever. The walls were lined with tools everywhere in neat rows. Every item had a number of nails or hooks suspending it or holding it in place.

'The hammer was one of six in a set, the entire tool range comprising forty in the Hard As They Come range.'

'They're a good make,' said Pete. 'If I was going to choose an implement to crack someone's skull in two, it would most likely be my choice.'

Unperturbed, Sophia carried on. 'If you look at the photographs of the garage, you'll see a gap where the hammer should have been. This is where Jenny was either brilliant, or very stupid.'

As Tom and Pete sat focusing on the telephone carrying the tale of Jenny's downfall from one incident room to another, they heard the voice change from Sophia's to Pierre's.

'The Hard As They Come range is available mostly

online and via reps in sales vans. It's very difficult to buy the stuff in the shops. In fact, there's only one shop in the county that has the exclusivity to sell them. And it's not many miles from where we are now. It's in North Downs. I made a couple of phone calls to them and the only hammer they've sold in the last couple of weeks was to a woman.'

'As luck would have it,' said Sophia, 'the shop assistant remembered her because she was particularly attractive and flirty. Fortunately, most of you men are alike. Well, not you, Pierre. I know that you and Frank are very happy together. I mean the likes of Tom and Pete.'

'That's a bit sexist, isn't it?' said Pete.

'Well, anyway,' said Sophia, ignoring him, 'Pierre's already asked if this woman's on CCTV. The store manager seems to think that the footage will still be there. So, if it's recorded properly, we're likely to have our murderer buying the murder weapon several days before she swore blind she ever held it in her hand.'

Chapter 64

Before she considered herself ready, Hazel was back with Travis at Una and John's dining table again. She was starting to feel exhausted and would have loved nothing more than to take a couple of days off. Even one of her scheduled rest days would have been enough to see her through the next stage. She knew how impossible that would be with two suspects in custody and, by the looks of it, one or both of them about to be charged with murder.

She knew that she would and should be Travis's first point of contact with the police, even though any number of people would have been more than willing in the circumstances to update him. There was little point in having a family liaison officer if everyone else was the point of contact. It didn't stop her hoping that she could step away from the tragedy for a moment. It was all about dealing with it, and that was her job – to help Travis deal with it as best he could manage.

The time would come for them both when the grief was under control, and when she could do no more for him Hazel would leave Travis with Victim Support Services and make her exit.

Right now, she had work to do.

'Are you sure you're OK to carry on with this?' she asked him.

'At least I'm doing something. It feels useful, even if it's not.'

'Everything you tell us will be useful, Travis, it's just that I may not be able to tell you why.'

She paused and gave him a wry smile, and then added, 'That's about all you've heard from me. As soon as I can tell you more, I promise that I will.'

'Do you like being a police officer?' he asked. 'I only say that because my dad loved it, but I know it's not for everyone.'

'I have good days and bad. What happened to your mum and dad was awful, and as a direct consequence, something terrible also happened to you. I get to help you as much as I can, so that part, I like. The helping aspect makes up for some of the unpleasantness. It has to, or else we'd all be insane.'

'What about doing what you're doing for me? The FLO stuff. Do you get a choice?'

'It's not a role that can be forced upon anyone. That's because it's not something everyone's prepared to do. It means putting yourself forward for it, completing the course and being considered suitable.'

'I keep crying on you every five minutes. I've sworn at you, I've lost my temper, told you to fuck off, rung you in the middle of the night. Why do you do it?'

Never had Hazel felt such a compulsion to tell the truth to a witness. This was a teenager who had lost both of his parents within hours of each other. A young man he might be, but he was no fool and perhaps by telling him something of her own life, it might show him a promise of a brighter future than he could currently glimpse.

'I was fifteen when my dad was killed in an accident on his way home from work. The truth is, I've never got over it. You don't get over it.'

Neither of them spoke for a minute or so.

Hazel hadn't meant to shock him or try to match his misery. Besides, that was in a league of its own. The only reason she told him was to let him see that he wasn't the only one to have suffered, there was always some way forward and out of today's mess. At some distant point, life would feel different, only now it was a long way off.

'No one will insult you, least of all me, by telling you that any of this will get better. It won't. You just find ways of dealing with it, getting through it. Grief and rage are exhausting. You'll be too worn out to hate for so long and wonder 'what if'. I've thought a hundred million times, what if I'd gone downstairs that morning and hidden my dad's car keys, what if I'd bunked off school and gone missing, meaning he came home earlier and missed the accident. I didn't do any of those things and I can't change it. I've learned to accept it.'

'Isn't accepting the same as giving in?'

'What would you be giving in to? Moving on and

putting everything behind you. Travis, it's far too early to be doing that at the moment. I'm not suggesting you even attempt it yet. Give yourself time, but please don't be too hard on yourself if in months', even years' time, you're still getting tearful. There's really no shame in it.'

He sat staring at the lacy doily on the table underneath the fruit bowl.

'I'm angry at all of them,' he said. 'I'm angry at Aiden and that bitch Jenny. I'm angry at my dad for having his accident, I'm even angry at my mum for getting herself murdered. How stupid is that?'

'It's not stupid at all.'

'What else do you need to ask me?' he said, nodding in the direction of her notebook.

'It can wait if you're not up to it.'

'No. Let's get on with it . . . Please.'

'OK. I need to ask you about the time that George Atkins came round and spoke to you and your mum about your dad.'

He looked up at the ceiling and said, 'You've been honest with me; I'm going to do the same with you. Up until now, I didn't want to tell you about that George fella, I'd tried to put it out of my mind, didn't want you to think I didn't love my mum and thought badly of her in any way. First, I have to tell you something unpleasant about my mum.'

Chapter 65

When Travis made eye contact with Hazel again, she held his gaze. It was too early to tell him about his mother's real family, a family of organized criminals she had fled from in the middle of the night in the back of an unmarked police car. That would have to wait for another day. The time was never going to be right for that, only at that moment she needed to let him talk.

His eyes were brimming with tears, holding back the flood. Neither of them was sure how much longer he could keep himself together.

'I know that you're not supposed to speak ill of the dead, least of all your own mother, but she had a spiteful streak to her. She could be really mean and unpleasant. I don't know where it came from. The thing was . . .'

As he trailed off, he gave a dry laugh and ran a hand through his hair.

'Well, the thing was, she didn't usually let people see it. It was as if she was always hiding something. She could be as manipulative as my dad if she wanted to be. In fairness to her, it might have been because of the way he behaved towards her.

'She flirted a bit. I suppose that we all do to an extent. I watched her flirt with Aiden and I've never been really sure that it never went any further. If it did, I certainly didn't know any details about it. She was a master manipulator. I even watched my mum flirt with blokes like Harry Powell.'

At the mention of his name, Hazel glanced down at her notebook, keen that her expression didn't give her away. She went back to concentrating on what he was telling her, frustration building that she wanted to specifically ask him more about Harry, and the guilty feeling that Travis was only unburdening himself to her because he considered that she had bared her soul to him.

'Most of all, Hazel, is that I wound Aiden up a bit about my mum too. I told him that she'd asked about him a couple of times, and did he have a girlfriend. That sort of thing. I could see that he was interested. Even worse was that I used to talk to my mum about him and how he couldn't get a girl to go out with him more than once. We even had a right laugh that he was probably still a virgin. It was something she seemed to find hysterical.'

Once again, Hazel paid attention to her notebook, not trusting that her eyes might somehow reveal the knowledge that Aiden's semen had been discovered in Travis's mother's bed.

'The reason I'm telling you this,' he said, 'is because both Aiden and Jenny are in a cell and I can't help but feel there must have been a reason why one or both of them killed her. It's not as if they turned up to rob the place and it went wrong. What could have made two people attack her like that?'

'That's what we're trying to find out,' said Hazel, drawing her eyes level with his again when she felt she couldn't keep looking away for any longer.

'That's why we have a team of officers with each of them, going over and over in interview what happened, when, how and why. You and I still have a lot to talk about too.'

'Me and Aiden used to try to outdo each other. We had a bit of a point-scoring thing going on with each other's mums. It seemed funny then. I think I told you that Jenny asked me to hang a photograph in the hall-way last weekend.'

He shook his head at the memory of something so seemingly innocent.

'I remember thinking at the time that it was a strange thing even for Jenny to do. Only reason being that it was a photograph of Aiden. I thought it was something she would automatically ask Aiden to do or wait until her husband came home from Dubai. She asked me to do it but Aiden got annoyed and grabbed the hammer off her, then went out and started banging a nail in the wall.

'Jenny then embarrassed him by saying he'd hung it— Fucking hell.'

That was the point that his hand flew up to his mouth, saliva absent, mouth gone dry.

'When we went to see my mum at the chapel of rest, you said she had head injuries. What caused those injuries?'

For only a second Hazel thought about telling him the truth. Today's witness might be tomorrow's suspect: so far they hadn't charged anyone with murder, and not every arrest meant the guilty parties were in custody.

She opted for discretion.

'When the pathologist carries out a post-mortem, they give a cause of death and what kind of instrument was likely to have caused the injuries to the deceased. Sometimes, they can't be specific. Only if we provide them with something we think was the possible murder weapon are they able to say whether it was likely to have caused those injuries.'

For the first time, Travis appeared to struggle with taking in what she was saying, seemingly not because of his anxiety or torment. This time it was because he was trying to lock on to her words and failing. She saw the opening and closing of his mouth and vacant expression and wanted to lean across the table and take his hand in hers.

'What I'm saying to you,' she said, voice as soft as she could make it, 'is that it isn't always possible so early on to say. It might have been a hammer, yes.'

She bit her lip as he said, 'Pretty fucking sick then, giving me the hammer she planned to kill my mum with. What was that about? It was only Aiden taking it from her that stopped me putting the picture up.'

Hazel's mind was also working overtime from a detective's forensic point of view as to whether Jenny Bloomfield had planned for Travis's DNA to be on the hammer all along.

Chapter 66

'Right then, Aiden,' said Pierre, DVDs recording their every movement and word in the interview room. 'Tell me about the hammer.'

The officer pushed a colour A4 photograph of the murder weapon towards Aiden and his solicitor. She craned her neck to see the picture, pushing her glasses up her nose as they slipped forward down her face.

'This is a photo of exhibit JS/282, found by senior CSI Styles. It's got your DNA and your mother's DNA on the black-and-yellow handle.'

Even though every one of them knew what a handle was, Pierre pointed with the end of his pen.

'And here,' he said, looking up so that he didn't miss the opportunity of seeing Aiden's expression as he moved his biro towards the hammer's head, 'this is the part that connected with Linda Bowman's skull as someone swung at her cranium more than once. Look, it's this smoother end here with the blood and hair on it, not the tapered end for pulling out nails.'

All colour from the suspect's face had long since fled.

'I didn't do it,' he croaked.

'Yet, you can't tell me how your DNA ended up on the hammer?'

'I put a picture up,' he said, suddenly weary and feeling that, whatever he said from now on, no one was going to listen. 'My mum asked Travis to put up a picture of me in the hallway and I said that I'd do it. It didn't seem right another bloke doing it.'

He slumped forward in his seat, elbows on the table, at a loss as to how he could get anyone to believe anything he said.

'Your mum and Travis have both confirmed that,' said Pierre, putting the photograph back inside his folder.

Now Aiden was off guard: he'd told them something, it checked out and they believed him. Perhaps he really could prove his innocence. He even felt his solicitor beside him as she sat back in her hard wooden seat, as though the difficult part was over with.

Then came a terrifying moment as Pierre unleashed something he really thought that he had got away with and hadn't been expecting.

'You've made it quite clear, Aiden, that you and Linda didn't have a sexual relationship. We've been over it a number of times during the last couple of days. Remember?'

All he could do was nod, parched mouth forcing him to keep silent.

Pierre resisted the urge to lean forward to maximize the impact. Apart from it being bad form, he didn't fancy his chances if Aiden decided to lean across the table and punch him. It was unlikely in an interview, but here was a young man who was facing life with a minimum of twenty years inside if charged and found guilty. Assault on police wouldn't even register on the scale.

'Tell me how your semen ended up in Linda Bowman's bedroom.'

Pierre remained neutral and heard from the absence of her pen scratching its way across the page that Sophia had stopped taking notes and was probably watching their prisoner too.

'My semen?' breathed Aiden.

He looked from Pierre to Sophia and back again, took a sip from the plastic cup in front of him and was prevented from speaking by his solicitor who said, 'Again, this is something I wasn't aware of—'

'Please,' said Aiden, 'I know you're trying to do what you think is best for me, but I want to tell them about this.'

The heat of the room had steadily increased, despite the air conditioning attempting to cool everyone. A trickle of sweat ran down Aiden's brow.

He wiped his face with the back of his hand and said, 'I'll come clean. I lied about that. I know it's a stupid reason only after everything Travis has been through, I didn't want him knowing that I'd been to bed with his mum. This was over a fortnight or so before she was murdered, I swear. I hadn't been up to her bedroom before and I certainly didn't go there again afterwards. It was one occasion only – that was it.'

Eyes darting from Pierre to Sophia, Aiden continued with his sorry tale. 'We liked each other and to
be honest with you, I thought, Why not? I wasn't the
one was who married with a son. I went over there one
night to meet Travis except he was off somewhere with
a girl, Linda said. She told me that he wouldn't be long
and invited me in.

'I'd been round there hundreds of times and sometimes I'd be alone with Linda. Travis's old man was
never about whenever I was at theirs so I didn't think
anything of it. This time it was different though.'

As soon as he said this, he paused and rubbed his
palms up and down the legs of his tracksuit bottoms.

'Linda seemed, oh, I don't know. Upset? Sad?
Lonely? I started talking to her, and one thing led to
another. She told me that some bloke called George
something had been to see her. Travis had been there
at the time and this fella, who was also a copper, was
shouting the odds about Milton and how he'd been
shagging his girlfriend. This police officer really got to
Linda and she told me it was the first time that anyone
had told her anything about the way he carried on. Up
until then, it had always been her suspecting him of
being up to no good.

'The worst thing of all for her was still to come: she
stood in the kitchen and listened to her own son say
that he knew all about it too. He'd even seen his old
man in a pub with his arm around another woman. I
wouldn't let my mum put up with my dad treating her
like that. It's disgusting.'

Aiden did a very bad job of stifling a yawn, an involuntary action that Pierre wanted to mirror.

'The thing I told you earlier,' said Aiden, 'about the condoms. That was true. Me and Linda ended up in bed together but I didn't have any condoms and Milton Bowman had a vasectomy years ago, so she told me. Christ, this is humiliating.'

He ran his hands over his face until they found his hairline to grab hold of.

'This is why I didn't want to tell you the truth. I came over the bed.'

Chapter 67

'Ready then,' said Pete Clements, the older and more senior DC, to Tom Delayhoyde when they were in the corridor, about to re-enter the custody area.

'Definitely. What's this latest information you mentioned?'

'There are a couple of interesting things back from the lab. I'll fill you in as we go.'

The two detectives made their way back towards the interview rooms, pausing well out of anyone's earshot whilst Pete got Tom up to speed on the developments coming in from the rest of the team.

They both knew that what they were about to put to Jenny Bloomfield had the potential to send her to prison for a very long time. Neither of them was prepared to have their conversation overheard either, so even when a chief inspector walked past them, they stopped talking, both said, 'Hello, ma'am,' and waited until she went into an office at the furthest end of the corridor before carrying on.

Each new piece of information Pete passed to Tom

made Tom's jaw drop a little further, until he was sure that he must have looked quite demented standing in the corridor completely open-mouthed at what he was hearing.

Finally, Pete said, 'Come on. The only reason we haven't sat in the office and gone through all of this is because we're running out of time on both prisoners' PACE clocks. We're trying to avoid running out of the extra time we've already been granted by the Magistrates. We don't have long so let's just go and ask her about it.'

Some days Tom adored his job. He felt a rush like no other. He knew that he would remember the next hour for the rest of his life.

He was about to catch a murderer out.

Back in the interview room, Tom and Pete remained the calm professionals and carried on as they had before. They checked that both their prisoner and her brief were prepared to continue with the interview and that Jenny was suitably composed. Once the DVDs were recording, Tom went over everything he was legally obliged to remind Jenny of, and he even covered how she was feeling and what the custody nurse had given her for her headache during the break.

It was unlikely that Jenny had any idea of what was coming.

'One of the many enquiries we've done, Jenny,' said Tom, 'is to take a look at your computer. The computer you confirmed only you use.'

Jenny said nothing.

'Our Digital Forensic Team had a look at your search history. You looked up the difference between murder and manslaughter on several occasions.'

Tom had the sheet of paper in front of him with the dates on. He broke eye contact with the ashen-faced Jenny to read out the dates.

'Have you got anything you'd like to say about that?'

'No comment,' she said.

'Why did you do that?'

'No comment.'

'Were you planning on going to Linda's house to murder her?'

'No comment.'

'Did you try to find out the difference between planning a murder and what could be considered manslaughter so that if you got caught and arrested, it would look like a spur of the moment thing?'

'No comment.'

'The prison sentence for manslaughter is likely to be a lot less than for murder. Was that why you looked it up on your computer eleven times?'

'No comment,' she croaked, looking down at her lap.

'Let's move on to CCTV,' Tom said.

A look of bewilderment took over Jenny's face and she snapped her head towards her solicitor, mouth open and the start of a word on her lips. His answer to her was to shake his head and put a finger to his own lips.

None of this went unnoticed, of course, by the interview team.

'This is a CCTV image, exhibit PR/4,' began Tom, enjoying himself. 'I'll put it down here so that you can see it clearly. It's been downloaded from the CCTV system at North Downs Tools in North Downs.'

If it was possible, Jenny's face took on an even whiter shade.

'Who is this in the picture?' said Tom to Jenny.

'No comment.'

'I would say that's you. It's a colour still too. That's unusual for a shop to have a system as sophisticated as this, but North Downs Tools sells some very exclusive and expensive stuff so they have a very good security system, Jenny.

'I'll go on a little further in a moment to explain more about that but for now, let's concentrate on the CCTV. I would say that woman in the still is you. She's slim, in her mid-forties—'

'I'm thirty—' began Jenny before her solicitor held up his hand to silence her.

Tom continued, inwardly amused by what would break her refusal to answer. 'The person on the CCTV I'm saying is you has bobbed, straight blonde hair, wearing a blue denim-style dress, buttons down the front.'

Tom took a sip of water before he said, 'When the search team were at your house, they seized a dress identical to this one. Anything you want to say about that?'

'No comment.'

'Here's another still,' he said. 'This one is PR/5 and

it shows you handing over cash for a hammer. The hammer here in the still is also identical to the one we found with Linda's hair and bone on one end, and your and your son's DNA on the other end.'

He leaned lower in his seat to attempt to look Jenny straight in the eye except she had shut down now and knew that the game was up.

'The date on this CCTV and from the shop's records of having sold the hammer was on the Friday before Linda's murder. You bought this hammer three days prior to going to Linda's house on the Monday morning, didn't you?'

'No comment.' This time it was barely a whisper.

'We've been through many times how you told me that the hammer was lying on the counter in Linda's kitchen and you picked it up, and before you knew what you were doing, you swung it at Linda's head, hitting her a number of times. Is there anything else you'd like to tell me now?'

'No. No comment.'

'Did you take the hammer from your house to Linda's?'

'No comment.'

'Perhaps there's a perfectly innocent explanation as to why you would go to see Linda at six or seven o'clock in the morning with a hammer?'

'No comment.'

'There's one last still from the tool shop, exhibit PR/6, I want to show you.'

Once again, all eyes in the room were on the

tabletop where Tom put down a picture of Jenny Bloomfield, showing her as she turned to walk out of the shop.

She held the hammer in one hand as she made towards the door.

'I've shown you this, Jenny, because I want you to look at the shoes you're wearing.'

Her hand gave an involuntary flutter in the direction of her throat before she remembered where she was and put it back down again.

Any hope she had had up until now that she might find a way out of this was well and truly dashed.

'I've been given a crash course in expensive women's designer shoes today,' said Tom. He pointed at the footwear in the still and said, 'These are Louis Vuitton shoes, and I'm told the cost of them is over £1,300. You're wearing them in this picture here and the search team also found a pair in your wardrobe. That's a lot of money for a pair of shoes so I can see why you wouldn't want to throw them away.'

Once more, Tom pulled a colour photograph out of his pile of paperwork.

'The final photograph I need to show you is of the shoes we took from your wardrobe. Both shoes are covered with thousands of tiny strass crystals. In between those crystals and covering the surface of them, the forensic scientists at the lab have found traces of Linda's blood.'

He paused to let his words sink in.

'It's no surprise that some of Linda's blood was on

them – you've told us yourself that you were there and hit her on the head at least twice with the hammer.'

'No comment.'

'What the scientist has told us is that this is airborne blood and this happens when wet blood becomes airborne. It's usually due to the application of force, such as hitting someone with something. For wet blood to travel from Linda's head injury onto your shoes, her head would need to have been fairly close to your feet when you were hitting her with the hammer. Did you hit her on the head with the hammer whilst she was lying on the ground?'

This time, the 'No comment' was accompanied by rigorous shaking of her head.

'As well as your shoes,' said Tom, 'blood-pattern analysis has been carried out in the kitchen where Linda was murdered. From the blood and the post-mortem, Linda Bowman was hit four times on the skull, breaking her head open. The way the blood splattered shows us two of those blows were more than likely delivered to her head as she was on the floor. Did you hit her on the head as she lay dying on the floor?'

'No comment.' But this time, the tears came and they wouldn't stop.

Anticipating that the interview was coming to an end, his prisoner about to be covered in her own mucus, Tom gave her his final line of questioning.

'You told me several times in earlier interviews that after you hit her, you left the house straight away in a total panic at what you'd done. Please explain how

Linda's blood came to be on the floor in the garage and on the wall where Milton Bowman kept his work tools?'

This time, she only shook her head and hid her face in her hands.

'Did you kill her and then go into the garage to take a hammer to make it look like someone attacked her with something already in the house?'

Jenny's solicitor passed her a tissue. She blew her nose and muttered, 'No comment.'

'It looks as though you took the hammer there, murdered Linda and then took a similarly sized and shaped hammer to cover what you've done. Is that correct?'

For the first time in several minutes, Jenny looked up to meet Tom's gaze. He could see how broken she was.

Chapter 68

Evening of Friday 9 June

As Hazel pulled up outside Harry's house, she tried her best to push all thoughts of Linda, Milton and Travis Bowman from her mind. It was easier said than done, and she knew that within five minutes of walking through Harry's front door, he would be asking her about the investigation.

The front door opened before she was halfway along the driveway.

'Hi, beautiful,' he called as she got within a couple of feet from him.

'Hello, Harry.'

Then came an awkward moment when they came face to face, both unsure if a kiss was right for their first official date in private, and if so, what kind of kiss. So far, not counting Hazel's first and only visit to his home where she took a long statement involving his discovery of a dead body, they had shared one less than average pub meal. That had felt so much easier and more casual because of the other customers in the bar. It had been totally natural to leave their greeting of one another as verbal, and the kiss goodnight on the cheek had been instigated by Harry.

Now, she felt as though she was walking into a lair, unsure of what was expected of her. Bringing up the subject of Linda's Witness Protection wasn't going to be easy either.

Harry leaned forward and placed his hand on one side of her face, brushing the other side with his lips. He stood back up and said, 'You'd better get inside. I think it's about to piss down.'

Seated at the kitchen table, Hazel watched Harry as he stirred saucepans on the stove, chopped ingredients and busied himself getting their meal ready.

'What do you fancy to drink?' he asked.

'Just a soft drink of some sort,' she said. 'I've probably got a long weekend at work ahead.'

'Do you mind helping yourself?' he said, opening the oven. 'I don't want to leave this lamb and let it overcook. It'll go as dry as old bollocks if I don't keep watch. Grab me a beer, please.'

Walking over to the fridge, and with Harry's back turned, she couldn't resist running an eye over the kitchen. Last time she had been here, there'd been a definite lack of attention. She couldn't fail to notice that the cobwebs on the clock had gone and Harry had made an effort to clear up. The place hadn't been dirty, more neglected with a sad air about it.

Now, it seemed to be brighter and more lived-in without looking abused.

She handed him his beer and took a can of lemonade for herself. He pointed towards a cupboard, which, she assumed, held the glasses.

'Have you always done the cooking?' she asked.

'Me and the wife shared it. I like cooking but by the time I got home, it would have been beans on toast or takeaway most days. I'm not really surprised she fucked off.'

'Do you miss her?'

Harry broke off mid-stir from the pot of home-made soup simmering away.

'I won't be offended if you say yes,' said Hazel.

'I miss having company, but that's not really the same. The kids were our focus and I suppose they kept us together. They're that bit older now, so I suppose it wouldn't have been too many years before they buggered off and did their own thing anyway. I guess it was a matter of time before it would have been me and her. Then I suppose the situation would have got worse.'

Hazel sat back down at the table and sipped her cloudy lemonade as Harry dashed from oven to stove to chopping board.

'Is there anything I can do to help?'

A look of puzzlement crossed Harry's face as he paused with the oven gloves in his hand.

'I mean with dinner, not your marriage,' she said.

'Thank fuck for that,' said Harry picking up a spoon. 'I don't want you to persuade my wife to come back but I do want you to try this soup and let me know if it needs any more salt.'

She got up and went over to where he was standing, spoon of pea-and-mint soup in one hand, the other underneath to catch any drops.

'Careful,' he said, standing inches away from her, 'it's hot.'

She leaned forward, lips slightly apart to take a sip. Harry watched as she closed her eyes and drank the soup. He made no move to back away from her in the cramped confines of the steamy kitchen.

Hazel looked up at him and smiled. 'You should try some. It's delicious.'

Throwing the spoon on the table, he bent his face towards Hazel and kissed her on the mouth, hands in her hair and their bodies now touching.

Chapter 69

If the smoke detector in the hallway hadn't started to sound, Harry would have carried on kissing Hazel until she pulled away from him.

Although they parted lips, they continued to hold on to one another, foreheads touching and both of them giggling.

'Are we literally smoking hot,' she said, 'or is it the lamb?'

'Little fucker's burnt to hell now,' he said, sad to let her go. He wasn't concerned that the food would go to waste if he held on to her, but he was a little worried that the house would eventually catch fire if he didn't do something.

He reset the alarm, opened a window, took the lamb from the oven and left it beside the stove. He then picked up her drink and said, 'I'll be through to join you in a moment. Follow me.'

It was a room that Hazel hadn't seen before. As Harry paused to hold the door open, she almost gasped. She didn't want to make him think she was amazed that he could go to so much effort. Clearly, he had.

The room was well enough lit by four table lamps, plus dimmed wall lights that gave it an atmosphere of relaxation, rather than making the impression he just wanted to get her into a darkened room. The coffee table held a small vase of fresh garden flowers and a bowl of large green olives.

She glanced further into the room and saw that it contained a huge dining table, laid for two at one end. The place settings were on top of a startling white, crisp tablecloth, and she could see from some feet away that the cutlery was gleaming and the crystal glasses were sparkling.

Suddenly, she felt a touch overwrought.

'Have a seat,' he said. 'Help yourself to olives. You told me the other night in the pub that green olives were your favourite. I'll go and get the dinner sorted.'

Left alone in Harry's living room, Hazel found herself wondering if she was there for the right reasons. She knew that she wouldn't get hurt if the relationship didn't take off or it was short-lived, but she wasn't so sure about Harry. He seemed to be going into this with an intensity that she wasn't sure was healthy for either of them.

Most of the furniture seemed to be good quality and little seemed to be spared as far as the television and other electrical items were concerned. It crossed Hazel's mind that if Harry's wife and children had left and neither come back nor laid claim to any of it, his ex-wife really didn't need the money. As much as she didn't want to get caught up in anyone's divorce, at least the fallout wasn't likely to involve Harry losing his home and wanting to move in with her. So she hoped.

That her thoughts had drifted to a time when they were so far down the line, ideas of moving in together more than a fleeting fancy, woke Hazel completely from her reverie.

The door opened as Harry walked in with two bowls of soup on a tray.

'Are you OK?' he said. 'You look a bit stunned, like you've only just realized where you are.'

'No, I'm fine. I've had a lot on this week and I think it's finally catching up with me. Let me help you with the starters.'

They each sat down at the table with their food, and fell into a comfortable silence.

'Are you sure I can't get you a glass of wine or a beer?' asked Harry, picking up the empty bowls on his way to get their main course ready.

'No thanks. I'd better not. I'll check my phone too in case there's anything new happening.'

On her way to her handbag underneath her jacket hanging on the coat rack, she took a second to be grateful that Harry hadn't asked her so far about Linda's murder or how things were progressing. He seemed to have made a conscientious effort to avoid it and the time didn't feel right to reveal the Bowmans' secrets.

Checking her phone, she saw that she had a voicemail from about twenty minutes earlier from Doug

Philbert. Hazel listened to the message and felt mixed emotions about the fact that at last they were going to be charging someone with Linda's murder, but sad for Travis that he had been betrayed by someone who was supposed to care for him.

All she had to do now was to tell Harry that as soon as she'd finished eating the delicious meal he was preparing for her, she would have to leave him to it for the night, while she went to see Travis.

Chapter 70

The evening hadn't gone as smoothly as Hazel would have liked. Harry seemed fine about her leaving without even eating the dessert he had made, though even if she hadn't had to go and speak to Travis in person, she couldn't have eaten another thing. Barbara Venice had offered to come with her, but Hazel hadn't wanted the young man to feel overwhelmed.

With a sense of dread, she turned off the engine, got out of her car and went towards the house.

Before she'd left Harry's, Hazel had sent Travis a text warning him that she was on her way and had received an *OK* text in reply. He knew that both Jenny and Aiden were still in custody so her dropping in on him at eleven o'clock at night wouldn't come as a complete surprise.

John opened the door to her and she couldn't help but notice that his shirt was buttoned up wrong and his hair was ruffled. She was already feeling surprisingly nervous and now she felt even worse to think that she'd got the entire household out of bed and dressed in a hurry.

With little in the way of greeting, he smiled and showed her to the dining room where Travis and Una sat with a mug of what smelled like cocoa in front of each of them.

'Can I get you anything?' said John.

'No thanks,' she said, before turning her entire attention to Travis, yet aware that others in the room had lost family members too. 'Travis,' she said, 'Aiden and Jenny are still in custody. Things have moved on a lot today and after discussing the evidence with the Crown Prosecution Service, the decision has been made to bail Aiden and charge Jenny with your mum's murder.'

No one spoke for some time, although the silence was filled with Una weeping and the noise of Travis's nails as they ran back and forth over the table.

Eventually he said, 'What's happening to Aiden? Did he do it or not?'

'For now, we don't have enough to charge him, and I have to tell you that it may never happen. We're about to bail him though, rather than refuse all charges, so he'll have to return to the police station at some point. We're also going to give him bail conditions not to contact you, so if he so much as tries to, let me know straight away.

'We took both of their DNA samples at the start of the investigation. At some point, they'd both held the weapon used on your mum. It's not totally clear when, but there was other stuff too.'

Hazel spoke as slowly as she could, realizing they weren't taking it all in. It would be impossible for anyone to under the circumstances. Training only went so far when it came to imparting news like this. Handling it correctly relied very heavily on the human touch, past experience and reading people's reactions.

Travis was showing all the signs of being about to be pushed over the edge. There was no possible way Hazel was going to tell him that Aiden's semen was on his parents' bedclothes. That was something she would have to explain to him when the time was right, if the time ever would be right. If Aiden was eventually charged with murder, she knew the staining would be spoken about in open court in about six months' time. Just as the wounds were beginning to heal over, the scab would come off and Travis would be in a tormented state once more, eager to get it over with, but morbidly fascinated and repelled by what he was hearing.

Many times Hazel had sat beside families whose lives had been torn apart by another's actions. She had supported them, driven them around, even broken up fights when they attacked the murderer's family waiting outside the courtroom.

She knew too well that the whole circus of a trial at court, complete with amateur dramatics by the defence barristers, would crush what little life Travis had left in him. When it did happen, she would do everything she could to help him, and that included picking her moment to tell him about the sexual relationship between his dead mother and his nineteen-year-old best friend.

'Travis,' Hazel said after several minutes had gone by. 'I think I should leave you with your aunt and uncle now. I'll be in touch tomorrow.'

'Fuck off and leave me alone,' Travis spat at her, fists clenching.

'Don't speak to her like that,' said John. 'I know you're upset—'

'No, no,' said Hazel, 'he's every right to be angry. I'll see myself out, as long as you're all right?'

She aimed the question at John more than the others: Una was far too upset to take anything else in and Hazel's concern stemmed from the possibility of the huge hulk of Travis losing control completely and going on the rampage.

In spite of the reassuring nod from John, after Hazel had left the house she sat outside in her unmarked car for over twenty minutes watching the three of them through the window.

The only picture they gave her was of three heart-broken members of a devastated family hugging each other and crying inconsolably.

Chapter 71

When Hazel did at last drive off, she was unsure where to go. She knew if she went home, she wouldn't sleep but didn't fancy the idea of returning to Harry's at such a late hour. The best use of her time seemed to be to go into work. Technically, she was back on duty now anyway, so she decided to head into the incident room and get her notes up to date.

The waft of Indian takeaway greeted her as she walked along the corridor towards the bank of desks and computers. Six officers sat around talking and eating a late meal, and all six said hello to her, most of them holding out containers of curry, rice and bhajis towards her.

'No thanks,' she said, 'I've eaten. I can't fail to notice that not one of you is eating at your own desk.'

'That's right,' said Pete, halfway through a bite of naan bread. 'Don't want my own work station stained yellow.'

'How was Travis when you told him?' said Barbara Venice.

'He was upset, ma'am,' said Hazel, taking a seat. 'That's natural. I'll go back and see him tomorrow, or at least call him. How did they react when they were given their news?'

'I bailed Aiden,' said Sophia, picking at a piece of chicken tikka and not entirely appearing to enjoy her dining experience. 'He shook the whole time I was explaining everything to him, but didn't say a word. The relief was written all over his face.'

'You sound as though you're almost pleased he was bailed,' said Hazel.

Sophia nodded, put the chicken down and pointed over at Doug Philbert.

'I was saying to Mr Philbert and Mrs Venice before you came in, Haze, that I'm not convinced he had anything to do with the murder. I'm glad that CPS's decision was to bail him. We still don't actually know that he was there at the time. His DNA on the hammer can be explained and he said that the sperm on the bed was from some time before the murder. Why Linda didn't change the sheets is another matter. We've got nothing other than him telling a few lies about going to the house and his sexual relationship with Linda.'

Chewing furiously so that he could join in the conversation, Doug wiped his mouth with a paper napkin and said, 'The point is though, that he did lie. We're not judge, jury and executioner. We find the evidence, CPS review it and it goes to court. It's the jury's job to find him guilty or not. It's not ours.'

'Mind you,' said Tom, putting his knife and fork

down, 'if Jenny's reaction when she was charged is anything to go by, I'm not convinced anyone would find her son guilty anyway.' He leafed through his notebook for a copy of the charge sheet and read out her reply after charge. '"I did it. It was me by myself. Aiden was asleep in bed when I left the house that morning."'

Pierre added, 'She hasn't helped him much there though, has she? Aiden told us that he went to see Linda early in the morning. He was either with his mum and they both murdered her, or Aiden's telling the truth and he was there in the kitchen when Jenny rang the doorbell. If that last part is correct, she's still a liar. She must have known her own son was in the house.'

'You OK, Hazel?' said the DI.

'I'm OK, sir,' she said. 'Travis has taken this hard and I've got to be honest, I know it's the least of his worries, but when this goes to trial, it'll come out about his mum's encounter with Aiden. He's probably going to hear that his best friend's semen was on his parents' bed.'

Pete was loading up his plate for a second helping of takeaway.

'Cheers, Haze,' he said. 'You've just put me right off the mint yoghurt. Can't say I really fancy the mango relish much now either.'

'Do you think that we'll ever have enough to charge Aiden? If we don't have anything else now, are we ever likely to?' Hazel asked.

Doug rubbed his chin between his thumb and forefinger while he considered the question. 'There's always the possibility that something'll turn up. If Jenny pleads guilty at the first hearing, takes sole responsibility and we get nothing further, Aiden may well be off the hook.'

Looking across in turn at the DCI and the DI, Hazel said, 'I was thinking of putting in for a few days off, if that's all right? Would it be OK if I took some leave at the end of next week?'

'Yeah, of course,' said Barbara, glancing at Doug.

'That shouldn't be a problem,' confirmed Doug. 'Are you thinking of going away anywhere or just in need of a break?'

'I'm not sure,' said Hazel, who had no intention of telling anyone before Harry himself that she had planned to make their day trip into something a little more serious.

Chapter 72

No sooner had Aiden been released from police custody than he started to worry about his father's reaction to what had gone on in his absence. He had only been out of the country for six days on a business trip to Dubai and now both Travis's parents were dead, his wife had been charged with murder, and his only son was on bail for the same murder.

Aiden stood outside the police station, shivering in the coolness of the night, waiting for his father's Jaguar to turn the corner from Lower Stone Street and pull up in front of the building.

The car slowed to a stop under the street lamp. He couldn't see inside but he knew that his father would be in the driver's seat, face set in stone. Whatever the occasion, Ron Bloomfield rarely pulled a facial expression. So often over the years, Aiden had heard Milton shout at Travis, tell him off for something trivial or praise him when he had done something good. He longed to invoke the same reactions from his own dad.

The thought that neither Travis's mum nor his dad

would ever tell him off or congratulate him again brought tears to his eyes once more.

He heard the sound of the car window lowering and glimpsed his father's deadpan expression.

With a sense of dread, he walked towards the car, all the while picturing a scenario where his dad threw open the car door and ran to him, asking him what had happened and was he all right. Telling him over and over again that it must all be a terrible mistake – the police had no idea what they were doing and of course he was innocent. Not to worry, his mum would also be home soon. She couldn't possibly have murdered someone, least of all Linda Bowman.

The saddest thing of all was not that there was no chance whatsoever of Ron Bloomfield saying any of that, but that not all of it would have been true.

His mother was going to prison for killing Linda and all because of him.

His father always knew the truth and he would see through his son within minutes.

Aiden opened the passenger door and got in, the scent of his father's aftershave hitting him. A pleasant smell after so long in a stale custody area with only his own body odour to distract him.

'Hello,' said his dad.

'Dad, I—' he said but was unsure how to continue.

In a rare act of compassion, his father placed his hand on his son's arm.

The shock of the touch caused the start of tears, but he couldn't cry in front of his dad. The last few days

had been bad enough without breaking down in front
of the one person whose approval really mattered. Self-
pity could wait.

He had much more important things to do once he
got home.

Chapter 73

Saturday 10 June

Within seconds of waking, Hazel made up her mind that she needed to speak to Harry as soon as she could get hold of him.

The last few days had taken it out of her, so she could only imagine how Travis was coping. Pushing all thoughts of work to the back of her mind, she brushed her teeth and tried to picture where she and Harry might go for a few days. He'd seemed keen to get away by himself so she hoped she wasn't jumping the gun by crashing on his trip. She mulled over whether they should head in the direction of Dorset so that, after a night or two with her, he could go and visit his children or whether they should keep the two matters firmly apart.

Having spent much longer on her oral hygiene than the recommended minimum of two minutes, she smiled at herself in the bathroom mirror, glad she'd managed to keep her mind distracted for at least a little while.

She went downstairs to put on the kettle and make a phone call.

From the background noise and acoustics when Harry answered, she could tell he was in a car and she was on speakerphone.

'Morning,' he said. 'How are you? Oh you fucking moron. Not you, Haze, the half-wit that's just pulled out on me. There are some twats on the road.'

'I'm good, thanks, Harry. Listen, is there anyone else in the car with you?'

'No, I'm on my own. I've been called in early to Riverstone as I'm covering for Doug Philbert. There've been a series of overnight creeper breaks and one poor sod just got a severe beating in his own home for trying to defend his family as they slept.'

She felt her heart sink. 'Does that mean ... Are you away for ...'

'You'll have to speak up a bit. This hands-free thing is total shit. What are you saying?'

Unsure of whether to go ahead with her plan of asking him to go away with her, she felt her opportunity slipping away as he said, 'I think there's another call coming through.'

'It's what you were saying the other day,' she all but shouted at him, so desperate was she to make him hear what she wanted to ask. 'You were talking about a trip somewhere. I need to take some time off, and well, I want to spend it with you.'

All she could hear was static. Even though she had no idea if he could still hear her or not, she continued,

'I'm sorry I had to rush off last night, but I'd really love to spend more time with you. Get to know you better and not get distracted by other people or work. What do you think?'

The problem with putting your heart on the line was that it was scary.

Hazel sat with the phone to her ear, eyes squeezed shut as she waited for his answer.

'I love the idea. Wherever you want to go. I'll leave it to you to find somewhere and we'll book it.'

Her spirits lifted, her eyes still firmly closed, but her mouth now set in a grin. Hazel felt better, she realized, than she had in a very long time.

Harry brought her back down to earth when he said, 'I need to get off the line and return that last call. It was the chief superintendent and the bloke's a wanker at the best of times. I'll call you later.'

Trying not to allow her mind to wander far from thoughts of Harry and a couple of days away together, she started on making herself some breakfast before she got ready for work.

It had been over two years since she'd had a boyfriend and she had enjoyed being single, going out whenever it suited her and not having anyone else to fit into her plans. She went to the cinema to see the films she wanted to see and most importantly of all, her remote control was always where she left it. But Harry was different from any of the men she'd been out with before. He was still married and a father for a start.

He also seemed to be refreshingly upfront, as well

as decent. She had her own perceptions of him, and nothing so far had shown him to be anything but straightforward.

Harry Powell was definitely a man Hazel could spend a considerable amount of time with. For now, she'd start off with a couple of days in a nice country hotel and cross her fingers that the relationship was heading in the direction she hoped.

Chapter 74

Harry had been expecting a call from Doug Philbert so he wasn't too surprised to see his name come up on the screen.

'Hello, Dougie,' he shouted over the hiss on his car's hands-free. 'Really glad I've covered your bloody on-call. I've been sent to Riverstone for some fucking creeper breaks. That'll teach me to help out a mate.'

'Sorry, Harry. I did hear this morning that things had developed on that one and it's now all hands to the pump. I'm grateful to you for helping out. Part of the reason I'm ringing you is to tell you that we've charged someone with Linda's death. Did you hear?'

'I did hear. Bloody Jenny Bloomfield. What a turn-up for the books. I'm pleased that you got someone for it.' He paused to check the road was clear as he pulled up to a roundabout and then said, 'You said "part of the reason" you were calling. What's the rest of it?'

He heard a sigh and noticed a drop in the volume from the other end of the line. 'Thing is, Harry, I'm a bit worried about Hazel. I don't want to speak out of line, but if you and her are getting serious and there is something happening between you, I'd ask a favour.'

Unsure where this was headed, Harry simply said, 'Go on.'

'She's been under a lot of pressure with this particular job. I must admit, I had my doubts about using Hazel, what with her own dad dying in a car accident when she was a teenager. Add to that the pressure everyone's under with all the problems and cutbacks and over one in twenty officers going off with stress or depression. I'm worried about her. I've asked for more staff though as usual it's fallen on deaf ears for now. Promise me one thing, Harry?'

'What?' said Harry, now giving him his full attention.

'Make sure she's OK?'

'Of course I will,' he replied. 'She's never far from my mind.'

'Give me a ring if you think there's a major problem.'

Harry said goodbye and sat staring at the steering wheel. He had pulled the car over as soon as Doug told him about Hazel's dad dying. Not only was it something he hadn't known about her, but it made him realize that he hadn't even asked her about her family.

For the first time ever, he wondered if he was doing the right thing. He hadn't asked her much about her background and, now he sat and thought about it, perhaps he had let it all go to his head and the affections of a younger, very attractive woman had blind-sided him into a relationship he wasn't ready for.

The last thing he wanted to do was hurt her feelings,

but better he did it now than six months down the line.

It hadn't passed him by that only a few minutes earlier he had told Hazel to look at romantic getaways for the both of them for the following week. He had a problem on his hands: spending time with a woman he wasn't married to hadn't been an issue for nearly two decades, he wasn't sure he was qualified for the new job.

Chapter 75

That morning, Aiden and Travis both lay awake in their beds longing to hear the sounds of their mothers moving about the house, preparing for the day, hoping to gain a few minutes' advantage by arranging cereal bowls and teacups for their family, before getting themselves dressed and ready.

What they would give to have their mum creep into their room and steal a look at her sleeping son.

All Travis could hope for was that his mum had known how much he loved her, because he knew he'd never get the chance to tell her again.

For Aiden, it was very different. He could do something for his mother so she would know what she meant to him and how grateful he was to her. He'd hardly slept and had watched the morning light slip into the room.

He was up and dressed before his dad, picking up his keys and rucksack and going quietly out of the house before most people were awake.

Unfortunately for Aiden, not everyone was asleep.

Several pairs of eyes were watching him. They saw where he went, how he looked over his shoulder every so often, mostly keeping to the edge of the path, trying to stay hidden. It was far too late for that, except he couldn't possibly know it.

When he reached the rented garage in the detached block about half a mile from his house, he stopped and glanced up and down the deserted street, making sure that he was alone. He took the key from his pocket and unlocked the door.

The police had no idea that his family had access to a temporary lock-up so close to their home. It didn't appear on the Bloomfields' council or tenancy records because it belonged to an elderly neighbour who had been in hospital for some months and had asked her kind next-door-but-one neighbours to look after it for her.

Mostly, it contained old lamps and chairs that Mrs Millett couldn't bear to throw away, and had asked her son to carry to the garage for her, but for the last several days it had also contained a black bin liner of clothing dumped inside an old tea chest.

He shoved the black bag and its contents into his rucksack, hauled it over his shoulder and slipped back outside, locking the door behind him. The whole thing had taken him less than ten minutes. Even though his heart was pounding, Aiden felt a huge wave of relief that the police would never have his mum's dress that had so much of Linda's blood on it. He knew that he was clinging to hope and doing the only thing he could think of to help her. If he could do this for her, she might stand a chance at court. Desperate. He needed it to be enough.

Then she could come home and they could put their lives back together.

During his almost sleepless night, Aiden had thought of the best thing to do with the clothing. Burning it would draw too much attention and neither he nor his mother had been entirely convinced that putting it in the washing machine would completely remove the blood. Leaving it where it was in the garage wasn't an option now that his father was home: he couldn't risk him telling the police about it, and confiding in his dad was definitely out of the question.

Had he been thinking clearly, Aiden might not have settled for walking to the local corner shop and stuffing the black bag down the chute of a charity clothing bank. Had he been thinking clearly, Aiden would have noticed the CCTV camera that watched his every move.

By now, he was dripping with sweat and shaking uncontrollably. He couldn't go home in the state he was in just in case his dad was awake. He would know that Aiden had been up to something and he couldn't face any more questions from anyone right now.

After spending so long in a police cell, he made the most of being free and took the long way back to his house.

At least his actions served a purpose, other than giving him a break from being cooped up. It gave the police time to contact the owner of the charity bin and get it opened up, and it also gave them time to assemble an arrest team for him.

Chapter 76

When Aiden got home, he could hear sounds of his father stirring upstairs. He took the opportunity to put his rucksack in the cupboard in the hallway, kick off his trainers and get himself some breakfast. It was important that now he maintained an air of getting up and going about his normal morning routine. Only of course, this morning brought his mum's first appearance at the Magistrates' Court. The officer who had showed him out of custody the previous evening had told him that his mum would be at the first available court the next morning in East Rise. He wished that he hadn't asked the officer if his mum would be coming home after she went to court. The reply he heard was, 'Don't hold your breath.'

He kept as quiet as could, stealing around his own home, all the while trying to act normally. His usual routine was to make tea, so that was the first thing he did, hands still trembling as he filled the kettle from the tap. In the silence after he finished sloshing water into the kettle, his father's footsteps sounded on the staircase. Aiden froze as he heard them stop halfway and, curious as to what had caused him to pause his descent, he put the kettle back down without switching it on. He knew that something was different to how it had been a couple of seconds ago, but exactly what it was, Aiden failed to fathom.

Then he realized what it was: the sound of several cars pulling to an abrupt stop in the street outside his front door. It made his blood run cold.

They were coming for him once more.

Slowly, he walked from the kitchen to the hallway, looking up at his dad's face as he peered down at him.

There were shapes moving the other side of the frosted glass of the front door, followed by banging and a voice shouting, 'Open the door. It's the police.'

'Don't open it, Dad,' said Aiden.

Ron Bloomfield placed a foot on the next step down.

'Please, Dad,' said Aiden.

'What in God's name have you done?' said his father.

'Please. I'm sorry. I was only trying to help.'

The banging on the door continued. Another voice called out, 'Aiden, we know you're in there. We'll force the door if you don't open it now.'

He watched as his dad ran down the last few stairs, pulled open the door and stood aside.

Five police officers in uniform filled the hallway, and were followed in by two plain-clothes officers, whom Aiden recognized as the two detectives who had spent several days interviewing him.

'Hello again, Aiden,' said Pierre. 'I'm arresting you

for attempting to pervert the course of justice. You do not have to say anything but it may—'

'Will someone please tell me why you're doing this to my family?' shouted Ron.

This was the moment that Pierre and two of the other officers went into the kitchen with Aiden so that Pierre could finish what he started, and Sophia attempted to calm down the irate parent demanding to know what legal powers they had to come into his home and arrest his son.

It was some considerable time before Aiden was led away in handcuffs to a waiting patrol car that would take him back into custody once more, the officers finished searching the house again, and Sophia was able to calm down Ron Bloomfield, who sat alone in his front room and wept quietly at what his family had become in his short absence.

None of this was Ron's fault; he was now as alone in the world as Travis.

Chapter 77

'Has he been nicked?' asked Tom when he got into the incident room at 8 a.m.

'Do you mean Aiden Bloomfield?' said Doug as he walked out of his office. 'If you do, the answer is yes. He was arrested this morning by Pierre and he's on his way back here. The overtime for all these working rest days is going through the roof.'

'Was he arrested for perverting?' Tom asked.

'Yes,' said the DI, empty coffee cup in hand, desperate to get a caffeine fix yet not wanting to walk away from a young DC asking questions, even though he knew they were about to become awkward. 'He tried to get rid of some clothing we think is connected to the murder in a charity bin.'

'So how did we know about that?' said Tom, straightening his tie as he caught the DI staring at it.

'Erm, we'll talk about it at the briefing. I need to call Hazel and let her know.'

He didn't really want to talk about it at all, except word would get out. It always did. The problem with police officers was that they were very nosy. Tell them they couldn't know about something or allow any air of mystery to a situation, it only made them more curious. At least Doug could rely on Hazel to accept what he was telling her. If she was nothing else, she was reliable and predictable.

That thought made him pause halfway through making his drink: Harry had never struck him as the sort of person to be attracted to reliable and predictable. He had always seemed to be the kind to pick more of a live-wire. Mind you, that was exactly the wife Harry had chosen and she'd left him as soon as she became financially independent. Perhaps Hazel was a very good choice after all.

'Morning, boss,' said a voice behind him. 'I hear there's news.'

'Hello, Hazel,' he said. 'I was just thinking about you. I was about to call you.' He looked around at her as he added milk to his coffee, spilling it over the counter top.

'What's going on?'

'Let's go to my office and I'll explain.'

Once the door was shut, Doug was more willing to speak a little more freely than he had a couple of minutes earlier.

'I couldn't forewarn you about this because we didn't know what Aiden was going to do or when he might make a move. We released him from custody, and please, Hazel, this stays confidential, a surveillance team was watching him. I didn't think he'd be so spooked that he'd act right away, but after twenty-five years, it's good to know I can still be surprised.'

'What did he do?' asked Hazel, desperate to know for herself, mind whirring over how she was going to tell Travis this news and how she was going to phrase it if she could only tell him half a story.

'The clothing Jenny said she was wearing at the time of the murder had no blood on it. We knew that couldn't be right because her shoes had blood on them and the blood-pattern splatters meant that anyone nearby or inflicting the blows would more than likely have had some of Linda's blood on them somewhere.

'Either Aiden, Jenny or both of them must have hidden her clothes in a garage that they had access to but wasn't a part of their home. At 6.30 this morning, Aiden let himself into the garage with a key, took a black bag of clothes and dumped them in a nearby charity clothing bin.'

'And he's been seen doing that and got arrested for attempting to pervert the course of justice?' asked Hazel before adding, 'What a total fool.'

She leaned back in the chair, wondering how Travis was going to react when he found out that his friend had been arrested again. No sooner had Hazel's mind turned the problem over and come up with Travis at least having an understanding of why Aiden would feel compelled to help his mum than Doug's next news dragged up something else hideous.

'The CSI's examining everything now,' he said, watching her intently. 'She thinks the clothes have got blood on them so we'll have to get them sent to the lab too. Again, if it's airborne blood from Linda, we should be able to show where Jenny was standing or possibly crouching over her on the floor when she was hit on the head with the hammer. I think that I or Barbara should come with you to tell Travis about this. He's bound to have questions, and possibly do a fair bit of shouting.'

Hazel shook her head in reply and wondered how anyone's sanity would come out of this intact.

Chapter 78

When the dust had settled, Jenny and Aiden having been charged and awaiting trial, the topic of conversation returned to Milton Bowman. Harry went along to the Coroner's Court with Doug Philbert, both aware that there was much speculation in the incident room about what happened to him that day. No one wanted to think that it was suicide and the forensic collision investigators examined his car and found no faults. There were three other important factors that played a part in explaining how Milton lost control of his car.

The Coroner's verdict came back, unsurprisingly, that Milton died as a result of an accident. Harry sat and listened, not previously aware of everything that was spoken about but he could at least put his own mind to rest that someone who had once been a friend hadn't taken his own life, especially with his wife lying dead on the floor at the time. It was little to be grateful

351

for, although under the circumstances, he would take anything that was being handed out.

Once the verdict was delivered, Harry and Doug took themselves off to a nearby pub for a pint to talk over the day.

'That was interesting, Dougie, about the plastic car mats.'

Doug nodded and took a sip of his lager. 'I thought I'd told you about that. Sorry, there's been so much going on. They weren't entirely sure because of the damage to the vehicle but it looked as though the mat got caught under the brake. It wouldn't have been enough by itself to stop him putting his foot on it, except the plastic was fairly thick and his mobile phone was jammed under it.'

'So the stupid sod was texting and driving,' said Harry, shaking his head. 'And he was texting Linda of all people.'

'He didn't actually press send though. That must have been when he dropped it. The message was *Sorry about the row this morning. There's nothing we can't sort out. Love you.*'

'Fucking hell,' said Harry. 'If he'd gone home instead of texting her, none of this would have happened.'

'I'm not so sure about that,' said Doug. 'You heard what that other witness said, the one who was driving in the opposite direction to Milton.'

'Oh yeah,' laughed Harry. 'That was about Milton's style, seeing a fit young woman in tiny shorts jogging towards him made him veer across the road.'

'It was probably her that made him drop his phone, bend down to get it and hit the accelerator rather than the brake.'

'It would be funny,' said Harry, 'if it wasn't so bloody tragic. Want another pint?'

'No thanks. I've got to get home. There's a parents' evening thing tonight and I'll be in the doghouse if I don't get back in time. You OK though? I haven't had much of a chance to catch up with you lately.'

'I'm OK. Just a bit weird not having the kids about. I suppose that the age they're at now, they'd be out all the time anyway and it'd be me and her stuck at home on our own. Me listening to her whinge.'

'How about Hazel? How are things going with her?'

'Not so sure to tell you the truth.' Harry scratched his stubbly cheek and contemplated what Doug had asked him. 'I think that I'm a lot keener on her than she is on me. Can't say that I blame her. I'm older than her, we haven't had the chat yet about how she sees her future and whether I'm in it, and I think that she's petrified I'm going to ask her if I can move in.'

'Why, are you moving?' said Doug picking up his almost empty glass.

'The fucking blood-sucking leech wants half the house as well. It's either find myself somewhere else to live or move in with my mum in her ground-floor maisonette. Neither appeals.'

'You going to be OK if I leave you here?'

'Course I will, Dougie. Get home and say hello to that gorgeous wife of yours.'

Harry got up to get himself another pint of bitter and watched from his space at the bar as Doug walked out of the pub, making a call as he went. He felt some resentment as Doug looked genuinely pleased to be talking to whoever was on the end of the phone. Harry assumed it was Doug's wife. She was the kind of wonderful woman that a man like Doug deserved.

He handed the barman a ten-pound note and tried not to feel too jealous of his friend's domestic set-up as he waited for his change.

He remembered all too clearly the twinges of jealousy he had felt during his last conversation with Milton when all along, he had no idea of what was going on beneath the surface of Milton's private life.

Harry learned the hard way to be careful of what he wished for.

Chapter 79

Harry's take on life had always been a simple one: treat others decently and play by the rules. Ever since he was a child, the world had been a straightforward place for him. Good behaviour was rewarded and bad behaviour was punished.

His best friend at school was Jimmy Matter. Jimmy Matter's father was a thief, a good thief, but nonetheless a thief. The police came for Jimmy's dad one day and he went away.

Harry thought that was how things should be. Mr Matter had broken the law and now he was being punished. What passed Harry by at the time, around his ninth birthday, was how difficult it must have been for Jimmy, his two brothers and three sisters, with no mother. The first time they met at infant school was in the playground watching the older children play British bulldog. His friend had told him, matter-of-factly, that his mummy was dead and his gran got their tea ready, but she wasn't all that well.

For as long as Harry could recall, he thought that if

he worked hard and did the right thing, he would be rewarded. Now he found himself in a pub alone on a Tuesday evening, an empty house to go home to and a Dalmatian-minding girlfriend at her own place, who didn't really seem all that convinced about their relationship. If that wasn't bad enough, his pint was cloudy.

He was certain that his life wasn't supposed to turn out this way, and couldn't think of one single thing he'd done to have everything go so wrong.

Chapter 80

Crown Court – Wednesday 15 November

The once huge bulk of Travis, now diminishing inside a suit that no longer fitted him, sat beside Hazel. She wanted to hold his hand to stop him from crying out as he prepared to sit for another day listening to the evidence surrounding the murder of his mother.

Part of Hazel's job was to get Travis there and to prepare him for what he was going to hear. What she had also taken care of was persuading the legal teams that he should give his evidence early in the trial so that he could sit in the court to watch the rest of the tragedy unfold.

Every police officer and civilian employee was primed to keep Travis away from any of the Bloomfields' family during the trial, whatever the cost. Since his mother's murder, Travis had turned twenty yet he didn't seem any older to Hazel. If anything, he seemed to have regressed in years. The Coroner's verdict for his father that he died as the result of an accident had knocked the fight out of him. She could see that his every pore leaked misery.

Whenever she looked at him, she couldn't help but feel saddened, and it was getting to her. The only light in her life was Harry. He had become someone for her to look forward to seeing at the end of every day when work allowed, someone she couldn't wait to tell good news to, and someone who whenever she shared bad news always put a positive slant on it.

Since the start of the trial, he'd kissed her each morning as she went out of the door and said, 'Good luck today. It's almost over.'

A beautiful little lie and she loved him for it.

Her heart sang a silent song on her daily walks along the driveway away from him, keeping her together for another tough day with Travis. He had never stopped being her responsibility, but none more so than at the start of the trial. He asked few questions, simply turned to her with pleading eyes on occasions too numerous to count whenever the defence counsel stood up to muddy the waters with their desperate attempts to stall for time.

The urge to stand up in court and scream, 'Whatever you say, they're going to prison,' bubbled below the surface from the moment she walked in the doors and bowed politely to the judge to the moment she backed out of the court, pausing to bow again at the judge.

It was the legal system and her job was to understand it, tolerate it and take Travis through it with the least amount of damage to his mental health as she could.

They would all come out the other side with a conviction for murder.

The problem was that Hazel was all too aware that there were two people on trial, and she had a sinking feeling that one of them would walk free.

Even if she'd been a gambling woman, she would have hated to say which one, and that wasn't because she hadn't been following the proceedings very closely from the jury selection and the opening speeches, to the witnesses and the experts brought in to explain about the cause of Linda's death.

She sat stock still beside Travis as the pathologist explained how Linda's skull had been hit with such force that it would have shattered. She felt Travis shiver beside her as he explained that whoever hit her would have had to pull the hammer back outside her head taking fragments of bone, tissue and hair with it. She watched two women on the jury, one a young girl of twenty or so and another in her sixties, pale and look away to their notes.

Then came the day for the forensic specialist, Freya Forbes, to come to court. A petite blonde woman dressed in a smart black trouser suit entered the courtroom and made her way to the witness stand. By now the jury had got used to watching one witness after another as they came and went through the heavy double doors. Most of them had probably made up their minds about each individual before they got as far as taking the oath or affirming. Freya's stride was purposeful but she stopped to give a short respectful pause in front of the judge. She looked confident and even the judge's face softened slightly.

Hazel had seen Freya give evidence on two other occasions and knew how well she came across. However, what the court was about to hear was going to be unpleasant, especially for Travis.

First, Freya held the room as she listed her impressive qualifications and explained her role in forensics and specialities. Most of it washed over Travis but the words that he heard loud and clear above all others were 'blood-pattern distribution expert'. Hazel felt him squirm in his seat beside her and followed his line of vision to the dock.

Jenny sat on the side nearest to the public gallery and Aiden sat beside his mother, head bowed most of the time while Jenny held her head high, looking straight ahead at whatever was going on around her. Throughout the trial, she had made notes as she sat in the dock, although rarely was she not scrutinizing whoever was giving evidence against her and her son.

Their time in prison since they'd been charged had altered them both in ways neither thought possible. Jenny had settled in and accepted her fate more easily than she might have, as if she knew she had done wrong and needed to be punished for it, so fighting it wasn't going to achieve anything. Aiden however had disappeared into himself, petrified of what was going to happen to him and what the next fifteen or so years of incarceration for murder might do to him.

Either a custodial sentence for Linda's murder or

for attempting to pervert the course of justice was a thought that made him want to weep.

The black bag he took from the garage and slid inside the chute of a charity clothing bank didn't only contain his mother's dress – it contained other blood-stained clothing. And that clothing belonged to Aiden.

The court waited and listened along with the two defendants on trial for murder as Freya Forbes explained her findings of exactly how Linda Bowman's blood got into the weave of Aiden Bloomfield's T-shirt, jeans and trainers.

Even though Aiden knew exactly what those findings were going to be, he sat transfixed as the expert witness explained how there was every likelihood he was present when Linda Bowman had her head smashed in.

Chapter 81

'Ms Forbes,' said the prosecution QC, 'please continue.'

'Certainly,' she said, nodding her head and looking at the jury. 'Bloodstain-pattern analysis is used to support or corroborate other findings, such as the post-mortem results. So in this instance, the pathologist determined the cause of death of Mrs Bowman as being trauma to the head. When I examined the clothing, part of my examination was to establish whether the pattern and volume of the blood spatterings were consistent with the victim being struck on the head.

'Again, I was made aware that the police had seized a hammer with blood and hair present on the head of the hammer and the injuries on the deceased were consistent with them being caused by such an instrument. The blood distribution on the dress would indicate that whoever was wearing it might have been in close proximity to the victim as some of the injuries to her head were inflicted.'

Only because she was sitting so near to Travis was Hazel able to hear him give the smallest of sighs.

As the witness paused to check her notes, Hazel took the opportunity to peek across at Aiden. He sat in the dock, eyes towards the floor, stealing an occasional glance at his mother, who was stock still feet from him.

The forensic scientist said, 'Airborne blood was found on the women's shoes, indicating that the victim breathed out, expiring blood onto the feet of the person standing close by.'

'Are you saying,' said the QC, 'that whoever was wearing the Louis Vuitton shoes, court exhibit four, stood next to Linda Bowman's mouth as she took her last breaths?'

'That is a likely possibility.'

'Are you able to say,' he continued, 'whether this same person inflicted the head injuries on the victim?'

'No, I am not. The presence of blood on both the dress and the shoes indicated that the person wearing them was nearby and traces of blood were on the dress and shoes as a result of being in close proximity to the victim during or after the attack took place.'

Several of the jury members sat up taller in their seats and one or two glanced at Jenny Bloomfield. They looked puzzled by what they were hearing. So far, she had been made out to be a cold and vindictive woman, spurned by Milton Bowman, angered by Linda's advances towards her son, but now they were hearing something new. Perhaps it had been Milton who had made a pass at Jenny. Perhaps she hadn't swung the hammer at the other woman's skull.

'If you'd allow me to explain as easily as I can?'

asked Freya, looking towards the judge who gave her the briefest of smiles. 'Blood-pattern analysis is taken into account along with everything else at a crime scene or from the victim. The clothing sent to the lab, in this case, Louis Vuitton shoes, a dress, a man's T-shirt and jeans and trainers, are screened for blood. Once traces of blood are discovered, they are compared to the victim's, Linda Bowman's in this case, and then once it's established that the blood is airborne, I carry out further analysis at the police's request to explain the blood-pattern analysis.

'So,' she reiterated, encouraging the jury to follow her on the simplest explanation she could manage, 'I look for blood, then find out who it belongs to and then if it's come into contact with the clothing through the air, rather than a direct surface, I establish the blood-pattern analysis. That's my area of expertise. However, in this case, I'm able to say that whoever was wearing the dress and shoes was nearby but I couldn't say categorically that the wearer was the person who used the hammer. All I can say is that that person was in close proximity to the victim at the time or shortly after the attack.'

Two of the jury members were staring at Jenny. For the first time, Hazel saw what she thought was doubt in their expressions about the female defendant on trial for murder. It was unusual, but not unheard of, for a woman to take another woman's life in such a brutal and personal way. Men and women alike wanted to believe that women weren't capable of such violence and were the fairer sex. Juries were made up of twelve members of society and a couple of weeks in a court-room, no matter how much attention they paid to the evidence and how careful they were to avoid being influenced by outside factors, couldn't alter the fact that for thousands of years violence had been mainly perpetrated by men. The concern Hazel had now was that the jury really didn't want to believe that Jenny had murdered Linda. They were listening and making notes, but juries were only human, and Jenny and Aiden's futures were in their hands.

Once more, she could feel Travis moving in his chair beside her, restless with nowhere to go. He put his hand up to his forehead and wiped his brow. She looked across at his hand, clammy with the perspiration he had wiped from his forehead, and wondered, not for the first time, how much more of this he could take.

'Do you want to step outside?' she whispered to him.

'No,' he mouthed back at her and she fought the urge to hold his hand, despite the sweat he was now wiping on his suit trousers.

By now, the forensic scientist had moved on to Aiden's clothing and was going through the same pro-cedures that had been applied to Jenny's.

The courtroom was filled with the sounds of the jury rustling through their jury bundle, a document containing dozens of pages of information and colour photographs and images depicting a myriad of horrors. The judge, counsel and Crown Prosecution did the same. Hazel was grateful she didn't have one to hand

and kept her fingers crossed that Travis didn't ask to see one.

'As you can see,' said Freya, referring to her own copy of the paperwork in front of her, 'from the amount of blood, the blood-pattern analysis on the T-shirt and jeans, taking into account the height and size of the defendant Aiden Bloomfield, the direction of travel the blood would have taken from the victim's head as the hammer struck the skull would be in keeping with this diagram here.'

She held up the colour image, not a photograph that might upset the jury too much, but a picture of a nondescript asexual head devoid of hair, complete with several skull injuries and lines to demonstrate the trajectory of blood.

'These lines here,' she continued, 'indicate that the blood would naturally go in this direction as the hammer connected with the victim's skull.' She pointed out the line on the diagram she was referring to before allowing the jury members any time to contemplate this as she then added, 'And this second line here would indicate that the next blow was inflicted on the side of Linda Bowman's head as she lay on the ground. Again, the blood pattern from the CSI photographs of the scene shows that, whoever struck this substantial blow, did it with a great deal of force, as the consultant forensic pathologist has confirmed, completely shattering the side of her skull. The concentration of the blood, its distribution and the direction it took are difficult to determine due to the overlap and messy patterns. In simpler terms, there is so much blood on court exhibit five, the men's jeans, it is impossible to be definitive. It's as though whoever was wearing the jeans literally kneeled in the blood from Linda Bowman's injuries.'

'Now, Hazel,' said Travis. 'I need to go outside now.'

Chapter 82

Each day, Hazel reserved two seats at the end of the front row of the public gallery for her and Travis. Each day he sat impassive beside her listening to the evidence being presented and despite the fidgeting and sweating, he seemed to take it all in with a determination to see it through to the end.

Today was too much for him.

It was too much for anyone and as much as Hazel had tried to forewarn him, support him and shield him, he was an adult and allowed to make up his own mind. What was unfolding in front of him in the legal system's playhouse was wearing him away one layer at a time, but this latest detail had gone straight to his core.

He didn't remember leaving the courtroom, walking across the well-worn carpet to the double glass doors leading to the public waiting and seating area, although he supposed that he must have. He was in a small side room with Hazel.

His head was full of anger and self-pity and hatred. They were all beginning to merge so he couldn't tell hate from self-loathing. He had no right to feel like this and every time he slept, every time he ate, every time he drank one of his aunt Una's endless cups of tea, he was letting his parents down. He should suffer. It was the only thing to do. He couldn't feel anything but misery.

At last Travis said, 'I don't think I can go back in there and listen to any more of that.'

His eyes were red as he looked at her for approval.

'It's up to you what you do. I promise you one thing and that's that no one, no one at all, will think any less of you for not going back in the court. You've been here every day and if that's what you want to do, you know that I'm here to help you and to support you in whatever way you want.'

They both sat still, hearing but not really listening to the sounds of a Crown Court with ten courtrooms, each having as many as four different sentencings, hearings, administrative hearings and trials on any given day.

'It's as though I can't stand to watch it,' he said, gulping air, 'yet I can't bear to look away either. From what that scientist woman just said, even if Aiden didn't hit my mum on the head, his clothes were saturated with her blood. Is that right?'

'Scientists give their interpretation of the facts and what she's said is that whoever was wearing the T-shirt and jeans, and we know that was Aiden, was likely to have kneeled or leaned very close to your mum's head as she was bleeding heavily. It's likely that Jenny was standing a little further away because the blood on her shoes was airborne.'

He started to speak through his tears, falling onto his tie as it hung draped around his neck. 'Aiden only got arrested the second time because he was stupid enough to go back for their clothing. He'd have got off scot-free otherwise.'

He wiped the back of his hand across his nose as Hazel fished in her bag for a tissue.

'You know the most stupid thought that keeps running through my head?' he asked Hazel.

She shook hers in response.

'If Jenny confessed in the police station to killing my mum, knowing that Aiden had done it all along, she loved him so much, she was prepared to go to prison for him. What did my mum do for me? Fuck my best friend and get her head smashed in.'

Chapter 83

Inside the courtroom, the forensic scientist turned to face questions from the defence teams. The jury were indicating a liking for her, so attacking her wasn't going to work on this occasion. As an expert witness, she knew what she was talking about too.

'Is it possible from your comments earlier relating to the enormous amount of blood on Aiden Bloomfield's clothing, and the "breathed-out blood", as it were, on the shoes, that you can rule out Jenny Bloomfield as having struck any blows?' asked Jenny's counsel.

Freya put her head to one side as she considered the question. 'In this situation, if I was to strike into a source of wet blood with a hammer, such as a person's head as they lay on the floor, I would have to bend down to do it.'

She made a half-hearted crouching motion within the witness box, encouraging the jury to think and imagine someone having to crouch to hit someone's head as they were prone.

From many years of giving evidence, Freya knew that

jury service could be heavy-going and did her best to give her findings in a way everyone could understand. Sometimes she became animated but she always got her point across in a rational and straightforward way.

'The action of bending or squatting down,' she said, 'exposes parts of me that would be different if I was standing and hitting someone. For example, if I bent down, my right knee might be presented to the impact site. When the men's jeans, court exhibit five, were examined, a large amount of bloodstaining was found on the right knee, consistent with whoever was wearing those jeans bending down and hitting the victim on the head.'

There was a pause whilst everyone took in this information and a few of the older jury members, no doubt many of them also parents, pondered Jenny's confession that would save her son. It also gave the QC time to get his thoughts together.

'Would you expect the person striking the victim's head with a hammer to have more or less blood on them than, say, an innocent bystander?' said the QC, leaning forward on his wooden note stand.

'For a blunt-force event, such as a hammer attack, the main things I would look for would be the size of the individual spatter stains caused by droplets of blood landing on an item, such as clothing, the spread of the spate, how each stain relates to others, and then finally the overall distribution of the bloodstains across an item. It's all taken into account but if I were to demonstrate to you with a meat tenderizer, some blood and a bit of pork – we use pork in training a lot as it behaves like human flesh – if you were standing close by, you would possibly end up with more blood on you than me, even if I was the one hitting the pork.'

Her last comment caused a small titter in a very tense room.

'So to speak,' she felt the need to add. 'Blood can fire off in a completely different direction too if the dynamics of an assault cause it to do so. So hitting someone with a particular shape of weapon, such as a hammer, will influence the spread of the resulting blood spatter. What this might mean is that the blood could all or mostly be forced away from the assailant. This might mean that a large amount of blood is deposited on a bystander and relatively little transferred to the attacker.'

'In conclusion,' asked the QC, scratching at his hair beneath his wig, 'from the blood-pattern analysis, you can't definitively say who struck the blows to Linda Bowman's head.'

If he wanted a 'no' answer, he was disappointed.

'The idea that the attacker would be heavily blood-stained is a misconception. Unless there is a lot of blood loss at the moment the blows are struck, there is a greater chance of there being no blood transferred at that time, or very little rather than lots. It's very easy to strike a bloodstained surface multiple times and walk away relatively or completely blood-free. I've hit hundreds of pork joints over the years and I've seen it myself in simulations.'

She paused and added, 'I can't be definitive about who struck the blows, but the right knee of the jeans, court exhibit five, has significant bloodstaining consistent with the person wearing them being beside the victim on the floor whilst blood loss was particularly heavy.'

This was what Jenny's defence team needed to do – show that Aiden was in some way responsible and get the jury to see things in a different light.

However, no one had yet asked the question of whether Aiden's jeans were blood-soaked because he was kneeling beside Linda to shield her from an attack.

Possibly from an assault by his own mother.

Chapter 84

Afternoon of Wednesday 15 November

For reasons he couldn't fathom, Sean felt nervous. He sat on the cheap material covering the cushioned sofa, his two-thousand-pound suit touching unspeakable horrors. He had thought about wearing something cheaper from his workwear collection, but then the sniffer dogs at the prison security checkpoint might have picked up on the Class A he came into regular contact with. Better to be safe, and besides, he wanted to impress Jack McCall.

It wasn't every day he got to visit one of the country's biggest organized crime bosses, definitely not one that had been grassed up and sent down.

Sean had made his mind up years ago that he was going to live an extraordinary life, so why not make peace with the past. He had known it would catch up with him, so he'd willingly run towards it.

He fiddled with his tie, pinched the creases in his trousers between his thumb and forefinger and kept a careful eye on the metal-barred door leading to the wing.

It wasn't long before the bulk of Jack McCall loomed into the doorway and was pointed in Sean's direction.

'What you dressed as, boy? You look like a fucking solicitor.'

'Good to see you too, Jack. You're looking well.'

The prisoner rubbed his hands over his stomach. 'Food's shit in here, unless you got a couple of quid, although I do get to go to the gym. Library's a bit light on the classics but it allows time for meditation and self-reflection.'

Sean wasn't sure if the last part was a joke so he waited until Jack laughed before forcing his own mirth to the surface.

'What you come to see your old uncle for then? You better not have ballsed up my business.'

Jack threw himself down in a chair so Sean warily sat down to face him.

'No, it's all going fine and I took a risk coming to see you. My name'll be linked to yours now on your prison records. The police aren't so stupid that they won't check.'

He jolted as Jack lurched across at him. 'Don't take fucking liberties. How's this a risk to you? You're enough of a dozy bastard that you risk the identity they gave you, Kelvin, to come and visit me in prison, so tell me how that's a risk to you? I'm inside and you're fucking about out there.'

Sean glanced around the room that was filling up

with prisoners and their visitors, opened his mouth to say something. Jack put up his hand to stop him, shot him a warning look.

'Let me remind you of something,' the family head said, 'take absolutely no risks about anything you say in here.' Then he held his forefinger up to his lips. He followed this up with a conspiratorial wink, then added, 'So whilst you're in town, have you managed to catch up with anyone? How about your sister?'

'That's not—'

'I always liked her. Thought she had more bollocks than you, real nasty cow when she wanted to be too. I saw a true McCall entrepreneur spirit in her. I always doubted my boys would take over the firm. It was a close thing between you and her. Why don't you drop by and see her? Bury the hatchet.'

Jack threw his head back and laughed at his own joke.

'Funny, Jack, real funny,' said Sean. 'The problem with my sister was that I didn't always like the company she kept. She should have been a bit more astute when it came to who her bedfellows were. Someone like her shouldn't have chosen to play such a dangerous game. It was pure and simple taking the piss.'

'I hope that's not the reason—'

Now it was Sean's turn to put his finger to his lips.

'Not in here, Jack. I'll let you know in eighteen months' time. I wanted to run a few work problems by you, but as you say, walls have ears. Still, I don't think this was an entirely wasted trip. In the meantime, I've got a few loose ends to tie up, so if you'll excuse me.'

He stood up, prompting Jack to do the same.

As a prison officer made his way towards them, Sean held out his hand and said, 'And by that time, you'll be blown away with my new business model.'

Chapter 85

After taking Travis home, Hazel couldn't wait to see Harry. Court was exhausting and she knew that there was a long way to go yet. She pulled up outside his house, relieved to be away from Travis and equally pleased to have a whole evening ahead with her boyfriend. He had texted her and told her that he was at home and asked if she fancied a quiet night in, a restaurant or pub plus a takeaway. 'Surprise me!' was her answer.

She was certainly surprised now as a second car was parked in the driveway alongside Harry's Honda. Her stomach gave a lurch as she realized that the brand-new Audi parked next to his six-year-old car was most probably his ex-wife's.

Engine silenced, she leaned forward over the steering wheel, thinking through her options. Hazel couldn't face any more confrontation today, yet she didn't think it was fair that a total stranger was stopping her from walking into her boyfriend's house.

That presented another problem: should she let

herself in with the key that Harry had given her some time ago, or ring the doorbell? The former seemed to be rubbing the other woman's nose in it but the latter made her the outcast.

It hadn't been Hazel who had left Harry at the first chance of financial independence, taking the children several counties away. She hadn't broken his marriage up, so why was she hiding in her own car outside his home?

Hazel made up her mind: whatever Harry's ex-wife wanted, she wasn't about to drive away again. Harry was worth hanging around for, and the near-panic she felt at losing him surprised her. Hazel opened the door to get out and had her key ready to show she wasn't afraid to make the point that things had moved on since Mrs Powell had left her husband to his own devices.

As she put one foot on the tarmac, she heard the front door open and a blonde woman, a very attractive blonde woman, came out of the house.

Transfixed, Hazel stayed where she was, scrutinizing the woman's neat choppy haircut, her long woollen coat, her designer handbag, her high-heeled beige suede boots and the way Harry was staring at her before she said something to him that made him laugh.

There was no mistaking that he gave a deep and hearty laugh that meant he'd found whatever she had said genuinely funny. Even the thought of the months of feeling secure and enjoying every moment with Harry, hardly a cross word, couldn't prevent her despair at what was unfolding before her very eyes. Hazel felt tears forming but couldn't stop watching. She had got there earlier than Harry was expecting. By the time she'd dropped Travis and driven all the way back across town again, court would have been finished. Now she wished she had gone back to work and not known that Harry's glamorous ex-wife had paid him a visit.

Then Harry did something so fantastic that Hazel let out a laugh between the fingers of the hand that had been about to turn the engine back over.

As his ex walked away from him, back turned, he extended both hands and gave her a very unmistakable middle-finger gesture. Just to make sure it wasn't wasted, he shouted, 'Oi, and next time, fucking ring first. I don't dance to your tune any more.'

Hazel took out her phone and texted Harry. *Decided pub and takeaway – my treat. Xxx*

Then she sat in the car outside his house for five minutes, never intending to tell him what she had seen.

Chapter 86

Friday 24 November

Since the day Travis asked Hazel to take him out of the court, he hadn't always made it there to listen to the evidence. It was the catalyst that allowed him to cut himself some slack. Sometimes he got out of bed determined to hear everything through, no matter how distressing it was, such as when Sasha Jones and former police officer George Atkins were called to give evidence, and sometimes he couldn't face getting up at all.

Once, they'd got as far as the steps of the court, and when Hazel looked round for him, expecting him to be following her, he was at the bottom of the steps, court staff and members of the public walking around him as he stood stock still, eyes shut, concentrating on breathing. She went back down to stand next to him and placed her hand on his arm.

'No,' was all he said and they walked to her car before she drove him home. She had her reservations about him staying during the trial on his own in the house where his mum was murdered, yet all she could do was talk to him about it. It wasn't something that she was able to influence even if she'd wanted to. He could legally live there and paying off the small mortgage wasn't a problem with the money his parents had put away, plus the insurance money.

Travis's actual problems were far less practically solved. He was in a living torment where every waking second was taken up with lamenting that he had ever agreed to go to the pub that evening with Aiden, that he'd stayed out and not gone home to his own bed, and more than anything else, that he and Aiden had ever had such a ridiculous bet as sleeping with each other's mothers. He felt as guilty as if he had killed her himself.

The weeks had dragged themselves on and the time had come for Jenny and Aiden to give their evidence. There was much talk in the poky police room along the corridor from court seven as to whether she actually would go into the witness box. Neither defendant was obliged to and the jury would be warned by the judge not to read anything into someone choosing to say nothing, but Travis wasn't on the jury. He could read anything he liked into it.

Warned by Hazel what might happen, he knew that he couldn't miss this, no matter how bad his mood was, how much he wanted to stay at home and pretend that his parents had gone out for the day and would be back at any moment, moaning at him for not tidying up or putting the rubbish in the dustbin, for leaving his trainers in the hallway. Strengthened by having not just his aunt and uncle around him, but the family liaison officer, plus half a dozen other police ranging from the exhibits officer to the detective chief inspector Barbara Venice, he sat still and waited to see what Jenny would do.

She was called to the front of the court and all eyes were on her as she walked to the witness box, security officer behind her.

Jenny held her head high and the only telltale signs, other than being flanked by a woman in uniform with keys on a long chain hanging on her belt, were the bags under Jenny's eyes. She took the oath in a loud and clear voice, Bible held high in her hand, and, in the way that came naturally to her, she held the room's attention.

'Why did you go to Linda Bowman's house in the early hours of Monday the 5th of June?'

'I wanted to speak to her – that's all,' said Jenny audibly, but managing to keep her volume down. The chances were that she had been told not to come across as too confident as jurors wouldn't like it. Confident women plotted to murder people. Women who kept themselves to themselves were more likely to be the poor unfortunate victims of circumstance. She wasn't slow to learn and smiled shyly at the jury on the two rows of seats to the judge's left-hand side, focusing mainly on the five women.

'That was all I wanted to do. Talk to her. She had been leading my son on. What mother wouldn't want to do the right thing for her son?'

She took a pause and looked humble, right on cue. Two of the women on the jury, both themselves no doubt mothers, leaned their heads to one side and their faces softened.

'And when you got there, what did Linda Bowman say to you?'

'She opened the front door and laughed. She said, "Oh it's you. You'd better come in too." I didn't know what she meant at the time by "You'd better come in too".'

'And later what did you take that to mean?'

'Well, it was obvious,' said Jenny, a little annoyance coming through in her voice, before she checked herself and carried on with her act. 'I realized before too long that she meant that my son, Aiden, was already there.'

'When did you first see him?'

'Not for some time – a couple of minutes, I suppose. Had I known that he was there, I wouldn't have felt so frightened of her and done what I did.'

'We'll come on to that in a moment. How did the conversation go between you and Linda Bowman?'

'I asked her to leave my son alone. To stop messing with him. I knew about it, you see, because I had overheard him on the phone talking to her when he didn't know I was about. I was worried for him and saw a change in him, chasing after her. Having a girlfriend is one thing, but this was an older, much older woman and his best friend's mother. It was wrong and disgusting.'

She bowed her head and added, 'What kind of a mother would do that?'

'What was Linda's reaction to you asking her to leave your son alone?'

'She got angry and she shouted at me. I've seen Linda lose her temper before and she has – had a tendency to fly off the handle to the point where I've thought she was going to hit someone. That day, she did slap me around the face.'

As she said these words to the jury, she tilted her head to look over her left shoulder in the direction of where Travis was seated. He in turn sat forward on his seat and opened his mouth as if to say something. Hazel whispered to him, 'You're doing OK, Travis.'

He sat back in his seat and used what was left of his thumbnail to pick at the cuticles of his bitten fingers.

He sat and listened, that morning's warning from Hazel still fresh in his mind. He wasn't to react, call out or give anyone any reason to think that he was attempting to win the jury over by his behaviour. Their job was to listen to the facts and be guided by the judge, but right now, he could see that Jenny was getting them on side and he couldn't stand to think where that might be heading.

'I was scared of her, to be honest,' continued Jenny, tearing Travis's world into smaller pieces than he thought possible. 'I saw Milton from time to time with scratch marks on him and once he told me that Linda did it. She said to me that morning that they'd had a fight before he left and I thought, if she wasn't afraid of a man, she certainly wouldn't be afraid of me.

'I'd gone there to reason with her, to ask her to leave Aiden alone, but she was threatening me and she had a hammer within her reach on the worktop. I could see it and she saw me looking at it. We both went for it at the same moment and I got there first. I hit her. I hit the back of her head to save myself. If I hadn't done it, she would have attacked me, I know it. It was self-defence.'

There were tears now, not only from Jenny but from Travis. Hazel passed him a tissue, not for the first time that day, and as she did so, she caught Aiden's eye, not fully able to work out his expression. It was fleeting but if she wasn't very much mistaken, he looked relieved.

Chapter 87

When the court broke for lunch, Hazel left Travis with his aunt and uncle. They had tried to get to the court for as much of the trial as they could, making their own way there and back. She needed to speak to DCI Venice and DI Philbert, but equally, she needed to get away from Travis at least once a day. He was her responsibility, but even so each day was draining her a little more.

She had the weekend off and was looking forward to spending it with Harry, although she knew now that the likelihood would be that Jenny wouldn't finish giving her evidence until Monday, leaving Travis very much in limbo for two days. There was nothing that anyone could do about that; the best she could hope for was that, when she texted the young man on each of her days off, he responded quickly and didn't give her too much cause for concern.

Squeezing herself into the police room, two walls lined with bookcases bursting with statement files, documents and lists of exhibits, and stepping over brown heavy-duty cardboard boxes containing all manner of paperwork, Hazel saw that apart from Doug Philbert and Tom Delayhoyde, the room also contained the prosecution QC and Harry.

'What are you doing here?' she asked.

It seemed a little wrong to see him at work but out of the usual context of the police station. He looked slightly awkward too as though he wasn't sure how to address her in front of another DI and a DC.

'I thought I'd come and see how things were going,' he said, coffee cup in hand. He waved it at her. 'And scrounge a free drink whilst I'm here.'

'If you're offering,' she said. 'I've got time. Travis has gone to get something to eat with his family.'

'Bloody hell,' said Harry. 'Pop in to see how you are and now I'm making a bloody brew.'

He got up to switch the kettle on and winked at her as Doug left the room to answer a call on his mobile. At such a stage in the trial, there was little more for any of the police officers at court to do, except watch the defendants give evidence, hear the prosecution and defence speeches, hear what the judge had to say in summary to the jury, and then wait for the jury to deliver its verdict. Tom was now the only other police officer in the room who wasn't making eyes at someone.

He mumbled something about calling his wife who was only weeks away from giving birth, and left the room.

Oblivious to what was going on between the two

officers, the QC removed his black gown and went in search of a sandwich, leaving the two of them alone.

'This is romantic,' said Hazel.

'You'll have to wait a moment,' said Harry. 'I can't hear you over this fucking kettle. What a noisy bastard it is.'

It reached boiling and switched itself off.

'What did you say?' Harry asked over his shoulder as he poured water onto a tea bag for her.

'It doesn't matter. Do we have plans for tonight?' she said.

'I've been thinking about this.' He concentrated on squeezing the life out of the tea bag and sought out the milk, sniffing the contents of the carton before pouring it into her cup.

Over the last few months, Hazel had got used to interpreting Harry's ways and felt sure she had cracked his code. He was about to tell her something that she wasn't going to think was a particularly good idea, and then he was going to use maximum effort to convince her otherwise. At least it heralded something he cared about, so she would listen and give it some thought before telling him why it was a terrible idea. She had learned that immediate refusal of his suggestions would only mean that he would go away, arm himself with the facts, albeit that they only showed his side of the argument, and wear her down until she gave in. Hazel's way meant that he thought she was giving it serious consideration, even though her mind had been made up before he'd finished his first sentence.

'I had this idea,' he said, handing her the tea. 'Hear me out before you say a word. I was thinking that we could ask Travis for dinner tonight.'

A pain crept across her forehead.

She closed her eyes and rubbed the bridge of her nose, wondering whether she could wash down head-ache tablets with scalding-hot tea.

This was the end of week five of the trial and Hazel was exhausted. She understood that whatever she was feeling Travis was suffering a lot more. Her stress would be over in a week or two, whereas his ordeal would follow him for the rest of his life. She fully understood that, to her, this was a murder that had destroyed lives, but at the end of it all, it would be another slice of human misery from the pie that would last her forty years of policing. Between now and the end of her service, hundreds more would be along. This one would stick in her mind, but it wasn't the first and it wouldn't be the last. She had survived for this long by distancing herself when off duty and limiting the time she thought about investigations. Harry didn't seem to get that.

'I feel it's the least I can do for Linda,' she heard him say. Only then did she realize that she still had her eyes shut.

Against her better judgement, she nodded and said, 'Sure. Ask him to dinner, but you're cooking.'

He stepped towards her and kissed the side of her face. 'You're a remarkably kind person, Hazel Hamilton,' he said into her ear.

That was the last thing she felt like right then. All she wanted to do was go home and put the day's emotion behind her. Inviting it to dinner wasn't helping her sanity one little bit.

Chapter 88

Evening of Friday 24 November

'Toad-in-the-hole,' said Hazel, peeking through the glass oven door. 'Good choice. Everyone likes toad-in-the-hole, Harry. Well, except for vegetarians.'

'And toads,' said Harry, opening himself a bottle of beer.

'As long as you haven't actually used real toads,' said Hazel, getting knives and forks out of the drawer and turning to take them to the living room.

He stopped her with an outstretched arm, folding her into his chest. She breathed in his scent, cutlery getting between them as they held on to one another.

'Thanks for doing this, Haze. I don't mean digging me in the nipple with that dessert fork.'

She laughed into his cotton shirt, face against the buttons.

'I know it's been a long few weeks for you,' he continued. 'I appreciate it and I'm sure that Travis does, or will one day.'

She sighed and moved her head back to look up at him. 'I'll be the first to admit that I could have done without this tonight. I've been with him for weeks on end and it's really wearing me down, but he doesn't really have anyone now apart from his aunt and uncle, does he? Is he going to be all right?'

'Yes, yes he is. We'll make sure he is. Now let's get on with this or he'll be here before we know it.'

When the doorbell sounded twenty minutes later Harry threw open the door and almost lifted Travis off the step before he pulled him into the hallway.

'So great to see you,' he said, pumping his hand before abandoning one greeting for another and embracing Travis to him again.

From the kitchen, Hazel saw the expression on Travis's face as he was bear-hugged by Harry. As she watched him digging his fingers into Harry's arms and forcing himself not to cry, she had an image of the three of them spending the entire evening crying if she didn't do her best to stop it right away.

'Hi there,' she said, walking towards Travis. 'Thank you for coming over.'

'Thanks for the invite,' he said as Hazel leaned over to kiss him on the cheek.

'Come on through,' said Harry. 'I'm sorting dinner so Hazel can get you a drink.'

'Oh, I bought a bottle of wine,' said Travis, holding up a hand up to his forehead. 'I must have left it behind.'

'Don't worry about that,' said Harry, calling back

to their guest as he walked towards the kitchen. 'Make yourself at home. Want a beer?'

'Yes please,' he said, following Hazel into the living room.

She held the door open for him and as he stepped past her he stopped and said, 'Ages ago, just after my mum was killed, we spoke about Harry. I'm not sure if you remember our conversation.'

She had no doubt where he was going with this, but chose to make out that she had no idea what he meant.

'Conversation?' she asked.

'I don't know if you were seeing Harry at the time but I told you that he liked my mum. I'm embarrassed now and realize that was out of order. I wouldn't have said it. I didn't mean it like that, it's just that he's a good bloke – one of the best. He always does the right thing, whatever the consequences.'

She listened, aware of how much the last six months had aged him, but not in a maturing and growing way. Rather in a manner that spoke of being exposed to too much far too soon.

'It's fine,' she said quietly. 'Beer, was it?'

At the second nod of his head, she went to get three bottles of beer from the fridge and to watch her boyfriend as he sang the *Pink Panther* theme tune and added carrots to a pan of boiling water.

There was no mistaking Harry's decency but one day it would get the better of him.

Chapter 89

Monday 27 November

The rest of the weekend rushed by and before Hazel knew it, it was time to go back to work. She made the journey to pick up Travis from his home and take him to court once more.

The drive was probably the most relaxed they had shared since the trial began, either because a couple of days before they had got to know each other a little more over sausages in batter mix, or because Harry had worked his magic and put Travis's mind at ease over a lot of the court procedures and likely outcomes. Hazel had explained everything to him but when Harry went over the exact same thing, Travis hung on every word with a look of reverence. It was to be expected, she supposed: they had known each other for a very long time and she knew from what he'd told her that Travis had loved being with Harry and his sons when they were all much younger.

Whatever the outcome of today, Jenny would finish

giving her evidence and they would all find out very soon whether she was about to be followed into the witness box by her son.

Hazel parked and they made their way towards the front of the building, up the steps to security. As she had done a couple of times before, she pulled Travis out of the queue when two members of the jury stood in line behind them. He had got used to the drill now and knew that under no circumstances should he speak to any of them, even if he found himself in the gents' standing at a urinal next to one of them. Although he had tried to point out to Hazel that in the toilets men didn't tend to strike up conversations with other men, especially if they were mid-flow.

As they stood waiting for a chance to join the snake of people waiting to be searched, Hazel said, 'Thanks for what you said on Friday about Harry liking your mum. I know it can't have been easy for you to talk about her that way.'

He shrugged and cast an eye over the diminishing line of people. 'It's OK. He is a good bloke. That's more than I can say for my dad. I'm gutted that he's not here, but there's no denying, he could be a bit of a dick. I'd even seen him trying to flirt around Jenny on occasion. Pretty ironic as it seems that she killed my mum and my dad was all but dead at the time.'

Hazel stood for a moment, envying smokers for having something to do with their hands in such a situation.

'My mum had been on at him for ages to fix

something in the loft,' said Travis, kicking a stone along with the toe of his shoe. 'He never had time to do that sort of thing but he went to Jenny's a couple of times to do stuff around the house and he went to help some woman across the street when she had a leak coming through her roof. No time for my mum though.'

Hazel looked down at him as he scratched the paving slab with the jagged edge of the stone.

'Shall we go inside now?' was all she said.

As Travis and Hazel sat in their usual seats the defendant on trial for murder sashayed her way to the witness stand and began to entrance the jury. The question and answer session was to grip everyone in the court as it had the previous Friday.

'How was your relationship with Milton Bowman?'

'Good, very good, I'd say. We'd known each other for some time, about the same time I'd known his wife Linda. My son and their son, Travis, were best friends from school so we all met up every so often. I saw more of Linda when the children were much younger, of course. Over the last four or five years, we hadn't seen each other as much.'

'The court is already aware of Mr Bowman's sad and tragic death as a result of a traffic accident, but prior to his death, when did you last see him?'

For the first time while under oath Jenny paused to give an answer.

'I think ... I think it was about a week before his horrible accident. I'd bumped into him one day in East

Rise town centre. I was in a bit of a state because I'd bought a new dishwasher and they were supposed to deliver it and install it. Because it had a hose extension or something, they wouldn't do it. The men who delivered it said that they couldn't do it in case it leaked. I had people coming over for dinner so I needed to find a hardware shop. I was hoping someone there might come out and fix it.'

'And what happened when you saw Milton Bowman?'

'He asked how I was. I told him and I was very flustered. He had always been kind to me and said that he would fix it. Then he asked me what tools I had at home.'

Jenny gave a small laugh and playing to the jury said, 'I'm a woman. As if I'd know that.'

'Quite,' smarmed the barrister, giving her a little smile in return.

'Milton then told me he could pop in that evening and he'd bring his tools with him. He arrived that evening with a toolbox of stuff and connected the dishwasher for me. I made him tea, kept out of his way and asked if I could return the favour. I remember very clearly that, as he left, he said that I could find his hammer for him. We had quite a laugh when he told me that the range was called Hard As They Come. That doesn't seem very important now.'

'What did you do about the hammer?'

'I decided to buy him one to replace the one he'd lost. It was the least I could do, so I found a shop that sells them and I went to buy one. On the morning I went to see Linda, I thought about taking it with me so that she could give it to Milton. Then I realized she might not know Milton had installed my dishwasher. The last thing I wanted to do was cause any problems between them. Besides, if I was going round there to confront her about Aiden it really wasn't a good idea. I left it at home.'

'Where is the hammer now that you bought for Mr Bowman?'

'I lost it.'

There was a titter from a couple of the jury members and from her sideways view of Jenny, Hazel saw her features snap into annoyance, before her face regained its composure again.

Even though the bottom half of Aiden was hidden by the wooden wall of the dock, through the top half of reinforced glass it was easy to see him squirm and wriggle in his seat.

No one was completely fooled that Aiden hadn't played a greater part in all this than simply trying to dispose of bloodstained clothing. His turn would soon come and then he could explain why he was kneeling next to Linda's bloodied skull when his own mother, who was taking full responsibility for the death, claimed he hadn't even been there.

It was clear to Hazel, who had sat through such a drama many times before, that the defence team were muddying the waters as far as Milton and Jenny's relationship was concerned. This was their attempt to try and give an innocent explanation as to why, only three days before the murder, Jenny went to a hardware shop and bought exactly the same make and size hammer that was already at the Bowmans' home. All the defence had to do was show the jury that they should doubt that Jenny's actions were indeed a premeditated act of murder, and she might get away with it.

What Hazel didn't pay much attention to, and what Jenny couldn't have seen as she stood in the witness box with her back to the courtroom door, was someone slip into the public gallery and listen to the rest of the defendant's answers as she gave her evidence.

It was someone with a lot more than a simple interest in the outcome of the trial.

Sean Turner was more ruthless than anyone had so far given him credit for.

Chapter 90

Evening of Monday 27 November

The trial that day had continued without Aiden giving his evidence and the judge pointed out that the jury shouldn't read anything into this.

Over a dinner that evening that Hazel barely picked at, Harry said, 'How about when the jury come back with their verdict, we go away for a weekend?'

She looked up at him from scrutinizing a prawn on the end of her fork and said, 'We could do that but it's difficult to predict how long they'll be out for.' She hesitated and added, 'You're right, though, a weekend away would be a great idea.'

Her face was drawn and her eyes hadn't danced at him for what seemed like eternity, yet they had only been in a relationship for a little over five months. Harry had messed up one relationship, and wasn't about to let another one go awry right in front of him.

'I've got a bloody good idea,' he said, watching her

smile at his enthusiasm. 'We can get a cab into town on Friday, get drunk and spend Saturday hungover.'

'It's probably not the most sensible thing to do, but I'll think about it.'

They carried on eating for a few minutes, Harry feeling relieved that Hazel was at least showing an interest in doing something together, even if it meant the pair of them feeling under the weather for half the weekend. He was also glad not to be talking about work for a while as it was all Hazel seemed to speak about lately. He wanted to make plans with her and make sure there was a future for them together. He wasn't sure if she could see ahead to spending years to come with a divorced father of three who was much older than her, but he wasn't too keen to point that one out. Also, he realized that he needed to cut her some slack until the verdict came back.

One thing he did know was that Travis wouldn't be the only one who was inconsolable if both Jenny and Aiden were found not guilty.

'Are you OK?' he asked her, picking up his beer.

'I'm fine. It's taken it out of me being at court for so long. That's all it is. I know this has been a really testing time for Travis. Even so, it's getting to me.'

She busied her hands by pouring some water from the jug into her glass. The truth was that, when the trial was over, she had no reason not to spend a lot more time with Harry, and he wasn't entirely convinced that was something she was looking forward to. Neither of them had expected the relationship to take off so fast and gather so much pace without them realizing what was happening.

Even though Harry had eaten enough seafood linguine to last him a lifetime, he continued to twirl pasta strands around his fork. The only reason was that he didn't want to look his girlfriend in the eye, and other than make it obvious by leaving the table, he needed to avert his gaze.

'You needn't worry so much,' he said, 'there's enough stuff, such as Jenny lying to begin with, the stuff on her computer she looked up about the difference between manslaughter and murder, the fact that she only admitted it when it was all stacking up against Aiden. Jenny will never get away with her claim of self-defence. There were too many injuries to Linda. I saw them.'

He crammed as much food into his mouth as he could manage and slowly began to chew. Right now, he wanted to avoid being drawn into a conversation about where they were headed: it was much easier to talk about murder than love.

'That's part of my problem though: she did only admit it when we had Aiden in custody, so what if she's merely taking the blame for something he's done to keep him out of prison?'

Verbalizing his thoughts was impossible at that moment, unless he wanted to spray linguine all over Hazel. He was no expert when it came to women, yet he didn't think she'd like a seafood coating very much.

'Either way,' continued Hazel, seemingly oblivious to Harry's desperate chomping, 'Jenny might have admitted to killing Linda, thinking it was Aiden when it wasn't him at all.'

'First off, Haze, we aren't looking at anyone else at all for this murder. It could only have been one of those fuckers that smashed her head in, the other one was standing there at the time. They helped each other to get rid of bloodstained clothing and threw the hammer with Linda's blood and hair all over it into a garden. A hammer, might I add, that was bought by Jenny and taken as a gift to the house at six in the morning. Even fucking Interflora don't deliver at that time of day. They're murdering fuckers. Can we leave it at that?'

Chapter 91

Things weren't supposed to go this way. Sean's plan had been a simple one: expand his business, recruit some door-to-door Class A dealers, make lots of money. It was a huge Avon round, except that instead of lipstick and perfume, they were taking orders for crack and heroin. It should have been so simple.

Then he found out that Karen was right here in East Rise. What the fuck did his stupid sister think she was doing being married to a copper, a bent one at that?

Anyone with so few brain cells that after keeping her identity a secret for thirty years allowed her photograph to go on Facebook, her standing next to her detective inspector husband, was too dumb to be allowed to live.

It didn't take much to find her – half an hour in an internet café and he had the address.

It wasn't quite the reunion he'd pictured. He knew there would be shouting, there always was. Even the day she upped and left Plymouth, not telling anyone where she was going. But for fuck's sake, to marry a copper? Was it some sort of sick joke? She didn't even seem to have a good word to say about him.

The red mist had come down and he'd acted in blind panic, anticipating the sound of the dull thud of metal on skull. He hadn't wanted to hurt her, he really hadn't.

He'd watched his own hand as he'd raised the hammer, horrified as it smashed against his own sister's head, hearing the sound of it connecting with bone as he hit her again and again. A sickening crunch that sounded much louder than it probably was, the blood flying in an arc as he used his strength to pull it back towards him, the bloody end inches from his face until he swung it again.

Over time, Sean had carried out similarly terrible acts of violence, only not against his own kith and kin. He hadn't gone to see his sister to do this to her. That wasn't the sort of person he was.

Although he couldn't explain to himself at what point before he picked the hammer up he slipped on the latex gloves he carried in his jacket pocket.

He had a couple of other matters to tie up, and although he would take no pleasure in it, it was all business at the end of the day.

Chapter 92

Afternoon of Wednesday 29 November

For the second day running, Barbara Venice warned all of those who were to be in the courtroom about their behaviour.

'Don't forget,' she said, 'when the jury come back, and it could be this afternoon, we remain professional and impassive. Whatever the verdict.' She scanned the faces of those jamming themselves into the police room.

'We won't always get the result we want,' she said. 'Nevertheless, we don't show it. OK?'

Her words were met with reluctant nods until someone offered to put the kettle on and it was back to business as usual, with the added edge of knowing that within an hour or so, they could be packing up the exhibits and paperwork and heading off to another murder. There had been another four in the county whilst the trial was going on and one or two members of staff had been released to rush off and deal with another family's anguish somewhere.

The world still kept on turning, even if it felt to Travis and the Bloomfields as though it had come to a halt far away from the light.

The difference was that Travis's predicament wasn't his own doing.

The tannoy had called all parties in the case of Bloomfield and Bloomfield back to court seven. Travis sat in his usual seat, next to Hazel, his aunt and uncle the other side of him. Every police and civilian employee who had worked on the investigation who could make time to be there took every last seat. Even a few that had nothing to do with the inquiry but had known Linda and Milton were in the room. Travis had seen Aiden's father outside the court and didn't have to turn round and scan the packed room to know he was behind him somewhere.

Hazel cast her eye over the other occupied seats and saw a couple of local reporters she recognized plus a few she didn't.

Everyone had anticipated that being called back to their places meant that twelve people who had been chosen from the local community, who had sat and listened to the evidence, and made notes throughout, were about to announce whether they thought that Jenny and Aiden Bloomfield were guilty of murder.

Both of his parents were gone so all Travis felt he had left was the words of the jury. It didn't seem to him as if it was about the evidence or the truth now, but still it all focused on this point. He had a thudding in his ears and barely registered what the court usher in her long black gown was saying as she checked with the jury foreman whether they had reached a verdict they all agreed on.

He tried his best to concentrate and not think about Hazel's explanation of what might happen if the jury couldn't agree. The word 'retrial' was as abhorrent to him as 'innocent'. Couldn't anyone see how he was suffering? How this was all weighted in the favour of those on trial?

His skull felt as though someone had replaced his brain with red-hot coals and they were burning him from the inside out.

He tried to concentrate on the words he was hearing and heard Aiden's name.

Travis closed his eyes, held his breath.

'Do you find the defendant guilty or not guilty?'

'Guilty.'

That was all he heard. He knew there was more to come but he had gone into sensory overload.

Jenny. They must have decided about Jenny only right now, feelings he hadn't expected to experience flooded him. He didn't want his best friend to be guilty. He knew that they couldn't ever be friends again, yet if twelve complete strangers had just said "not guilty" instead of "guilty", it wouldn't have been Travis's decision. He could have then put all of his efforts into hating Jenny and all the times he and Aiden had spent together over the years would count for something.

Now that was gone too.

'Do you find the defendant guilty or not guilty?' he heard again.

'Not guilty.'

He couldn't believe what was happening. He looked around wildly at the faces of the jury then the faces of Aiden and Jenny as they stood in the dock. Hers paler than death, his, an open-mouthed stare of disbelief.

'It's OK,' Hazel said, tilting her head towards his. 'Do you understand what happened?'

His eyes, staring yet not seeming to focus, were unsettling and leading her to believe he hadn't grasped what had just happened.

'Yeah,' he rasped, 'they said my best friend murdered my mum.'

Chapter 93

Feeling as though she had lost everything in a very dangerous game, Jenny Bloomfield stood outside the court building, utterly bewildered and unsure what to do.

She had seen her husband in the public gallery from time to time throughout the trial, although he had never once made contact with her in prison, wouldn't take her phone calls and failed on each occasion she looked his way in court to return her gaze.

It was as though she wasn't even there. She knew that he was there for Aiden and not for her, that idea reinforced by his rapid exit as soon as the jury announced her innocence.

Traffic was heavy and the air had a sharp bite to it. It was the time of year she usually had her Christmas shopping out of the way and could start to enjoy the holiday season. This year, she wasn't even sure where she'd be living.

Without any other plan, shivering, Jenny made her way to the town. She had never envisaged that, if she was found not guilty, they would kick her out there and then with only the clothes she stood in. She had no money, no credit card. Everything she had was at the prison. She hadn't even been able to find her barrister after the verdict. Feeling herself start to panic, she toyed with the idea of going back into the court to ask one of the police officers for a lift home, then realized how preposterous that was: they had put her inside in the first place, and for something she hadn't done.

She waited at the lights to cross towards the taxi rank, not thinking through how she would pay for her fare home, wherever home was. Her mind still turning over the events of nearly six months ago and how her actions of that morning were all down to one single act of love for her son.

What mother wouldn't have done the same?

Her feet took her past where the CCTV cameras used to be until the council decided it had to save £80,000 and remove two thirds of them, and out the other side in the direction of the waiting area for cabs. Except it was empty.

Lost in the thought of how Aiden was the whole reason she had been at the Bowmans' in the first place, she stood miserable and vulnerable at the side of the darkened street, the biting wind keeping most people in the shops and pubs only a couple of roads away. Her only crime had been to creep from her own house at an ungodly hour to plead with Linda to leave her son alone, partly fuelled by her pillow talk with Sean during afternoons at the Grand.

She had arrived at Linda's house expecting to be

laughed at, although not ignored, so after she'd rung the doorbell for the second time, she tried the door and let herself in, making her way to the heart of the house, the kitchen.

Hindsight was a wonderful thing, and if only she had gone back home again, forgotten the confrontation she had practised in her mind.

The sight of Linda on the floor, the noise of gurgling coming from her lips and blood from her mouth as Jenny stood over her and watched her take her final breath.

She would never have confessed to a murder she wasn't responsible for if she had known for one second that her wonderful, sweet, kind son would instead be found guilty.

Now she was terrified and alone, teeth chattering, and completely at a loss as to what she should do.

Jenny called to mind the battle she had had with herself deciding whether to help the dying woman on the floor and call an ambulance, or whether to get herself away as fast as possible. She closed her eyes and remembered the tentative step forward she had taken, her head next to Linda's head.

Then self-preservation had kicked in. And her love for her son.

If she ran, she'd reasoned, no one would know she'd been there. Linda would soon be dead and not plaguing her family.

The worst thought of all was that Aiden had done this himself. Jenny knew that he wasn't in his bed when she'd left that morning, and here was the same make of hammer he had made such a fuss about using to hang that bloody photograph.

With her arms wrapped round her in an attempt to keep warm, she blinked back tears, now realizing how stupid she had been. All she had to do was turn round, go back and find one of the police officers and tell them. She and Aiden had never spoken about it, too numb with terror at what the other had done, too horrified that they considered each other capable of standing there and watching another person's life's blood trickle away.

Wasn't that what she had done? Didn't that make her as guilty as her son?

Now it was too late: she had lied for the sake of her son. Jenny would gladly have spent the rest of her days in prison if it meant that her boy was set free.

Only he hadn't been.

And now she was in a part of town she couldn't remember going to before. Despite the cold late afternoon air, she broke out in a sweat.

Then the headlights of a car came towards her. She shrank back into the shadows, moved closer to the unlit closed-up shop fronts.

The car slowed, pulled over a few feet from where she cowered.

Unsure whether to run or scream, she stood rooted to the spot as the driver's window opened.

'Sean?' she said, unable to keep a relieved laugh out of her voice. 'What are you doing here?'

'Looking for you,' he said. 'I heard your good news. Jump in and we'll go somewhere warm and quiet, away from everyone else.'

Chapter 94

Most of the team that had worked on the murder went to the pub after the jury's verdict. On her way to join them for the first round, the DCI stopped at the bottom of the Crown Court steps to make a statement to the waiting press. To make sure that she set aside an hour to congratulate her team and didn't sneak off home, Doug Philbert had relieved her of her credit card for the first round of drinks, promising she would get it back as soon as she had a slimline tonic in her hand.

Hazel had waited until the corridor was empty and taken Travis out of a side security door to her car. He hadn't said very much, only told her how grateful he was for everything.

She decided to leave him at his aunt and uncle's house with the little family he had left.

Right now, she had a neglected boyfriend to get home to.

As soon as she pulled up outside Harry's house, saw the lights on and could make out movement through the front window, Hazel put her head back against the rest, closed her eyes and took a long, slow breath out. Somehow, she'd managed to get through it all. Somehow Travis had managed it too.

Now it was over and she was relishing getting back to normal. Whatever that was.

When she opened her eyes again, she saw Harry's face at the bay window, peering out at her. The sight of him with the hem of the net curtains on his head, draping down on either side, manic grin on his face, was enough to make her smile. What couldn't fail to lift her mood was that the hand that wasn't busying itself beckoning her inside was waving a bottle of champagne at her.

She waved back, got out of the car and trotted down the driveway towards him.

The door was slung open and Harry all but hollered, 'You're not only beautiful, you convict murderers.'

Even the danger of dropping a bottle of champagne on the doorstep didn't stop Harry from kissing her before she made it inside the house. They stood where they were for over a minute, lost in their embrace, Hazel's hands in his hair, Harry kissing her mouth, so pleased to have his girlfriend back.

She made herself promise that, at least for now, she wouldn't bring up the subject that had been at the back of her mind for so long, lurking, waiting to take a hold as soon as the trial stopped. What was she going to say to Harry if he asked to move in with her now his ex-wife was insisting on their selling the house?

'Everything OK?' he asked when they drew apart.

'Of course. It's a brilliant result.'

'Let's have a glass of this before I manage to smash the bottle,' he said, holding up the champagne.

'Shall we toast to justice and a lengthy custodial sentence?' Hazel said.

Harry smiled at her. 'How about to less work and a lot more time together?'

Chapter 95

Still numb from the shock of the verdict, Aiden quietly did as he was told and followed the dock officers to the cells buried beneath the court building. Throughout his time in prison, he had given no one any cause for complaint about his behaviour. He did what was asked of him, when it was asked. He had even given most of his money and phone credit to other prisoners, allowing them to make calls on his phone account. Nothing mattered to him any more. He should have told the truth when he had the chance. No one would ever believe him now: he was a convicted murderer.

Aiden sat immobilized in the cell as he waited to be taken back to prison for the first night of what would probably be the next two decades of his life.

That was the moment he closed his eyes and remembered every vivid detail of putting down the hammer his mother had bought for Milton on the kitchen worktop as Linda laughed at him and walked away. He'd brought it over as an excuse if anyone found out he was there, only now the temptation to pick it up and swing it at her skull was almost irresistible, except somehow, somehow, she'd turned to him and flashed her heart-melting smile at him, beautiful green eyes beckoning him.

There was a torrent of teenage hormones as she pulled him to her, kissed him, let him murmur how much he wanted her, then he was kissing her mouth, her face. Suddenly, she pushed him away, and he watched her put her index finger to her lips to silence him.

'The doorbell,' she said. 'You'll have to go out through the kitchen door.'

That had been the last time he had seen Linda alive.

Aiden barely registered that he was being taken from the court cells, put into the prison van and driven back towards what might be his final destination. The temperature in the van was stifling after the damp cells, early evening traffic bringing them to a stop every couple of minutes.

It made no difference to him: he wasn't going anywhere in a hurry.

He was still lost in thought when the enormous gates of the prison were opened, he was let out of the van, searched and booked back in, and then led to his wing.

He couldn't have left things like they were with Linda. She might not have felt the same way, but he had had to find out. He remembered his sprint back to the Bowmans' house and bursting through the kitchen door, frantic to tell Linda how much she meant to him, that he couldn't stop seeing her and she had to give him one more chance.

Except the scene that met him had filled his nightmares ever since.

Aiden had stepped across the kitchen, taken in the bloodied weapon, and looked down at Linda's broken body on the floor. Incredulous but fascinated by the sight of blood sprayed up the wall, along the floor, on her clothes, he had found himself kneeling on the floor beside her, blood spreading closer to him. The sound of someone else in the house jolting him to full alert.

That was when he did the worst thing possible – he got up and ran. He was too frightened to stay and confront whoever it was. He just wasn't that sort of man. He couldn't tell the police, even his own mother, never his best friend, that he had been so scared, he got up and ran home. He ran home to his mum, who wordlessly led him to the bathroom, put his clothes and trainers in a black sack and pushed him towards the shower.

'This is your cell now,' said the prison officer, jolting Aiden back to his present torment.

'And this is who you'll be sharing with for the time being.'

'Hello, boy,' said his new cell-mate. 'My name's Jack McCall. I think we've got a couple of mutual friends.'

Acknowledgements

As ever, I am grateful to so many people for their help. The final version of this book is vastly different from the first draft. One huge change was after a conversation with retired DC Dave Frampton, where once again we talked about policing, both today and in another age. I'm indebted to Dave for his expertise and advice regarding a particular aspect of the plot, something I would otherwise have guessed at and no doubt would have got wrong. In case you've skipped to this page I won't give too much away but thanks to Dave for adding another dimension to Linda Bowman's past.

My thanks also to Jo Millington, forensic specialist in all things relating to blood pattern analysis for the help and vivid image of hitting joints of pork as part of a working day. I'm so very grateful to you.

Thanks so much to Diane Ashworth and Sarah Gillen for wading through an early draft. It's safe to read it again now, honest.

Without readers, there would be no point to any of this, so again, I'm so grateful to anyone who takes the time to read my books, and to the book club members and reviewers who have been so supportive.

Huge thanks to my wonderful agent, Cathryn Summerhayes of Curtis Brown for having faith in me from the beginning.

Mega thanks to Jo Dickinson, superb editor who always knows the right thing to say and suggest.

Many thanks to the team at Simon & Schuster for everything they do behind the scenes and for the constant assistance whenever I've needed it.

Last but not least, to my husband, family, friends and colleagues who have been so supportive throughout. Impossible without you.